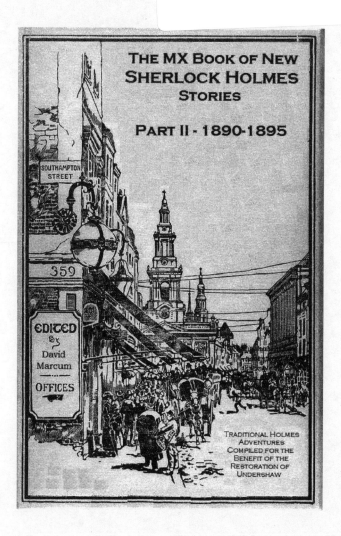

THE MX BOOK OF NEW SHERLOCK HOLMES STORIES

PART II · 1890-1895

SOUTHAMPTON STREET

359

EDITED By David Marcum

OFFICES

TRADITIONAL HOLMES ADVENTURES COMPILED FOR THE BENEFIT OF THE RESTORATION OF UNDERSHAW

SHERLOCK HOLMES

The VERSE *of* DEATH
and other stories

DAVID MARCUM, EDITOR

JAICO PUBLISHING HOUSE

Ahmedabad Bangalore Bhopal Bhubaneswar Chennai
Delhi Hyderabad Kolkata Lucknow Mumbai

Published by Jaico Publishing House
A-2 Jash Chambers, 7-A Sir Phirozshah Mehta Road
Fort, Mumbai - 400 001
jaicopub@jaicobooks.com
www.jaicobooks.com

© MX Publishing

Published in arrangement with
MX Publishing Ltd
335 Princess Park Manor
London, N11 3GX

SHERLOCK HOLMES
THE VERSE OF DEATH AND OTHER STORIES
ISBN 978-81-8495-912-3

First Jaico Impression: 2016

Page design and layout: Special Effects, Mumbai

Printed by
Replika Press Pvt. Ltd.

COPYRIGHT INFORMATION

All of the contributions in this collection are copyrighted by the authors listed below. Grateful acknowledgement is given to the authors and/or their agents for the kind permission to use their work within these volumes.

Contents

The years between 1890 and 1895 were times of upheaval for both Holmes and Watson. While Watson continued to enjoy married life with his wife, Mary, Holmes faced an ever escalating battle with the Napoleon of Crime, Professor James Moriarty. The contest between the two culminated on 4 May, 1891, atop the Reichenbach Falls. While Watson was decoyed away, Holmes and Moriarty met and fought on the slippery ledge. Moriarty fell, and Holmes did not. However, seeing the opportunity to continue his work in secret if he was thought to have died, and also as a way to protect Watson and his wife from the last remains of the Professor's organization, Holmes allowed Watson to believe that he, too, had fallen. Watson returned home heartbroken, while Holmes journeyed all over the world, carrying out missions for the British Government and his brother, Mycroft. From May 1891 until April 1894, Holmes traveled to various locations, including Lhasa in Tibet, Mecca, Khartoum, and Montpellier, France (as recorded in "The Empty

House".) *In addition, he also visited many other locations that are not recorded in the Canon.*

While Holmes was away from England, Watson faced both the grief of losing his best friend, as well as the death of his wife Mary in 1893. When Holmes returned to London in April 1894, Watson was amazed to learn that his friend was alive after all, and he soon returned to sharing rooms at 221b Baker Street. The years that followed, particularly 1894-1895, were extremely busy, and the cases literally tumbled upon them, one after the other....

The Bachelor of Baker Street Muses on Irene Adler

by Carole Nelson Douglas

Kings do not impress him, especially from Bohemia. Women do not obsess him, with their vapors and anemia.

Watson is wrong. His brain thrives on opium dreams and smoke. Yet sometimes they unite against him, and, uninvited, invoke

A vision of The Woman.

He brushed off a monarch's hand, but when it comes to her now, He remembers a kindly touch to an aged clergyman's brow.

His injured cleric now seems a shabby trick, thought nothing of, When she was fighting for her freedom and the cause of true love Always paramount to The Woman.

Yet such cheek! Feminine features under muffler and bowler hat, His own name appropriated at his very doorstep, audacious that!

His name, with the honourific "Mister" muttered

*in a youthful male tone. He should have known.
Not a former Baker Street Irregular grown,*

But a woman in wolf's clothing.

*All is fair in crime and punishment, and disguise
a commonplace. So she mastered it herself, but
she was fair in more than face,*

*Accepting only her own honour from the prideful
and possessive King, Leaving her true adversary
an eternal portrait of her leave-taking.*

He too refused the Royal ring.

*He smiles as he fingers the gold "sovereign"
dangling on his watch chain.*

*Him she tipped. The King she slipped. What an
ironical refrain.*

*To sum up the same old story, that last letter left
for him lingers near.*

*She called him hers, she called him dear, terms he
had never longed to hear*

From any woman.

*And then Baker Street reclaims its own. He will
no longer be alone. Knocking at the lower door,
footsteps pounding up a floor to his own.*

*His blood is up, his pulses race, he wonders what
new enigma he will find.*

He banishes past and pipe dream, leaps up from his chair. And leaves behind

The Woman on his mind.

Kings do not impress him, especially from Bohemia. Women do not obsess him, with their vapors and anemia. He still finds his muse in opium dreams and smoke,

And the not unwelcome recollections they provoke Of The Woman.

The Affair of Miss Finney

by Ann Margaret Lewis

t was in the third week of June, in 1890, that Sherlock Holmes encountered a case the likes of which he'd never before had the misfortune to solve. Women had always been a puzzling topic for Holmes. After my marriage to Mary, he exhibited no overt ill will toward my bride, and yet made it clear that he was not happy about our nuptials. It is with the Miss Finney affair that I believe he came to see my wife with new eyes.

That day, I'd stayed late into the evening with one of my patients. In fact, I returned home at such an hour that I was certain Mary had gone to bed. The house was dark, save for a solitary gas lamp in the front hall that she left up for me so I could find my key in the dark. I did my best not to wake her, but instead turned the corner and surprised her in the hall, candle in hand. She wore her lavender dressing gown trimmed in white lace, and her hair fell to one shoulder in a single, blonde braid.

She gasped. "James!"

I smiled and kissed her cheek. It was a personal affection of ours that she'd address me in a form of my middle name. "I'm sorry, dear; I didn't mean to startle you."

She placed her hand on her breast and sighed with relief. "That's all right. I wasn't expecting you to be there. My, but you were quiet."

"I thought you were asleep." "Did you have anything to eat?"

"Yes. The housekeeper insisted on feeding me after the baby was born. Child gave us a bit of a fright, but ultimately it all went well."

"Boy or girl?"

"Girl." I smiled. "Charming little thing." Suddenly, the bell rang downstairs. "Who might that be?" Mary asked.

"There's only one person who would ring at this hour." I charged with a stiff gait down the stairs and swung open the front door.

Sherlock Holmes stood on the step. "I'm glad you are here, Watson. I see your wife is still awake. Excellent. May I come in?"

"Of course."

Mary looked askance at me as I led my friend up the stairs. I gestured for her to precede us into our parlour. "Is something wrong?" she asked as I closed the door behind us.

"Mrs. Watson," Holmes said. "I came here to find you, especially, in the hope that you might assist me."

"I'm always happy to be of help, Mr. Holmes."

He began to pace the carpet, his nervous energy evident in his stride. He removed his hat, and I realized his hair was mussed as if he'd been asleep. Whatever it was, it had apparently awakened him.

"In my entire career," he said, "I have been fortunate that I have never dealt with a case such as this. I have always known it was possible that something of its ilk might walk through my door, but I'd hoped I'd never see it." He stopped at my fireplace and continued in a hoarse voice. "It is heinous, monstrous, depraved, and vile. It is pure evil."

"Whatever is it, Mr. Holmes?" Mary asked.

"There is a young lady, who waits for me now at Baker Street. I came here, leaving her in the care of the maid. I fear she has been ill- used."

"Ill-used?"

"In a most unspeakable way."

Mary's fingers went to her mouth. "Oh...." "Good Lord," I whispered.

"She does not know the man who attacked her. He abducted her, rendering her unconscious with chloroform. The man gagged her, put a burlap sack over her head so she'd not know where she was, and later held a knife to her throat as he did...what he did. After, that he beat her and left her alone in this fashion for three days in some sort of prison, giving her only marginal food and drink, if any at all. Around 10:30 this evening, she managed to twist herself free of her bounds and crawl through a coal chute to escape.

"A cabby named Preston, whom I know from other cases, brought her to me tonight believing I might help her. Even so, I have sent word to Stanley Hopkins at the Yard. He is a compassionate sort, someone a woman in this state might find consoling." He shook his head. "Meanwhile, I have tried, in vain, to interview the lady at length, to glean more definitive details about her ordeal, but her upset renders her unable to speak of it coherently. Much of what I've told you I was able to deduce by observation, but when I attempted to examine the blood under her nails, she recoiled from me as if my hands were laced with acid."

"The poor girl." Mary shook her head.

"Mrs. Watson, I have the faculties to help this young lady, but she cannot reveal what she must to me because...." He paused, his lips turning downward in a troubled frown.

"You are a man," she finished for him.

He nodded. "Despite her desire for my assistance, she is not entirely...comfortable...in my presence, which I understand completely given the circumstances." He continued in a subdued voice. "Mrs. Watson, you've read your husband's narratives and you know that I have not always spoken of the fair sex in the most sympathetic terms. Nonetheless, I would never wish to see such grievous harm done to a woman."

"I know that, Mr. Holmes," Mary said in a gentle voice.

My friend averted his gaze from her and turned to pace the rug again. "The loathsome vermin who did this must be found, but without more data I am in the dark. There is grain powder and saw dust on her dress, along with mechanical oil, indicating she was kept at a mill or some similar place. Where, that is the question. I need her to reveal more. She fears me, though, which, while irrational, is, as I said, understandable."

Mary nodded. "What would you have me do?"

"I would like you to interview her while the doctor and I listen from the adjoining room. Mrs. Hudson may have helped, but she is with her son this evening. Besides, I think someone close to her own age may comfort her. The housemaid would be of little use in this regard, for I need someone with a quicker intellect."

"But, Mr. Holmes, I am not a detective. I am hardly qualified – "

"On the contrary, you are uniquely qualified for what I am asking. You are reserved, but not shy. You are also personable, and what she needs now is a friend. I believe she will respond to you better than I because, in addition to being female, you have a genuine, sympathetic character. And yet...." He leaned on the fireplace mantel and pressed his knuckle to his lips.

"What is it?" Mary asked.

"You have never done this before. Perhaps I am asking too much of you. It is just that I can conceive of no other way."

"If there is no other way that you can think to manage this situation," Mary replied, "then I must do it, must I not? At the very least I should do the very best I can."

Holmes looked from my wife to me, and back again. "All right, then. If you feel confident enough to try."

"I confess, I am not entirely confident, but I will find my

way. What sort of questions must I ask?"

"It is best to concentrate on her senses, what she smelled, heard, etcetera. Anything that she can remember to describe this man, for she could not see him. Also, the location is important. He took her someplace she'd never been before, to her knowledge."

"Did she not come to your rooms from there?" I asked.

"She hid under a tarpaulin in barrel cart that was next to the building and allowed it to take her away, so she was not aware of the path she took. When that stopped, she apparently came upon Preston, who immediately thought to bring her to me. He wondered if he should to take her to a hospital, and in truth, that may not have been a bad idea considering her condition."

"I should examine her, then, Holmes," I said. "She will no doubt have some serious injuries with the treatment she's received."

"I agree, but given her reaction to my touching her hand, doing that may be difficult at first. You should wait until your wife has won her trust."

"Should I write down her answers for you?" Mary asked.

Holmes pursed his lips thoughtfully. "That would be a fine pretence. As I said, I plan to eavesdrop with your husband from my bedroom. I'll make an excuse and pretend to leave the house, perhaps that I am going to find the doctor. She need not know he is even there – you'll wait in my room, Watson – then I'll enter my bedroom from the hall. When I've heard enough, I'll return as if I'd returned from the outside. You may then show me what notes you have, so she does not suspect that I was listening through the wall."

Mary sighed. Her clear blue eyes glistened once more with uncertainty.

"This will certainly be a challenge, Mrs. Watson," said my friend. "Yet you say you cannot convince her to speak to you."

"No," he said. "I am afraid this case is doomed to failure

at my hands alone."

"Very well, then." Mary nodded. "Let me dress and we shall go."

After a few moments, Mary emerged from our bedroom dressed in a simple, emerald green gown accented with ivory, with her hair neatly wrapped in a bun. She carried over her arm two other gowns and personal linens.

"I thought perhaps she might like some clean clothes. These dresses are different sizes."

"Very good, Mrs. Watson," said my friend. "Let's be off."

We summoned a hansom cab. As we made the short drive to Holmes rooms down the street and around the corner, Holmes gave my wife some additional guidance on the sort of questions to ask. He then added, "You should be aware that she is in the condition she was in when she arrived. The maid wanted to clean her up, but I asked her to wait until you have seen her."

Holmes led us up the stairs, gesturing us to be quiet. He directed me to enter his bedroom door, and when I did, I went immediately to the small peep hole Holmes had created in the wall to see into the sitting room. In the room it was hidden by a moulded glass wall decoration that expanded the field of vision so one could see the entire room laid out. As I peered through the hole, I froze for a moment, mortified at the site that met my eyes.

A young woman around the age of 23 sat in the chair at Holmes's hearth. Her pale red hair was ratted and dirty, and her fair skin layered in grime. Her dress, a soft pink calico, was ripped in several places and soiled with oil, muck, and dust. She was missing a shoe and her stocking was rent, leaving her foot nearly bare. A crocheted afghan blanket of red and blue had been laid about her shoulders, and yet she still shivered as she lifted a cup of tea to her swollen lips with fingers cut and covered with dirt and blood. Black and blue bruises coloured her right eye and cheeks, the sides of her mouth, her arms, and red, raw burn wounds circled her wrists.

I looked at my Mary, who had preceded Holmes into the room, and I could see alarm in her opened lips and widened eyes.

"Miss Finney," Holmes said in a quiet voice.

The young woman twisted in her chair as if stung. "Mr. Holmes?" Her voice had the lilt of Irish.

"This is Mrs. Watson. She is the wife of my dear friend, Doctor Watson."

"The gentleman who writes of you?"

"Yes. I thought she might keep you company while I find the doctor. I am hoping he will assist me with your case."

"Oh." She blinked at Mary with pale blue eyes that seemed lifeless. "Thank you, Mrs. Watson."

"You are so very welcome." Mary walked across the room and tugged the bell rope. "Why don't I have the maid bring up a wash basin with warm soap and water, and we can clean your wounds a bit? Won't that make you feel a little better?"

"I think that's an excellent plan, Mrs. Watson," said Holmes. "Meanwhile, I shall be on my way. Good-bye, Mrs. Watson, Miss Finney." He nodded his head and stepped into the hall, closing the door solidly behind him. He then entered his room silently from the hall and came to stand beside me near the wall, to listen.

The maid answered the summons and brought Mary's requests. Mary then sat before the young woman on the ottoman to ring out a towel with warm water and soap.

"Thank you, Mrs. Watson," Miss Finney whispered. "You are very kind."

"Why don't you simply call me 'Mary'," my wife said. "We are about the same age, are we not?"

"I am 25," Miss Finney said. "My name is Melinda."

"Melinda is a beautiful name." Mary smiled warmly. "Let me start with your face, dear." She began to clean the young woman's cheeks with gentle touches.

"Mr. Holmes is a good man," my own lady continued as

she worked. "On our ride here he told me he wants to help you, but you'll need to tell him more of what happened to you."

"I know," Miss Finney said with a quivering voice. "But... it's so difficult to...talk about it...there's so much...."

"I cannot imagine," Mary agreed. She patted the young woman's face with a dry towel. "But perhaps if you and I break the whole ghastly thing up into tiny, little pieces, discussing it won't be so trying. In fact...." Standing, she went to Holmes's desk and took up a piece of foolscap, pen, and ink. "I shall write some notes, and we can tell him these little pieces when he comes back."

"Little pieces? What do you mean?" Miss Finney's pale eyes were wide.

Mary set the paper next to her on the side table. "Thinking about everything at once is just overwhelming, so we focus on one little thing at a time. For example, when you were in the room alone, I understand your eyes were covered so all you could do is listen. Did you hear anything?"

"Yes."

"What?"

Miss Finney swallowed hard. "The rats."

My eyes shot over to my friend standing across from me. He winced.

"Good God," I whispered.

Holmes again held his finger to his lips and I went silent once more to listen.

"Shall I roll up your sleeves, dear, so I can wash your hands?"

Miss Finney tenuously put forward her arms, and allowed Mary to wash the dirt, blood, and ichor from her arms and fingers.

"Did you remember hearing anything from outside?" Mary asked as she worked.

"Church bells."

"Church bells? You are certain it wasn't a clock tower?"

"Yes. The bells didn't ring every quarter hour, but every few hours. I am sure it was the Angelus. I prayed it...."

Suddenly, the clock on the mantelpiece chimed midnight. Miss Finney started, but Mary soothed her by placing a firm hand on her shoulder. Dropping her face into her wet hands, Miss Finney sobbed.

Mary pulled the young woman to her shoulder and let her cry there. She rocked her gently, stroking her tangled hair. I turned my gaze to my friend, who stood by the door wearing a thoughtful expression.

"It's all right, dear," Mary said finally. "It's another little piece that'll help him find where you were imprisoned. It could help lead him to...to the one who did this."

"Y-yes. I see." Miss Finney sniffed.

Mary brushed loose hair from the woman's face. "Did you hear anything else that you recall?" Mary asked, she dabbed Miss Finney's tears away with the towel, and returned to bathing the young woman's wrists and fingers.

"A gurgling and swishing, like water in pipes...only louder."

"Excellent. That's another thing that Mr. Holmes might find useful I'll write that down." Mary set aside the rag a moment to write on the paper.

I looked over at Holmes and saw a gleam in his eyes. This had apparently indeed triggered a thought in his mind.

"Now, in this room...did you smell anything that stands out in your mind?"

"Oh." Miss Finney rolled her eyes. "That I shall never forget. It smelled so foul there. There was waste...some of it my own, I fear. But mostly it smelled like...bread yeast... only the strongest I have ever smelled. It was mixed with the scent of beer. It was overwhelming. I don't know that I shall make bread or smell beer for an entire year after this."

I saw a slight smile curl at the edge of my friend's lips.

"Did the...man who attacked you smell this way, too?"

"Yes, he smelled strongly of it. That, and tobacco. A very

acrid tobacco, much like what I smell here. I'm afraid when I entered Mr. Holmes's sitting room, I wanted to retch."

Holmes sighed. He closed his eyes and rested his head against the wall.

"He put a gag on you, I understand," Mary prompted.

"Yes, it was...so horrible."

"I don't doubt it," Mary said gently. "Did the cloth he use taste of anything?"

"Oh, it tasted rank. Like stale beer."

Holmes nodded, as if he expected to hear this. "Now the man," he murmured. "Ask about the man."

"Now here's one more thing, and I think this may be the most difficult of all, dear." Mary shifted her seat closer to the young woman and taking the younger woman's hands in her own, held them tightly. "Was the man who did this... could you tell if he was large or small in size?"

"He...was...broad shouldered, average build, I think. But not so tall."

"Were his hands rough, or smooth?"

"S-smooth. If I'd not known him otherw-wise, I'd say he was a gentleman. And the way he spoke was educated. He had a rasping voice, not very deep."

"So he spoke to you. Did he say anything that stands out in your mind? Something specific?"

"Not much I'd repeat. He said such foul things."

"But you'd recognize his voice if you heard it again."

"Yes. I don't think I can ever forget it."

"Melinda, you are doing brilliantly. See how much easier it is to take it piece by piece?" Mary wrote these down on the paper she had beside her.

"I feel badly that I could not tell Mr. Holmes this. He asked some similar questions, but I just c-couldn't..."

"It's all right, dear. I'm sure he understood. But you see? We have all these notes here that will help him."

"There's one more thing you might write down."

"What's that?"

"He had a beard. A short one. It was very strange... coarse, like horsehair. He had a moustache, too, but it was not as rough."

"Very good. I know that will be helpful."

Holmes patted me on the shoulder and gestured with his head for me to follow him. He went out into the hall, walked quietly downstairs and led me out the front door.

Once downstairs, he reopened the front door noisily and walked up to the landing, taking care to walk heavy on the stairs. I did the same. Holmes knocked lightly on the door, and heard my wife say, "Come in."

"Hello again, Miss Finney, Mrs. Watson," Holmes said, entering the sitting room. "I have located the doctor."

"I think Miss Finney is doing better, Mr. Holmes," my wife said. "She shared some things about her ordeal that I recorded for you."

Holmes took up the paper my wife held out to him and glanced over it. "Ladies, this is marvellous. It will help tremendously." He folded the paper and put it in his pocket. "Miss Finney, I assume you live with relatives?"

"Yes. My father."

"Do you wish me to contact him to let him know where you are?"

"Yes, please. He is the proprietor of the Celtic Knot Public House, on Surrey Row in Southwark."

"If I may," I interjected. "I'd like to examine her injuries."

"Of course, Watson. Miss Finney?"

I sat before the young woman, and when I reached out to touch her chin to inspect her bruises, she shied away, pressing against my wife who sat beside her. Mary placed her arm around her shoulders reassuringly. "It's all right, Melinda," Mary said. "My husband is very gentle."

With Mary's reassurance, she allowed me to give a superficial inspection of her injuries. She needed a more thorough exam, but I determined that she would be all right for the time being.

Mary then said to me, "Do you think I could have the maid draw a bath for Miss Finney? Then I can finish caring for her?"

"That is an excellent idea, dear. I can give you some ointment and bandages for her wounds."

"Meanwhile, the doctor and I have some other work to do," said Holmes. "Thank you for your help, Mrs. Watson."

"You are very welcome, Mr. Holmes."

After Mary led Miss Finney from the room, Holmes went to the mantel to fill his long clay pipe from the tobacco slipper. Halfway through this process he paused, set aside the pipe, and took a cigar from the coal scuttle.

"Holmes, this is simply monstrous."

Holmes lit his cigar and paced the floor, puffing and thinking. "Southwark." He stopped in his tracks.

"Southwark?"

"Anchor Brewery, Watson. It is right next to St. Saviour's Church in Southwark. That is where she was imprisoned. I'm certain of it. The smell of yeast and stale beer. The gurgling pipes, rather loud from her description. A good deal of water, malt, and hops. Clearly a brewery. The Celtic Knot Pub is also in Southwark, and her father would likely order from a local brewer. I believe this monster works for her father's beer supplier. He probably kept her in the brewery's cellar. The closest supplier is Barclay's Anchor Brewery."

"It cannot be that simple, Holmes. Can it?"

"Usually it is. Most victims of this crime know their attackers in some way. Human nature, really. We covet what is most familiar to us. The difficulty lies in finding the man within a brewery establishment that fits her description, but I believe I know where to start."

There was a knock at the door. "Come in, Hopkins."

The youthful, primly-dressed Scotland Yarder stepped through the door. "How the devil did you know who it was through the door?"

"I was expecting you, and you have thick knuckles."

"Of course." He gave my friend an amused grin. "What's this about then, Mr. Holmes?"

As Holmes explained in delicate terms the situation at hand, Hopkin's expression clouded.

"Dark business," he said. "There was a report this morning of a missing young lady from Southwark. It wasn't my case, so I don't know the details, but I wager it's the same one. I can send word to the Yard." He pulled out a notebook. "So you want to look in at the brewery? No one will be there at this hour."

Holmes went to the closet and took out a dark lantern. "Which is precisely when I wish to go, my dear fellow."

"Now, wait just a moment. There are laws to follow."

"And you should follow them, of course. I place all the legal formalities of entering the building in your capable hands. You shall meet us there when you have papers."

"Meet you there? You mean – ?"

"The rest shall remain unsaid, Hopkins, lest you find yourself in a position of having to lie to your superiors. Here is the address. Join us as soon as you can. Watson, I trust you have your revolver? Right then, let us be off."

As we made our way to Southwark in a hansom, Holmes asked, "What do you make of it, Watson?"

"As I said before – monstrous."

"What about the description of the man?"

"Medium build, I think. With a beard."

"Yes. She said the beard was like horsehair. What does that suggest to you?"

"It was fake?"

"I believe so."

"Then the man would be clean-shaven."

"Most likely. Ah, here we are." Holmes tapped the roof of the cab with his cane.

The brewery loomed dark and large in front of us as we approached it. Holmes lit the lantern in his hand, and began to walk around the building.

"Wouldn't it be better to see what's here in the daylight, Holmes? Why did we have to come at night?"

"Seeing evidence would be better during the day, I admit. Now, however, our quarry will not be here. He took her in the evening, left her alone late at night, and abused her, I would surmise, earlier the next day. She was gagged so she could not be heard as he left her here. That's why she took the late night opportunity to escape, for she knew he'd leave her to herself. I wanted to find this prison now and inspect it before he can return."

"Will you have enough light?"

"I've found clues in less light than this, my friend. Hello, here is a coal chute." He held his lantern over the rusted entryway and crouched. From the edge of the rusted metal chute door, he removed a tiny piece of fabric and thread.

"Hold the lamp won't you, Watson?" I did as he asked, and he examined the fragment closer to his eyes.

"Pink calico. This is where she crawled out of her prison. The room is beyond this wall."

I walked a few steps along the building. "There's a window here, Holmes, but it seems to have been blacked over on the inside."

He looked over my shoulder. "Close the lantern."

"Why?"

"A precaution. Let me see if we can open this window." He bent down in the dark, and I could see his shadow moving in a pushing motion. "Ah, for shame. It is a crank window, locked from the inside. Very well, then, I must break it or find another way in."

"Someone will hear you if you do that."

"Yes, I'd rather find another way." We walked together down the length of the wall, and around the back of the building. There we found a simple wooden door, which was locked with a padlock. I opened the lantern slightly so he might inspect it.

"This Aquire model is not much of a challenge." From

his the pocket inside his coat, Holmes pulled out what I recognized as his lock picking tool kit, selected and instrument and went to work. It wasn't long before we were inside and making our way down a set of creaky wooden stairs into an unused portion of the giant brewery cellar. I say "unused" in that it didn't seem to be currently employed for the brewing and ageing of beer. It was, however, filled with old barrels, equipment, bottles, sawdust, and tools which were layered in dust.

Holmes took the lantern from my hand and stood gazing at the slate floor. Footprints were clear in the dust, leading to the end of the room and another singular, wooden door, which was bolted shut.

Holmes slid open the bolt and stepped into the chamber beyond. A foul odour struck me first as we passed into what had been the young woman's prison. I took my handkerchief from my sleeve and pressed it to my nose and mouth to block out the stench. Holmes held up lantern to illuminate the entirety of the grim space.

"Here are her bonds," he said, touching bits of thick rope with his cane. "Being a tiny woman, she wriggled free of them. What have we here?" He handed me the lantern, and bent down. He then lifted up a small glass bottle in his gloved fingers. Opening the top, he sniffed.

"Spirit gum. That confirms the fake beard, Watson."

"He put it on here?"

"I think not. Most likely he carried this small bottle in his pocket to re-affix the hair piece as necessary. They fall off with oil from the skin and perspiration when worn too long. This bottle is not empty, so he probably did not drop it on purpose."

"He then left the premises wearing the beard."

"I think so."

"We are aware," said Holmes. "That's why we are here. My name is Sherlock Holmes, and these gentlemen with me are Inspector Hopkins of Scotland Yard, and my associate

Doctor Watson."

"Sherlock Holmes – Scotland Yard." He nodded. "You are quick, gentlemen. I only submitted a missing person's report today, as they'd not let me do it sooner."

"Shall we go inside?"

"Surely, surely." He led us into the pub, and locked the door behind us once we were inside. It was a clean, bright establishment inside, not as grim or dark as others I've visited. In fact, I'd say that while the establishment was one a man would frequent, it had the prim, orderly touch of a woman's influence, with shining glassware, well-swept floor, and dust-free artwork and lamps.

"Would you like a pint, gentlemen, or anything else to drink?" Mr. Finney ushered us to a large table at the centre of the floor and we sat together. "*Gratis*, of course. You're here to help, and I'll not take a farthing."

"I'm on duty, so nothing for me," said Hopkins. "Though Holmes and the doctor can indulge."

"If I had something now, it may put me to sleep," I said. "Holmes?"

Holmes shook his head. "I think you might want something for yourself, Mr. Finney. What we have to tell you might be a shock."

The barkeep paled visibly and sank into the open chair beside Holmes. "It doesn't serve to drink the profits," he said in a subdued tone. "You might as well tell me what you must."

"First, let me begin by assuring you that your daughter is alive."

"Oh, thank God." Finney rested his face in his hands.

"But there is more," my friend continued. In a gentle tone, he revealed the facts of his daughter's misery, and as he spoke the barkeep's eyes welled with tears.

"Dear Lord in heaven," he muttered, when my friend finished. He wiped his eyes with his fingers. "My sweet Melinda. Where is she now?"

"The doctor's wife is caring for her at my residence. She's sleeping in the guest room now, I hope. We shall bring her home tomorrow, late in the morning."

"Why late?"

"She must identify the culprit, and you also may help with that goal. The man who did this worked for Anchor Brewery and would have been here regularly. Do you know anyone that fits that description?"

"There doesn't seem to be much else here," I said, walking the length of the room to the coal chute. "Other than that burlap sack, which you say covered her head, and this cloth." I picked it up off the floor. "Her blindfold, I'd assume."

"Yes, and this is the gag." Holmes said, pointing with his cane to another crumpled, stained rag. "No, nothing much else, Watson. He brought her here three days ago, used her, and left her here for his next convenience. Ultimately he would have killed her, I believe."

A slight movement near my boot caused me to jump. "Good heavens. The rats. I'd forgotten. It seems we've startled them." I looked up at Holmes, and saw he was gazing at me with a peculiar glint in his eye. And yet it was as if he was not seeing me. His jaw and fists were clenched tight and his lips were pressed into a firm line.

"Holmes – " I began.

"Let's go, Watson. I have had enough of this atmosphere."

I followed him outside, and, as we returned the way we had come, we encountered Inspector Hopkins with two constables.

"There you are, Holmes. You've been inside?"

My friend described the inner chamber we found, and handed Hopkins the bottle. "You might want to leave a constable here in case he returns."

"Are you off then already?"

"Yes, to the Celtic Knot Pub. The owner is Miss Finney's father, and I suspect he knows who this villain is, though he might not realize it. The villain works for this brewery, and knew Miss Finney already. He knew when she'd be vulnerable, and he followed her. He also knows where that room is, knew it was abandoned, and that he could use it with impunity."

"You don't mind if I come along, do you?"

Holmes smiled. Hopkins was a student of his methods, if an imperfect one.

"Of course, Inspector. Let's hail a cab, shall we? The pub is in Southwark but too far too walk."

When we reached the pub, we encountered the owner turning down the gas lamp outside the shop. He was a small man, whose pale face and shock of white hair betrayed his own Celt heritage.

"Ach, fellows, I cannot help you tonight. As you see I'm closing the doors a bit early. We've had some family trouble."

The elderly man dabbed his eyes once more with a handkerchief. "There are three that I know. Charles Hamming is the nephew of the owner and the salesman who takes my orders. The delivery driver is Paul Somersfield, and then there is Joshua Gable. He's an odd fellow, a bookkeeper for the brewery, and he comes here frequently after he leaves work. He doesn't say much, but he has a queer look in his eyes."

"Are any of these fellows clean-shaven?" I asked.

"Clean-shaven? Yes, Gable is clean shaven. The other two have moustaches, and Hamming has a beard after a fashion."

"After a fashion?" I asked.

"He's been trying to grow one, it seems. It's not filled in."

"This has been a helpful interview, Mr. Finney," said my friend, rising from his chair. "Let's leave you to your rest, I am confident that your daughter will be returned to you tomorrow."

"Thank you, gentlemen," Mr. Finney said, shaking our hands. "Thank you so very much."

As Holmes and Hopkins stepped outside, I paused a moment with Mr. Finney. "Sir," I said, "Your daughter will have great difficulty returning to your pub, I think. It is where she was taken, and the memories of her experience will be quite raw. Does she have anywhere she can go to stay for a time to calm her nerves? Somewhere in the country perhaps?"

Mr. Finney nodded. "I have a sister in Yorkshire. I'm sure she'd be happy to have Melinda to stay with her for a while."

"Excellent," I shook his hand once more. "And if there's anything I can do to help in anyway afterward, pray, let me know."

When we arrived at Baker Street, Holmes, Hopkins, and I found Mary in Holmes's sitting room, sleeping in the chair by the fire. I touched her shoulder and she woke with a start. "Oh! You've returned. I am sorry. I tried to stay awake."

"Do not apologize, dear," I said. "Is Miss Finney in bed?"

"Yes. She's clean and her wounds are bandaged. The maid gave her one of her nightgowns and put her in your old room. I stayed with her until she fell asleep."

"I think sleep is a fine idea for all of us," I said. "I don't believe we can do much more until morning. Or, rather, later this morning."

"I'd rather not leave her, though. The maid said there was a room downstairs where I might sleep, but I wanted to wait until you came back before I went to lie down."

"I hope you would both stay if you can," said Holmes. "Tomorrow morning may be a trial for her, and your presence would be a great help to me."

"That room will accommodate both of us, as I recall," I said. "I'll send a boy over to our flat gather some clean collars for me and some things for you as well, Mary."

"Hopkins," Holmes turned to the inspector. "Those three men can be collected when they report for work in the morning. Do you think you could bring them here?"

Hopkins shrugged. "We've done it before, so I cannot see

why not. With some good constables with me, I believe we can have them here around ten o'clock."

"Then you should all go get some much needed sleep. I will stay up a bit longer and smoke – " He paused. "A cigarette or two."

I smiled. "Very well, then. Good night, Holmes."

The next morning, I awoke at eight o'clock. Mary had already risen, dressed, and gone to look after Miss Finney. I washed and dressed quickly, and, upon entering Holmes's sitting room, discovered a breakfast laid out for us. Holmes, Miss Finney and Mary were already seated at the table. One of the windows, I noticed, was opened slightly, allowing a fresh morning breeze to billow the curtains.

"The maid has anticipated our needs, Watson," Holmes said. "Come join us."

I did as he suggested, and we ate together in silence for a few moments, until Holmes said, "Miss Finney, there is something I must tell you."

She looked up at him, her right eye more a vivid blue in contrast to the grey-blue bruise that surrounded it. "What is it, Mr. Holmes?"

He placed his napkin and looked around at all of us. "This morning, Inspector Hopkins will be bringing three men here, one of whom is most likely your assailant."

Miss Finney set her fork down on her plate with a *clink*. "Oh."

"Do not fret, dear lady. I will not ask you to face him. However, if you desire justice, you must identify him for the police."

She shook her head. "But I did not see him."

"You heard his voice. Therefore, I will interview the men in this room. You will listen to the conversation from my bedroom, which is adjacent to this one." Her eyes widened at the suggestion of being in his bedroom, but he held up his hand. "Mrs. Watson will stay with you, will you not, Mrs. Watson?"

"Of course," Mary said.

"There, on my chemistry table, you will see that I have an Edison light bulb in a lamp stand. I have attached it to a switch that I'll give to you. When you hear a voice you recognize, you will flip the switch to signal to me."

"Will they not see the light go on?" Miss Finney asked.

"They may, but that need not concern you."

Miss Finney looked to Mary, who, in turn, placed her hand gently on her arm. Miss Finney straightened her shoulders and turned back to my friend.

"I can do it," said Miss Finney. "I *will* do it."

"Capital. There is only one thing more." Holmes leaned forward with his elbows on the table and asked in a voice that was most gentle. "Are you certain that there is no particular word or phrase that the man used, nothing he said that stands out in your mind? Anything he said may be of help to us."

Her delicate lips turned down in a frown. "Patience."

"Patience?"

"The first morning, just before he left me, he said that. He mocked me by saying 'patience is a virtue.' It was horrible... he made it sound as if I wanted...." She covered her mouth and wept once more.

Mary rested her hand on her shoulder. "Mr. Holmes – "

"No more, Miss Finney. I have precisely what I need. Watson, would you escort the ladies next door? I have set some chairs in there so they may be comfortable. I'll ask the maid to clear these dishes, then I'll prepare the light switch."

I did as he asked, and when I opened the door to his room, I was surprised at the site that met my eyes.

It was tidy to the point of being pristine. Holmes had, no doubt, spent a better part of the night cleaning it. The window was also cracked open like that of the sitting room, allowing in the fresh air. He'd set two padded chairs near the wall where he and I had stood the night before to listen to Mary's conversation with the young lady. There was also a small side table with a pitcher of cool water and drinking glasses.

"Well, then," I said. "Here you are, ladies. Is there anything else you think you might like?"

"I may close the window later if there's a chill, but I think we're fine for now."

"I'd recommend a book," I said. "But reading the detailed lives of criminals might be a bit much."

"I think we'll be all right," Mary said with a smile. "What time do you expect Inspector Hopkins to arrive?"

I glanced at my pocket watch. "Any time now. He said he would be here around ten o'clock."

"Then we haven't long to wait."

Suddenly the door to the closet opened, and Holmes stepped into the room.

"Good Lord, Holmes," I said. "What...how did you...?"

"I'm sorry, ladies. Watson." He held up a bit of rubber-coated wire linked to a small black box with a switch. "This is for Miss Finney. I had to pull the connection through."

"But your closet...what did you do?"

He glanced over his shoulder. "Oh, that. After you married and moved, I knocked a hole in the back of my closet, and another in the sitting room which is covered by those additional drapes. Having a hidden way into my room is useful, especially when one must string wire." He smiled and placed the box in Miss Finney's hand. "Simply flip this switch. Watson, let's you and I go in the other room and test it. We have little time."

I followed him back to the sitting room. There he stood in the centre of the room and called out, "Miss Finney, flip the switch please." The lightbulb on Holmes desk lit. "Excellent, you may turn it off now."

"Will you interview all the suspects at once, Holmes?"

"Of course, Watson. If a man is interviewed alone, his voice isn't natural. Put him in a conversation with three or more people, and he'll speak normally. That is what we want. Ah, I believe that is Hopkins' ring downstairs. Watson, sit over at my table near the lamp, won't you?"

Holmes then paced back and forth as we heard several men tramping up the stairs. "Come in, Hopkins," Holmes called out, before the officer's knuckles had struck the door.

Hopkins entered followed by three men and two constables.

"Sit, gentlemen, please," Holmes said, gesturing to the chairs at the dining table. "I fear I haven't much time. I have more pressing matters to attend to today, but I promised the inspector I'd assist him with his case, so let's get on with it."

Hopkins raised an eyebrow at Holmes, then turned his gaze to me. I shrugged my shoulders, wondering what this meant.

"Now, gentlemen, you have been asked here by the inspector because a crime has been committed, and we wish to know if you were involved." Holmes paced around the table, not looking at the suspects. It appeared to me as if he were not interested in them at all. "You sir, are a bookkeeper are you not?"

This question was posed to the man who sat at the end of the table. He was not overly tall, but his eyes were squinting and his mouth turned in an awkward scowl. Clean-shaven and of middle years, he did not meet my friend's gaze.

"I am. How would you know?"

"I was told one of you was a bookkeeper. You seemed most likely, with the mark of a pen on your thumb and forefinger, ink stain on your cuff, and the wear on your sleeve. You also have indentions from a pair of spectacles which are currently in your breast pocket. Your attitude is also lacks the confidence of a salesman. Therefore you are Joshua Gable. This man here," he pointed to the bearded young man who sat beside Gable, "has that confidence. You are Charles Hamming, are you not? Nephew of the owner of the Anchor Brewery?"

"I am. But I fail to see – "

"Of course you do. And that means you," he said to the third, moustached, muscular fellow, "are Paul Somersfield, the delivery driver. Your build belies that line of work."

"Aye, that'll be what I do, but I have no idea why I am – "

"You are here because a young woman was abused and assaulted in the brewery basement."

"Good God," said the bookkeeper. His scowl softened. "Who would do that?"

"One of you three. All of you have association with the Celtic Knot Pub, and all three of you work at the brewery. It can only be one of you. To be frank, I'd rather one of you simply confess and spare me the agonizing tedium of working it out of you. I swear, Hopkins," he turned to the inspector suddenly. "Could you have brought me a less interesting case?"

"I...bring it to...you?" Hopkins repeated. He crossed his arms. "What do you – ?"

"I grow tired of having to solve the simplest little problems for Scotland Yard," Holmes interrupted. "Is there not one that you could puzzle for yourselves? Why must I be the one to labour for you when the answers are always so obvious?"

"Well if the answer is so obvious," said Hopkins, his voice dropping to a growl, "why don't you just give it to us now?"

"I think you should be patient," Holmes snapped in return. The salesman snickered.

"Why are you laughing?" Holmes said.

"You're asking him to be patient. You are the one who needs patience."

"I need *what*?"

"Patience. You do most of the talking, you cut others off, and do not let them finish. Who do you think you are?"

I felt heat on my left hand. Glancing next to me, I saw that the bulb was lit.

Holmes did not appear to notice. He leaned over

Hamming as if examining a bug under a microscope. "Tell me, Hamming. What happened to your cheeks?"

"My cheeks? What do you mean?"

"There are small abrasions on your skin, just above the line of your beard. It looks to me like the skin has been ripped away."

"I'm not used to shaving above the beard line and I scraped it by accident."

"No, no, that is not from shaving. That injury happens when one pulls off a fake beard affixed with spirit gum. If you remove it after a short time without solvent, it hurts like the devil. I know what that injury looks like, as I've done it to myself a few times. When did you do it? Two, three days ago? It's not quite healed. Do you see it, Hopkins? I must admit, hiding a real beard under a fake one shows some cleverness, but if you're going to use a disguise, you might at least learn how to remove it properly."

As Holmes spoke, the light went on and off several times next to me, then finally remained lit.

"Here now," said the delivery driver. "What the deuce is wrong with that bulb there?"

Suddenly the door burst open and Miss Finney entered, followed by a rather anxious looking Mary.

"Mr. Holmes, did you not see the light?" Miss Finney cried with some exasperation.

"I did," Holmes replied. "I was merely confirming your identification."

Jumping to his feet, Hamming spat a word toward the young lady that I shall not record in this memoir. It was so vulgar that everyone froze with shock.

Everyone save Holmes, however. He sprang forward with a solid right cross that sent teeth and blood shooting from the man's lips. There was also a loud *crack* when he connected, and I surmised he'd broken the man's jaw. Spinning from the force of the blow, Hamming crashed to the floor in an unconscious heap.

Releasing a contented sigh, Holmes straightened his jacket, then turned to the women in the doorway.

"I apologize for that, dear ladies. Though I must admit it did give me tremendous satisfaction. I hope it did for you as well, Miss Finney?"

She gave him a slight smile. "It did, indeed."

"Well, there you are, Hopkins." He waved at the unmoving lump on the floor as if it were a fly. "Pray, have your men drag this vile refuse from my sitting room."

"With pleasure," said Hopkins. "I admit I thought you'd lost your mind for a moment there. All that about bringing you boring cases...."

"It's often true," said Holmes said with a smile. "But not in this instance."

Hopkins gave Holmes a wry grin as he followed his constables and the others out the door.

"Holmes, Mary and I would be happy to take Miss Finney to her father," I said. "If there's nothing else you'll need from us...."

"No, Watson. We are finished here."

Miss Finney went to my friend and, with a slight hesitation, laid her hand on his forearm. Holmes's eyes widened slightly at the gesture. He did not shrink away, but remained still at her touch.

"Mr. Holmes, I know that I wasn't the easiest client for you – " Holmes shook his head. "It is all right."

"Yes, but, I want you to know. You've helped to restore my faith in men and you have given me hope. Thank you."

"You are welcome, of course. Be well."

As we helped Miss Finney into a carriage outside, I heard Holmes's violin playing a sweet, melancholy melody. From that day, I noticed he seldom made negative references to women or marriage in my presence. I wonder now if seeing Mary's effectiveness in this case amended his point of view, not only of her but of all women, or if seeing Miss Finney's strength in her suffering made him less apt to deride them.

If it is either, I can only say that he's has become, and always will be, a better man for it.

The Adventure of the Bookshop Owner

by Vincent W. Wright

As I look over the files concerning the cases in which Sherlock Holmes and I became involved, I find a particular one from the summer of 1890 that had initially presented itself as fairly conclusive on all points, but like many others turned out to be less so.

I had not seen Holmes for some weeks, and found myself in a recurring state of longing for a telegram or visit that would spark an adventure once again. My practice kept me busy, and while I was perfectly content with my work, it could turn dull quite quickly and become routine. My loving wife had lately spent a good deal of time visiting an ill friend in Birmingham, and I felt as if I were a bachelor once more. The recent sun-bathed mornings encouraged me to amble through the streets and listen to the bustle of life, while nights were when I ignored the hubbub and enjoyed Tennyson. Still, I pined for the days when my pulse quickened from the ceaseless, yet unpredictable, cases London would deliver to our door.

On the morning of July 1st I received a short message from Holmes requesting my attendance that evening. No other hints or clues were to be found in the terse missive, but I was certain a visit would be worth my while. My appointments for the next few days were trivial and light, and I arranged for a capable colleague to attend to the cases while I made plans to be gone until at least the weekend.

It was a perfect, cloudless late afternoon when I set out. An occasional breeze carried with it the smell of wet soil from last night's rain. The hansom came to a stop in front of 221, and I stepped down onto the damp street. Mrs. Hudson greeted me with her usual cordiality, and I hurried up the familiar steps. As I entered our old sitting room, I found Holmes already engaged with a visitor.

"Watson, so very nice to see you. Six o'clock! Perfect. Please join Inspector Chamberlain and me for what promises to be a most intriguing conversation," Holmes declared, gesturing toward a strapping young man.

"Hello, Holmes. It's always good to see you. Inspector Chamberlain," I said, turning to him. "I've followed your exploits in the papers. Allow me to offer my congratulations on attaining your position at only 30. Putting away that sadistic animal Parker and his assistant was indeed a feather in your cap."

Chamberlain rose to greet me. He stood as tall as Holmes but cut a much stouter figure, and bore the large, roughened hands of a man who preferred to use them. His patent leather shoes and dark brown Scottish tweed suit indicated a man of business and professionalism, as did his neatly groomed beard and moustache.

"Thank you, Dr. Watson," Chamberlain said while shaking my hand. "It's a pleasure to meet you and Mr. Holmes. I trust between the three of us we can come to some conclusion about a most curious affair."

As I took my usual chair, I could see a fire in Holmes's gray eyes. It was a familiar sight, but given the unkempt state of the room, it had been some time since he had experienced it.

Newspapers were strewn about, some sliced to ribbons, and no doubt articles had been clipped out for his files. Books teetered in uneven piles on chairs, spilling onto the floor like some miniature mountain range. The humidity that had muffled London for the past few days had left the room stale and musty. A haze clouded the front windows, doubtless due to the acrid smoke from Holmes's preferred mixture of shag. He had not had a case in weeks, but to my relief I saw no evidence of the damaging syringe. In the middle of the room sat the dining table, surprisingly clean, upon which rested a small wooden box partially wrapped in torn paper.

"This will be a welcome change from summer colds and dog bites." I sat, rubbing my hands together in anticipation.

"Chamberlain was providing the details about a murder that happened in Harrow. If you would be so kind, Inspector, could you start over for my friend?" Holmes sat opposite me in his faded dressing gown, crossing his legs. He lit a cigarette and slowly blew a column of smoke toward the ceiling.

"My pleasure, Mr. Holmes," Chamberlain said, sitting down and re- opening his notebook. "Yesterday at 8:45 a.m., I was called upon to investigate the murder of one Jacob Collier. A neighbor found him face down in the mud behind his house. He was killed by a single stab from behind, angled upward to the heart. Hunting knife, seems to me. Other than those of the neighbor that found the body, there was a single set of footprints that led straight to Collier from the road and back. The rains made some of the prints visible in the muck. Sharp new edges on them. Had an imprint on the sole. I could make out the name F. Pine. That and a lion, I believe."

"F. Pinet. It's a French brand," Holmes said.

"Right. Pinet. Well, the tracks went back to the road, then disappeared. Got in a carriage, no doubt. I don't think we can gather anything from them, though."

"Pray continue," Holmes said quietly.

"I searched the home and found a business card. Collier owned a bookshop on Uxbridge Road in Southall – a place called Falstaff Books. Near as I can make out from some papers I found in his desk, he left Manchester three years ago. After I finished having a look around the home, I headed for the bookshop." He sat forward and shook his head. "What I found there was quite odd. The door was unlocked, and the shop appeared open for business. There weren't any signs of a robbery, though, as the register still had a few pounds in it. But there was no one tending the shop. While we were giving the place a look over, a young boy came in. He said he worked for Collier from time to time, pushing a barrow of books. He confirmed that the place had been opened by Collier that morning, and that he had spoken to him before heading out to push his cart."

"What time did you go to the shop?" Holmes asked. "I arrived at half past ten."

"And when was the last time someone saw Collier there?"

"A gentleman across the street runs a little haberdashery – a Mr. Arnold George," Chamberlain said, looking at his notes. "He recalled seeing a postman enter the place around ten. I confirmed this with that postman once I found him."

"So this postman saw Collier?"

"Well, according to the postman, he didn't notice who signed for the package. Seems he was busying himself with a volume about photography. A little hobby of his, he claimed. Now I figure it must have been the murderer who was behind the counter. He obviously went to the store to rob the place with the owner out of the way."

"What of the delivery signature?" Holmes asked.

"Unreadable. Shaky. Seems as though the murderer made a poor attempt at Collier's signature, for it appeared to read Jack, not Jacob. The two names look enough alike, I guess. Nerves, perhaps."

"Perhaps. Were there any receipts in the register?"

"None. The gent across the street said business was slow that morning. Not much foot traffic to speak of."

"Thank you. Please go on," Holmes said, closing his eyes and rubbing his temples.

"Well, I found nothing at the shop that would indicate what happened to Collier except for this package. It was on the main counter." Holmes handed it to me, and I turned it over in my hands. How many times had I watched Holmes take a mundane object such as this and deduce its history? Sheer repetition should have left an impression, but I was unable to discern anything useful. It was a simply built wooden box wrapped in plain off-white butcher's paper, tied with twine. The paper had been ripped open, one end of the box was pried off, and any contents had been removed.

"There was blood on the box," Chamberlain continued, "as you can see. The blood was far from fresh when I arrived there. Some had dripped down to the papers under it. Inventory papers that were dated from the same day. Someone opened the box and then left it sitting there. I thought it might be important, so I brought it with me. One thing I noticed was that the handwriting on the package matched perfectly with that on the papers under it, and to other papers about the place. The high loops and slant made it easy to identify."

"You have a good eye, Inspector. What do you make of the box, Watson?" Holmes leaned forward.

"I can see nothing about it that would lead to any conclusions," I said. "It's of simple construction, about the size of a small cigar box, and the address of the shop is in a man's hand. The paper has been torn away rather savagely, and the twine is still knotted. Strange that the box wasn't fitted with a hinge or panel, so the only way to open it is to destroy it."

"There isn't much to be gathered from the box, that is true, and unfortunately the postmark has been smudged. I can make nothing of it," Holmes said as he took the box back. "However, there are a couple of minor points. The person who made it has little experience with carpentry, is right-handed, enjoys black sausages, and may have spent time in the Navy. The last point is purely speculative, I'm afraid."

I frowned at the box. "Once more I am at a loss about how you come to these conclusions," I said.

"Allow me to enlighten you. The box is made from scrap wood, unevenly cut, with nails much too large for this size box. They have caused the wood to split in one or two places." Holmes pointed to cracks in the side panels. "Add to that the marks of a hammer from a right-handed man who missed his target several times, and you can conclude this was not made by an experienced woodworker. The paper and twine are types regularly used by butchers, and you can just smell the hint of sausage – a rather unique recipe, I might add. There were no contents in the box, so we must conclude that someone took them."

"And the Navy?" I asked.

"Again, this is pure speculation, but the type of knot used to tie the twine is called a figure-eight knot. It is used primarily by sailors, but can be found anywhere there are boats. I cannot see a sailor making the box, however, for that well-known nautical neatness of hand is contradicted by the shoddiness of construction."

"I'll be, Mr. Holmes," Chamberlain said, shaking his head. "I've heard of your abilities when it comes to reading things, but I'm glad to finally see it for myself."

Holmes eased back in his armchair.

"Can you describe the dead man?" I asked. Holmes shot a quick glance and smile at me.

"Mid-forties, 15 stone or so, about five and a half feet, with graying hair. Had a scar on his left cheek just below the eye. He was wearing working clothes, and his muddy boots were old. Certainly not the ones that made the footmarks. Blood had pooled on his back and ran down both of his sides. Mud caked his pant cuffs."

"What can you tell us about the home?" Holmes inquired.

"Quiet place. Small. Country furniture. Local items.

Nothing of any terrible cost." Chamberlain again opened his notebook. "A kitchen table and chairs, a writing desk, a small fireplace, one large bed, wardrobe, and a couple of parlor chairs. One big room for everything. Sits on about an acre or so with a small barn in back. A few pigs and chickens. No signs of a wife or children. Simple, really. Rather fond of his own face, though. Had a painting of himself hanging on the wall. Scar and all. Nice frame, too."

"Did you look in the barn?" Holmes asked.

"Of course, sir. Found some work clothes like the dead man was wearing hanging on a line in the loft, and a small unmade bed in there, as well. Curious as the one in the house was perfectly made. Looks like Collier preferred to sleep near his animals. Outside of that it was a standard barn. I should also add that there were no witnesses to the crime."

"What of the bookshop? Any footprints?" I asked.

"Several in the store, but only one person's behind the counter, Doctor. The light rain last night left enough mud to leave tracks, but I could find only the one set past the counter and down into the cellar," Chamberlain said.

"No signs of a struggle? No forced entry?"

"Nothing."

Holmes clutched his hands together, closed his eyes, and leaned his head back against the worn fabric of the chair.

"What do you make of the blood on the counter, Inspector?" I asked.

"It must have come from the man who opened the box."

"Yes. The blood," Holmes interrupted, "was from the man cutting himself when he opened the box. He was desperate to get at what was inside, and in his haste caught his skin on the splintered wood. There is nothing more to be learned from it.

"This case certainly has some curious points about it, Inspector. I should like to contemplate it further. Thank you for stopping in," Holmes said as he stood and walked to the door.

"Very good, Mr. Holmes." Chamberlain's brows rose. "I do have a murderer to catch. I'll inform you if we find anything more, but, to be honest, I was hoping for better tonight."

"I'm afraid there is nothing more I can tell you. Goodnight, Inspector."

Chamberlain shook our hands and made his way to the door. "Good evening, gentlemen," he said with a tip of his bowler.

The door closed behind him, and Holmes smiled at me.

"An excellent case to end my dreary days. What do you make of the whole business, Watson?" Holmes asked as he retook his chair.

"Perplexing. It seems to me that the murderer certainly could be the one who signed for the package at the bookshop. He must have gone there looking for something. Who else would have known the place would be vacated?"

"It is a possibility," Holmes said softly. "He could easily have assumed the role of an employee. And if he were searching for something, it could very well be whatever was in that box." Holmes sat forward, put his elbows on his knees, and pressed his fingertips together. "Curious that it has the murdered man's handwriting on it. He must have sent it to himself to avoid having it found. But why? Why not just take it along with him when he went to work? It is paramount that we find out what was inside."

"I must confess at being absolutely befuddled. What do you think we should do next?"

"Dinner and a walk. What do you say, Watson – are you up for a little night air? I find it most restorative to the senses."

"I should be delighted."

We dined and passed the time in splendid conversation. Many and varied were the subjects we spoke of. I talked about the newest advances in medicine, and how I was enjoying my married life, after which Holmes thrilled me by recounting the recent championship boxing bout between Dixon and Wallace in Soho. The evening was brought to a close with both of us lounging at Baker Street with pipes in hand, and enjoying the occasional recollection or memory. Not a word was spoken about the case. We retired early, both ready for the resumption of the case the next day.

The next morning dawned fair. I made my way down to breakfast to find Holmes already dressed and drinking his coffee.

"Good morning, Holmes."

"Ah, Doctor. I trust you slept well."

"Very. Thank you," I said as I picked up the newspaper. A small article had been emphatically circled.

"The piece you see there is about the murder. Nothing new to be reported. It reflects everything we already know. However, I have a few items I would like to look into concerning the matter. Would you care to join me?"

"Certainly. Where are we going?"

"The paper that wrapped the box is nothing special in itself, but the smell of the sausage it had once covered was a particular type that is only made in one or two places in the city. I have some questions I would like to ask the proprietor."

"Sounds like the perfect way to spend a morning," I smiled.

"Excellent. Let us finish Mrs. Hudson's fine eggs and toast and we'll be on our way."

Within the hour we were in a cab headed for Southall. Our ride, like many before in our partnership, was spent in silence.

We stopped on High Street in front of a butchery. The windows displayed the rather grotesque and elongated carcasses of numerous hogs and fowl. A breeze carried the smell of cooking animal flesh. The bakers, confectioners, and brewers that lined the street added their own unique smells, resulting in an aroma that confused the senses but roused the appetite.

We stepped inside and found ourselves between two long glass counters which contained all matter of headcheeses, rumps, and shoulders on mounds of ice. Sausages and hams hung from hooks above, and bones for soup and stock were in buckets on the floor in front of the display cases.

"Fancy a taste of somethin', gents?" From behind a curtain stepped a small, thin man with large sideburns and liver spots beneath the remaining strands of hair on his head. He took off his bloodied gloves, tossed them behind the curtain, and wiped his hands on a clean corner of his spattered apron.

"My name is Sherlock Holmes. This is my friend, Dr. Watson. I was hoping I might take a moment of your time and ask about a customer of yours."

"Mr. Sherlock 'Olmes. Pleasure to meet you, it is. Stevens is my name. C.L. Stevens." The man gave a nod to Holmes. "Fine work on that nasty murder of the Prime Minister's cousin. Read about it in the paper, I did."

"Thank you. Now, to the matter at hand, my good man. It is my understanding that you have done business with Jacob Collier."

"'Ow come you be needin' to know that?" the man said, cocking his head to the side.

"Forgive me, Mr. Stevens. Collier is an old acquaintance of mine. Back to our college days, actually. Rugby players. I'm responsible for the scar under his eye."

"Scar, Mr. 'Olmes?" Stevens asked in some confusion.

"Well, that was many, many years ago. Perhaps it has healed up completely." Holmes pointed at the links around the ceiling. "Mr. Collier said your black sausage was the best in the city."

"Best anywhere. Recipe passed down for several generations," he said smiling.

"Excellent," Holmes said. "I was hoping you could tell me the last time you saw Mr. Collier. His shop is closed, and

I can't seem to locate him."

Stevens rubbed his chin. "Always odd for someone to up and leave without tellin' no one. Can't say, though, if that's the case for Jacob. Been a customer of mine since 'e bought 'is shop. Nervous little man. Likes to live the peaceful life. Tends a small farm. Supplies the 'ogs for the sausage, 'e does. Just did some dealin' with 'im a couple days ago. Monday, it was."

"Can you tell me what time you saw him that day?" Holmes asked. "Oh, 'e sent a runner with a note. Does that sometimes. I'll 'ave the time in me ledger." He stepped into a side door and back out a moment later. "Well, 'ere it is. Just as I told you," he proclaimed, pointing to his ledger. "I wrote it in me book at a quarter to ten. 'Ere's the note 'e 'ad brought in," he said as he thrust the paper toward us.

Holmes took the paper and studied it carefully. "Does he ever send one of his workers?"

"'E only 'as the one, Mr. 'Olmes. Young boy. Pushes a cart for 'im."

"When was the last time you actually saw Mr. Collier?"

"Oh, it's been since the week prior. Often comes in 'imself. Once a week. Really loves me sausages. Must eat them and nothin' else. Orders enough for two people."

Holmes placed a half-crown in the butcher's hand. "I would like to thank you for your time and bid you a good day."

"Well, sure, if that's all you be needin'."

Holmes tipped his hat and started out the door. We stepped out into the sunlight of the day and stood silent for a moment at the edge of the street.

"Holmes, Collier was dead an hour before that. How can this be?"

"There is something most foul here, Watson. Nothing is at it seems. That note had Collier's handwriting on it. He must have sent it."

"A forgery, perhaps."

"But about sausage? To what end? No, there is something deeper here. Something we haven't seen." Holmes tapped his cane impatiently on the ground.

"Perhaps we should take a look at his home in Harrow," I said.

"I do not believe there is anything more to be learned there. Chamberlain's notes were extensive enough. Also, there is no doubt that the place has been carelessly searched and the grounds tromped over.

"There are a number of things about this case that make it quite unique, my friend. I suspect that we will find out more about Jacob Collier than he ever wanted known."

"So what now?"

"Back to Baker Street. I am expecting a telegram – a response to one I sent this morning before you rose. It will confirm an idea I had this morning concerning a case in Greater Manchester."

Upon our arrival Mrs. Hudson met us in the hall.

"Mr. Holmes? There's a gentleman waiting to see you. Been here about 20 minutes."

"Thank you. Could you send up some tea, please?"

We entered our sitting room and found a gentleman standing before our fireplace. He was dressed in a worsted suit with high black boots, and on the table lay his top hat and yellow leather gloves. He turned to look at us, clutching his lapels. One of his hands was bandaged, and the wrapping had loosened.

Holmes hesitated for a barely perceptible moment and then walked over to the man. "My name is Sherlock Holmes. This is Dr. Watson. Who do we have the pleasure of meeting?"

"My name is not important," the man said curtly. "I am not one to mince words so I shall get to the point. I understand you have some interest in the murder of a bookshop owner named Jacob Collier."

"I'm afraid I'm not at liberty to discuss the matter.

Perhaps you should approach Scotland Yard with your concerns," Holmes said.

"Then you *are* looking at it."

"Without making an admittance of any kind, I will ask how it is that you believe I am familiar with this murder at all?"

"Everyone has a price, Mr. Holmes, including a constable ordered to guard the door of his bookshop."

"Sir, whatever I may or may not know about the situation, I will not be discussing anything with you or anyone else save the Inspector who has been assigned to the case."

The man's jaw tightened and his fists balled.

"Your bandage is tattered," Holmes said. "Watson, would you be so good as to change the dressing for him?"

"Leave it be," the man barked, hiding his hand behind his back. "Jacob Collier was a friend of mine," he continued. "He disappeared, and I've only recently found him. I hear, however, that he has been murdered. As I am still acquainted with his family, I am interested in conveying any news I can. I can make it worth your while to tell me what I want to know."

"I am terribly sorry, sir, but I cannot help you. I am certain that Mr. Collier's family appreciates your concern, and I ask you to give them my condolences. Thank you for stopping in," Holmes said with an insincere smile.

The gentleman scowled and breathed deeply through flared nostrils. Without another word he grabbed his hat and gloves and hurried through the door. His steps checked, and he slowly descended the stairs. The front door slammed closed.

"Well, that was unsettling. What do you make of him?" I asked. "What I make of him is that whomever we were just addressing is not who he says he is. Also, he was wearing lifts in his shoes to make himself appear taller. His high-heeled boots added to that deception. Did you notice how slowly he descended the stairs? He is not comfortable wearing the lifts."

"Incredible."

"His moustache was real enough, but it and his hair were dyed darker."

"So, who were we talking to?"

Holmes peered out the window. "I have a suspicion, but I cannot commit at the moment."

"Should we follow him?"

"No. I saw the unmistakable shape of a revolver in his right-hand pocket, and any man who is brazen enough to pay off a policeman and then bribe others for data regarding a murder is not a man to be taken lightly. "Watson, I need to step out for a few moments. I shall return shortly." Holmes grabbed his hat and was downstairs in seconds.

Mrs. Hudson appeared with a tray. "I apologize for the delay, Doctor. Where is Mr. Holmes going?"

"Thank you, Mrs. Hudson. He'll be back soon. I'll keep the pot warm for him until he gets back."

No more than 15 minutes passed before Holmes reappeared. "I think we should have this little problem unknotted by tonight, at least if my sources don't fail me."

"Where did you go?"

"When one wishes to know what happens on the streets of London, one has to go to those streets."

"Ah. You've been to see the Irregulars, haven't you?"

"They are the most valuable institution for information, next to the press. As you know, they have been helpful on a number of occasions. I have Wiggins and his friends gathering some data for me, and if my suspicions are correct, we should have an answer to my query in no more than a couple hours."

"And until then?"

"I have sent for Inspector Chamberlain. I would prefer having an official member of the Force with us. Unless I am very much mistaken, he will have learned nothing about the murder of Jacob Collier. Ah! I see you've kept the tea warm.

Excellent."

As the clock on the mantel sounded four, we heard heavy footsteps climbing our stairs. The Inspector appeared at the door.

"What's this all about, Mr. Holmes?"

"I was hoping you might bring us up to date on what you know concerning the murder of Mr. Collier," Holmes said.

"I'm afraid there isn't much to tell." Chamberlain sat. "Since we have no witnesses to give us a description of the killer, no usable evidence left at the crime scene, and no way to know what happened at the bookshop, my men have come up with nothing."

"Any theories?" Holmes asked as he rose and stood at the window. "I still believe the man in the shop who signed for the package was the murderer. It all went so. Collier left for work that morning and arrived at his usual time – probably about seven, as I understand it. Sometime around eight he realized he had forgotten something important at home and returned to retrieve it. In doing so he unintentionally left the shop door unlocked. When he arrived home he must have interrupted a robbery and was stabbed while running away. The killer then went to his shop to rob the place, and was nearly unmasked when the postman arrived. After that he disappeared. I've yet to find him, but I will."

"Excellent, Inspector. However, I believe there is more to this story than you may have realized," Holmes said as he gazed down at the busy street. Suddenly a slight smile crossed his lips and he started across the room. "And unless I am mistaken part of the answer should be coming through our door in seconds."

Holmes opened the door just in time for a young page to enter.

"I have a message for you, Mr. Holmes," the boy said, holding out a folded sheet of paper, and trying to catch his breath.

Holmes took the paper and opened it. His smile grew and

he dug into his pocket. He handed the lad a coin. "Thank you. Your expedience is very much appreciated."

"Thank you, sir. Good day," the runner said. He turned on his heel and left.

"Well, gentlemen, one half of the mystery has been cleared up. Now we only have to wait for the answer to the second half. I suspect it will be here very soon."

"Out with it, Mr. Holmes," Chamberlain scowled. "We *are* talking about a murder here, you know."

Holmes handed the paper to Chamberlain. As he read it his brow furrowed. "What's the meaning of this? We already know this," he exclaimed.

"Read it aloud for the good Doctor, if you please."

"'JACOB COLLIER IS DEAD.' If this is some kind of joke, Mr. Holmes, I'll have you spend a night looking through bars."

"I assure you it is nothing of the kind. What the note *doesn't* say is confirmation of a clue you didn't even know you had, Inspector."

"You little rascal, you!" Mrs. Hudson's voice was shrill. "I'll take my broom to your breeches to teach you some manners!"

Seconds later a scruffy ragamuffin burst through the door.

"We found him, Mr. Holmes. We found him," the boy said with excitement. "Here's the address."

Holmes glanced at the message.

"Good work, my boy." Holmes scribbled on a new sheet of paper and handed it to the boy. "Please take this to the man."

"Yes, sir."

"Here is your promised sixpence. Make sure to have each of your associates who aided you stop by for theirs tomorrow, will you?"

The boy smiled, gave a quick salute, and left.

Holmes turned to Chamberlain. "Inspector, if you would

care to accompany Dr. Watson and me to Southall, your name should appear in the papers once again by tomorrow."

"This best work out, Holmes," grumbled Chamberlain as we descended the stair. "Valuable time has already been wasted."

In Southall, our brougham pulled up to the curb. We climbed down. Before us rose a fashionable, narrow-windowed building of five stories.

Chamberlain frowned at Holmes. "All right, Mr. Holmes. What are we doing here?"

"Isn't that Collier's bookshop across the street?" I asked. "It is," Holmes said, "and it's under observation."

"By the murderer?" Chamberlain asked.

"Patience, my good man. Note that we are standing just down from The Grand Garden Hotel? Inside is a man with whom you will need to speak. If my calculations are correct, he should be in the lobby very soon. I would ask that you have your revolver ready, as he may not go easily."

We entered the doors of the hotel and found a quiet spot in the corner on a pair of Chesterfields. After several minutes Holmes quietly pointed to the stairs at the far end of the room. We stood and followed closely behind him along the wall and columns, getting to within about ten feet of the man.

"Jack," Holmes said in a low tone.

The man – the same one we had spoken to a short time ago at Baker Street – spun around with a look of sheer horror on his face, his hand already slipping into his waistcoat pocket.

"That'll do you no good, sir," said Chamberlain, pulling his pistol and pointing it at the man.

Holmes walked over and stared hard at the man. "Gentlemen, I would like for you both to meet Mr. Jack Collier – brother to Jacob Collier."

"What?" cried Chamberlain. I shared his confusion.

"Let us find someplace more private, shall we?" Holmes

asked. "We need not put this man in any more danger."

Chamberlain took Collier by the arm. "Don't do anything stupid, Mr. Collier. I'm a quick shot, I can assure you of that. In fact, I'll have the piece in your pocket," he said as he gently pulled the gun out. Once we were ensconced in a private room, courtesy of the hotel proprietor, the Inspector shoved Collier into a seat and turned to Holmes. "Now, Mr. Holmes, what is the meaning of all of this?"

"Gentlemen, let me start by saying that Jacob is the poor soul who was murdered in Harrow," Holmes began. "He was mistaken for his brother Jack here and lost his life as a result. This killer had discovered the whereabouts of Jack and went to his home to exact revenge for a past crime. He mistakenly killed the brother. Jack was at work and was not aware of the situation until the mysterious package arrived at his shop. That package was a signal that something was amiss."

Collier shifted in his seat and glared up at Holmes. Chamberlain's grip tightened on the man's shoulder.

"Jack is the identical twin of Jacob," Holmes continued. "Thus the mistaken identity. The only true way to tell them apart quickly was the scar on Jacob's cheek. The painting in the house in Harrow was of your brother. Is that correct, Jack?" Holmes looked down at the man. Collier stared straight ahead and said nothing.

"I first began to suspect the existence of a twin when I spoke to your butcher, Mr. Stevens. I made a passing mention of the scar, but he had no knowledge of one. It was also impossible for someone to send a runner with an order an hour after he was dead. The thought of a twin had not occurred to me before then, but it seemed a plausible theory after that. By using this possibility, I was able to construct a timeline of events. At ten a.m. the postman entered your shop with the package. You recognized it immediately, cut your hand forcing it open, removed the contents, and were so shaken that you left the shop without even locking the door.

From there you put into motion a plan already conceived."

"What was in the box, Mr. Holmes?" asked Chamberlain.

"Money, Inspector. Enough to disappear again if necessary. It had been stolen from Jack's old boss, Mr. Benjamin Tower."

Collier looked at Holmes, his mouth hanging slightly open.

"Jack here found it necessary to use Jacob's name in place of his own because he had declared, just before they disappeared into London, that Jacob had died. There was even a funeral. All this was necessary to fool the Tower family into believing they no longer needed to hunt Jacob. If they saw that name they wouldn't think twice about it. Jack was the name they would be looking for."

"My gracious, Holmes. Why?" I asked in astonishment.

"Mr. Tower is a well-known criminal. His power and money have maddeningly allowed him to slip the bonds of justice. Politicians and judges may be swayed, you see, and as a result of some of his more monstrous crimes. I have kept a file on him. A number of things associated with this case seemed familiar, so I sent a message to a colleague in Manchester, asking him to look into the facts of a three- year-old case."

Collier's shoulders sagged.

"Your brother killed one of Tower's sons in a heated exchange – an exchange about missing money that *you* were suspected of taking. It got out of control and Jacob stepped in and beat the man to death. For his protection, you faked his death, and then you both disappeared into London. When you arrived, you changed your name to your brother's. Shortly thereafter, you bought a bookshop. Meanwhile, Jacob led a hidden life in Harrow. No one knew he existed anymore."

"I'll ask you not to think ill of my brother, Mr. Holmes. He did what he did out of loyalty. He was merely protecting me. The only sin he ever committed was being born a little slow in the mind, and without the ability to stop when he was angered. He was all I had in this world. Our mother died when we were very young. I took care of him, and vowed to always do so. Jacob was the reason for the money being taken. I had emptied our reserves. Our father died from consumption, leaving us nothing. It drove him mad that neither of his sons would follow in his footsteps as a Navy man."

I looked at Holmes and saw a slight grin on his face.

"I used Jacob's name out of my love for him," Collier continued. "Tower's people thought he was dead, and we had moved over 200 miles away. I even went so far as to purchase passage on three different ships to three different countries under my actual name to throw them off my trail. For three years I never suspected a problem. I was certain we were safe and would never be found."

"How did you come to be discovered then?" Chamberlain asked.

"A simple slip of the tongue, sir. Nothing more. A customer in town on business was looking at a book about Manchester, talking about being from there, and I made a few careless references to my past. He must have put things together once he knew that I was from the area and saw the name on the business cards on the counter. I have talked to so many people, but never once made a mistake in talking about myself. Overconfidence or stupidity, I suppose. That devil, damn the fortunes, must have been one of a thousand men in Tower's network. He alerted them, and by that night they had probably found out all they needed to know. They came to the house early thinking I wouldn't have left for the shop yet. Found poor Jacob out back feeding his hens. Mistook him from behind for me. Had they seen the scar, which the Tower boy created with his knife during their struggle, they would have known. But, they didn't." Collier let out a deep sigh and lowered his head. "Jacob made that box for me, and I filled it with all the money I could afford.

I had to wrap and tie it, though. I saw it at your flat, Mr. Holmes, and even though I wanted it back, I thought it best to leave, as I didn't want to give you any clues as to my true identity. "I would put the box out every morning for the postman, and Jacob would bring it back inside before the man was scheduled to arrive. That was the arrangement. If the package shipped it meant that something was wrong, and that I needed to flee. If I didn't see it by lunch I could rest a little easier that the morning had passed uneventful. When I saw the package I left immediately. I jumped in a hansom. There is a room I keep in Brentford should I need it. Near the docks."

Holmes nodded. "Of course. But as you were leaving, you saw Thomas Cady lurking about."

Collier straightened and once again stared at Holmes in disbelief.

He sat for a moment in silence and then cleared his throat.

"Tower's money has long arms," he said, nodding. "Cady would stop at nothing for him. I knew it was Cady, though I only caught a glimpse of him. He prefers to do his work in the mornings. That's the reason a signal between Jacob and me wasn't necessary later in the day. After I saw Cady, I hurried back to the shop. I quickly made my way into this hotel here and got a room that gave me a view of the shop. I watched it constantly. Every moment I was awake. I was going to wait until I saw no one I might even slightly recognize, but with my nerves being on edge it seemed everyone looked suspicious. My mind was torn between staying long enough to see my beloved brother buried, and leaving the city for my own self-preservation. I could not even claim Jacob's body for fear of being seen. It has torn my heart apart. I have, however, paid to make sure he gets a proper burial. Anonymously, of course."

"How could you be certain that the package arriving meant his death?" I asked.

"It would almost have to be," Collier said. "Jacob was

very healthy, and as strong as Samson. He lived a clean life. Never had a vice. Didn't know of them. He had put on a few pounds recently because of those awful smelling black sausages. Still, it wasn't a concern."

"And when you came to Baker Street earlier, you thought perhaps I wouldn't realize I was talking to someone in disguise?" Holmes asked. "The lifts in your boots were a clever touch, but merely made you look clumsy. I will compliment your attempt, however, as you managed to add four inches to your height."

"I needed this disguise. I'm thinner now than my brother, but we still resemble each other. I couldn't risk being seen. I would have been a dead man for sure. So, I dyed my hair and moustache this morning and then went out to buy the shoes. I did it just so I could come to see you and find out what you knew. I had no idea what was happening with my brother's murder case. I went out bundled up late last night and spoke with the constable across the street at the shop. That's how I came to know about your involvement." Collier removed his hat and used a jacket sleeve to dab his brow. "I must say, I was shocked to get your message. Figured I must have given myself away again. However, I was on my way."

"It was necessary to draw you out," Holmes said. "The closeness of your room here would have been dangerous for everyone involved."

"How did you ever find me? I gave you no idea of who I was," Collier said.

"I took note of the cab you used as you left. The mare pulling it was brown and white, the rear legs themselves being completely white. The cab itself had damage to the right side window. It was easy enough to have found. I could only hope you didn't stop and change carriages, but I suspected you wished to get back to wherever you were staying and take off those uncomfortable boots. It took my informants only a couple of hours to determine where you had been taken. After that, they only had to wait to see someone matching your description."

"That seems to be everything, but who is this Cady fellow you talked about, Mr. Holmes?" asked Chamberlain.

"He is one of Tower's henchmen, and the murderer of Jacob. I know of his crimes, even though his name is always kept out of the paper. However, he does have a fondness for a particular brand of French boot."

"I'll track him to Hell's doorstep if needed," Chamberlain said. He lifted Collier up by the arm. "I'm afraid I'm going to have to take you in, sir. I believe there's a charge of embezzlement you'll have to answer for."

It was some weeks later I read in the Times that Chamberlain had shot and killed Thomas Cady on a foggy morning in Derby. The murderer of Jacob Collier, as well as countless others, was dead. Chamberlain was unable to connect him to Benjamin Tower, and so Tower was never brought to trial for any of the crimes of which he was suspected. Upon speaking with Holmes afterwards, I had the impression that he was unlikely to stop trying to make sure he paid for his offenses.

Jack Collier had pleaded his case before a Manchester judge. He was not allowed to go free, but instead was given a sentence of two years at Wandsworth and ordered to pay back any money he had left that had belonged to Tower. Upon his release he promptly disappeared again.

The Singular Case of
the Unrepentant Husband

by William Patrick Maynard

f the many adventures that I shared with Sherlock Holmes, the case I record here may well stand as the most troubling. It began, unremarkably, with a telephone conversation. My wife had come to rely upon that infernal device which so often disturbs a man's thoughts at the most inconvenient hour for the most mundane reasons. It was not unimportant in this instance, as it happened, and my wife insisted that I pay a visit to my old friend as a consequence.

It was half past 12 in the afternoon of the following day when I arrived at the great house on Baker Street. Mrs. Turner answered the doorbell and I saw a glimmer of relief flash across her features.

"Good afternoon, Mrs. Turner. Is he home?"

The matronly Scotswoman rolled her eyes theatrically as she stepped aside to allow me to enter.

"Where else might he be, Doctor Watson? Where else could he conduct his odious scientific experiments or pace the floor at all hours of the night? How my sister tolerates that man is beyond my ken. I'll be the one needing the holiday once she returns."

"Right you are. Silly of me to have asked in the first place, I suppose. Well, never mind. I'll soon have him out of your hair."

"You have a case for him, I hope?"

I detected the hint of anticipation in her voice and knew that Holmes must have driven the poor woman to her limit.

"If all goes well, I do, Mrs. Turner."

The last I saw of her was the smile creasing her lined face as I made my way upstairs to Holmes's rooms.

My old friend lay sprawled upon the davenport. Street maps were unfolded and lay strewn over the table and on the floor. An empty tea cup was overturned on top of the map nearest the front legs of the table.

"What is it this time, Mrs. Turner?"

Holmes did not even glance up as I entered the room. His toneless voice betrayed his boredom with his enforced solitude. I was relieved he had long since broken his addiction to that awful drug that so often claimed him at times such as this. I cleared my throat pointedly.

"Watson! What an unexpected surprise!"

His face registered what appeared to be genuine delight at seeing me.

"It shouldn't be unexpected, Holmes, I have rung you three times since yesterday morning. You told Mrs. Turner on every occasion that you had no wish to speak with me."

"Did she tell you that?" Holmes asked as he sat up, stiffly. "The woman's incorrigible. It's high time I had her put down for distemper. Perhaps I'll have her stuffed. I could keep her in the hallway next to the hat stand. She'd make a lovely conversation piece."

"One must entertain visitors if one is to have conversations, Holmes."

"That is a fair point, Watson, and a welcome reminder that you have business to attend to unless I'm very much mistaken."

"Did I say anything of the sort?"

"Well, I certainly didn't extend an invitation."

"That's perfectly beastly of you, Holmes, but also oddly appropriate."

"Is it? Pray tell me more."

"I have a case for you to consider taking and, coincidentally, it involves an acquaintance of mine who will not stay dead."

"You interest me, Watson. Go on; go on...while I search for my socks."

"Try looking at the end of your feet."

"Not these socks, Watson!" he shot me a reproachful glance as he wriggled his toes. "I mean the socks I removed when I retired last night – or this morning."

"Alfred Habersham is the gentleman who refuses to rest in peace."

"Habersham...Habersham..." Holmes muttered as he leaned over to peer underneath the davenport.

"Yes, the late Alfred Habersham was a patient of mine. Not a particularly lucrative one, but respectable nonetheless. He was an author as well, although I daresay he couldn't have made a go of it had he not been fortunate enough to come into a princely sum of money at an early age which allowed him to indulge his passion without fear of wondering where his next meal was coming from."

I had started to wander about the room as I spoke. It was the only way to keep my concentration while Holmes continued to be preoccupied with his missing socks. I spied the stray animals resting on the small writing desk by the window. Lifting them gingerly, I brought them back to Holmes, who was on his hands and knees like a hound upon a scent, peering intently under the davenport. I dropped them on his back as I continued.

"Very conservative fellow our Habersham was. He spent precious little of his wealth except when absolutely necessary. He married well. A nice sensible girl, although I fear she left her girlhood behind quite some time ago. No children, but he did have a ward. A distant relative he sent to a boarding school in Switzerland."

Holmes sat upright suddenly and the socks fell from his

back and onto the floor in front of him.

"Ah! There they are! Darn socks!"

"Really, Holmes, such humor is beneath you."

"Humor is beneath everyone. That's what makes it humorous."

"Are you paying attention? I daresay you haven't heard a word I've said."

Holmes's brow furrowed in irritation at my rebuke. "Of course I have! Alfred Habersham died leaving a widow and a ward well off since he was a miserly old sod, and you have yet to get to the interesting bit about how he is refusing to stay dead. Not very respectable behavior for a chap you seem to consider so respectable."

I smiled with unhidden amusement.

"Well said, Holmes. Although I should make it clear that it is the claim of Mrs. Habersham that her husband is not resting peacefully in his grave. She claims he has appeared to her twice during the past week. The first time she thought she was dreaming. The second time she says she was wide awake and had only just retired for the night."

"Sounds like her nerves are frayed."

"There is little question of that, yet somehow...I believe her." Holmes raised an eyebrow quizzically.

"You see, there's more to it than just seeing her late husband. He speaks to her."

"He speaks to her?"

"Yes, he speaks to her. Confesses might be the more appropriate word. He apparently cannot rest with a guilty conscience and has told her some rather terrible things."

"What sort of terrible things?"

"Crimes he claims he committed when he was younger... indiscretions that she knew nothing of during their long marriage."

"Are these claims credible?"

"Well, his wife certainly thinks so."

"What do you propose I do about it, set a trap to catch a

ghost?"

"What I expect you to do, Holmes is to restore peace to a poor widow. Prove that these ghostly visitations are the result of nervous excitement or grief. She is beside herself with the thought that the man she loved was a blackguard. Imagine her pain to hear that he wronged others when he was a young man and, worse still, was unfaithful to her for decades. She could scarcely keep from crying when she told Mary about it."

"Ah, your scheming wife put you up to this. I might have known." "That is uncalled for and you know it, Holmes. Mary merely relayed the story to me and I sought your aid on my own."

Holmes sighed and sunk back in the davenport, arms folded across his chest.

"You're being disingenuous on that last point at the very least."

"Oh for heaven's sake, Holmes, I've known Alfred and Olivia Habersham for ages, and Mary and Olivia have become quite close since we've been married. You have only to speak with her and make her see reason."

"Watson, the woman sees and converses with her husband's ghost. She is not likely to be receptive to anything approaching reason."

Silence hung over the room. I stood still and stared at the well-worn carpet beneath my feet.

"Oh, all right. I'll come along, but not more than 20 minutes, do you understand? If she has not come round to the idea by that time, I want to hear no more about the matter."

I shook his hand effusively.

"Thank you, Holmes. Mary will be thrilled."

He grumbled in response, but I caught the flicker of a smile cross his sullen face.

"You know...you're not nearly the curmudgeon you pretend to be some of the time."

My old friend snorted derisively.

"I fear that I never mastered the art of disguising my feelings."

"That is hardly true and we both know it, Holmes."

He sat there silent for a moment before breaking into a hearty laugh.

We arrived at the modest Praed Street residence of the late Alfred Habersham a short while later. Olivia Habersham answered the door to their apartment. She was an attractive woman whose beauty remained undimmed by the passing years. I noted that her eyes betrayed both exhaustion and emotional fragility. Her eyebrows arched in irritation, a tell-tale sign of her Irish heritage, at being disturbed by unwelcome visitors, but her features quickly softened when she recognized my face.

"John! My word, what brings you here? Do come in. You should have telephoned first. Oh dear, I must look a fright. Is Mary with you?"

Olivia's mouth quivered as she caught sight of Holmes standing to my left, just out of sight of the door.

"Good afternoon, Olivia. Allow me to present my dear friend, Mr. Sherlock Holmes of Baker Street."

Olivia stared at him a moment, her mouth curling into a look of mild repulsion.

"Oh dear," Olivia repeated, listlessly. "You're that consulting detective everyone talks about, aren't you?"

Holmes responded with a slight inclination of his head.

"If it isn't too much trouble," I asked, "might we come in, Olivia?" She stepped aside for us to enter, but never took her eyes off Holmes.

"I can't understand the need for it myself, what with Scotland Yard and all."

"Yes, well that's why we've dropped by you see. Mary mentioned to me this morning that you have been troubled of late, and while Scotland Yard would not be of much use, I do believe Holmes, who has considerable experience handling some fairly peculiar cases such as yours, might be of some assistance."

Olivia blinked a few times, her mouth hanging agape.

"I don't know what to say, John, other than you really should have telephoned first. I don't wish to be rude, Mr. Holmes, but this is a difficult time right now, and I don't see what you could possibly do that would...."

"Mrs. Habersham, I beg you..." Holmes's tone was calm and conciliatory, "please at least share with me in your own words what you have experienced and then let me judge whether or not I can prove to be useful to you."

The Irish eyebrows arched once more as her cheeks flushed with emotion.

"I'm sure you both mean well, gentlemen, but this is hardly a matter for Scotland Yard, much less consulting detectives. However, should I find myself in need of such services as you render, I would not hesitate to call. Good day to you both, gentlemen."

Without a further word, we were ushered back out into the hallway as the door promptly closed in our faces and was bolted shut.

"I'll be damned!"

"Oh, I shouldn't go so far as to damn you for this wasted trip, Watson," Holmes sighed, "so long as you listen to me and not your well- meaning wife the next time round."

The incident left me in a foul mood the rest of the day. I was sullen and ill-tempered with Mary and retired for bed early, instead of staying up late reading as was my fashion. I awoke dreadfully early the next morning to an unexpected phone call.

"John?" the voice on the other end trembled.

"Yes. Who is this, please?" I asked, bitterly rubbing my bleary eyes. "It's Olivia."

"Olivia...." I repeated the name, momentarily puzzled, "... of course, Olivia! Good morning! What can I do for you?"

"Your detective friend...."

"Holmes?" I asked, genuinely puzzled.

"Yes. I need him. I don't think I can stand another night in this house. I don't know whether I'm going mad or whether Alfred really is speaking to me."

I scratched my uncombed hair, absently. "Olivia, please try to relax...."

"John, do me the favor...the tremendous favor of bringing your friend round right after lunch or sooner still. I must know what is happening. I must know the truth. I cannot bear the thought of another night of Alfred coming to me and telling me those ghastly things he's done."

Her voice trailed away in uncontrolled sobs.

"Keep your spirits up, Olivia. We will get to the bottom of this, I promise you."

I returned the receiver to its cradle and sank back in the bed. "What was that all about?" Mary rolled over and asked, groggily.

"Poor old Alfred is still appearing to Olivia and confessing his misdeeds. She wants me to retain Holmes's services to set things to right."

"Well isn't that a good thing?" Mary asked.

"I don't relish the thought of convincing Holmes to make the trip a second time. You know how he is about having his time wasted. Add to the fact that Olivia treated him as if he were a leper and you can imagine why I am dreading speaking to him."

Mary clicked her tongue at me as she rolled back over in bed, "I don't know why you insist on sticking your nose in other people's affairs, darling."

I sat there a moment, dumbstruck, before replying, "It is what a doctor is paid to do, dearest."

"I am not paid to be insulted, Watson."

To say that Holmes was obstinate this morning was a considerable understatement.

"If you have nothing further to say to me," he said burying his eyes in the newspaper, "then I suggest you return home and leave me to my own work."

I sat there a moment, considering the best course of action before settling on righteous indignation.

"What work, Holmes? You haven't taken a case in weeks. You told me so yourself!"

Holmes slapped the newspaper down on his table in irritation. "You bring up an excellent point, Watson."

"Thank you," I nodded my head, hopefully. "Olivia Habersham personally requested that I ask for your help. I'm sure that you won't be insulted in any way now that..."

"... now that she knows she needs me," Holmes finished my sentence, ruefully.

"We could still make lunch if we hurry," I said quietly.

Holmes stared at the newspaper again before sweeping it off the table with a hurried gesture, "Oh, botheration! I'll never enjoy a moment's peace until I agree."

He wiped his mouth clean of the crumbs from his morning toast as I clapped my hands together jubilantly.

The Olivia Habersham who quickly ushered us into her apartment that afternoon was a very different woman from the one we had last seen. Her hair was in complete disarray, and the dark circles under her eyes betrayed the fact that she had slept very little. She had a haunted look about her, and her lower jaw trembled a bit as she spoke.

"Thank you so much for coming, Doctor Watson...Mr. Holmes. I feel as if I'm coming apart at the seams."

"Why don't you start at the beginning, Olivia?" I asked as we sat down at her kitchen table.

"Well...the beginning of it all or...."

"The beginning of when your husband's ghost first appeared to you, Mrs. Habersham," Holmes said, bluntly.

I blanched as I watched Olivia visibly wince at his words.

"I am not a hysterical woman, Mr. Holmes nor am I given to flights of fancy involving ghosts. If I appear rattled today it is because I have good reason to be."

"Quite. Now kindly explain what occurred the first night."

Olivia gave vent to a deep sigh and shut her eyes, composing herself before speaking.

"It isn't so simple, Mr. Holmes. It started with voices... or maybe they were just thoughts...or dreams while I was still awake. I would hear Alfred speaking to me as if he were in the room chatting as we are now. He would speak of a specific incident, a memory we both shared only...it would go all wrong."

"All wrong...in what way?"

She placed her hands before her on the table and played with her wedding ring in nervous agitation.

"He would say to me, 'Remember the time we did such-and-such?' A picnic or a holiday or something...and then he would tell me how he went off with the maid or...or with some other woman he met in passing. It was...it was awful."

She was fighting tears, but Holmes stayed focused.

"These were dreams you say where you were not quite asleep?"

"Yes, it was as if he were whispering in my ear. No, that's wrong. Not as intimate as that. It was more as if he were in the room with me...speaking softly."

"Did he apologize to you for what he had done?"

She paused for a moment and appeared lost in thought before answering.

"No, no, he didn't. He was rather matter-of-fact and detached about it all. It was as if it were some horrible joke he was choosing to share with me now that he is...gone."

"Was your husband given to such ill humor?"

"No, Mr. Holmes. Most assuredly he was not."

"Have you considered the possibility, Olivia, that this is simply your grief manifesting itself in this queer fashion?"

She looked at me sharply and I felt compelled to explain myself better.

"You and Alfred had a good life together. It would not be uncommon in your sadness to experience...doubts...about his integrity. Fears perhaps that you have harbored over the years and kept silent and unspoken that may now be coming to the fore."

"You should give up medicine to follow Doctor Freud, Watson," Holmes chuckled.

"There were no doubts, John," was Olivia's stern response. "I understand why you might suggest that and I would be half-inclined to agree with you, if only to offer some form of rational explanation, but I assure you it is a theory without basis in fact. These...experiences continued on this way for some time...not every night, but most of them. Then...I started seeing him."

Her voice trailed off. I couldn't tell if she was fearful of the memory or doubting her own sanity. Perhaps it was a bit of both.

"I heard him calling my name. I lay there for a few moments, hoping it would stop, but it didn't, so I got out of bed and went out into the corridor. He was at the opposite end, by the stairwell. He stood there looking at me and said, 'Olivia, I have been a sinful man. I have ruined others for my financial gain'. And then he would proceed to tell me the most...heartless stories imaginable."

"What did you do?"

"What could I do, Mr. Holmes? I cried. I told him to stop. I asked him why."

"Did he approach you? Did he take you in his arms and reassure you?"

Her jaw quivered terribly and I marveled at her endurance.

"No, Mr. Holmes. He simply backed up a step and vanished into thin air."

"How many times has this happened?"

"I don't know. I lost count. Seven, maybe eight times if we count the dreams where he only spoke to me...four times now that I have seen him...last night was the worst by far."

"What was different about last night?"

"He stood over my bed, leaning near me. He was

young again. Younger than I had seen him in years...and he said, 'Olivia, I killed a man. He threatened to ruin me so I bludgeoned him to death in his stable and doused him with kerosene and threw a lit match upon his body and let him burn. I am not sorry, Olivia. I am glad I did it.' Oh, God, Alfred, how could you do such an unconscionable thing?"

She put her head down on the table and sobbed. It was clear she had been fighting for too long to keep her emotions bottled up, and now she gave vent to tremendous pain. Her sobbing was so great that she took in great gulps of air in order to breathe and appeared to rock back and forth as she did so, like a child in its cradle. For half a minute, I worried she might require medical attention, but presently she regained her composure and sat upright in her chair.

"There you have it, gentlemen," she laughed humorlessly. "Now tell me, what am I supposed to do?"

"Wait until nightfall and let us see your ghost for ourselves."

"You mean to stay here all day?"

"I suggest no impropriety, Mrs. Habersham, nor have I any intent of causing a scandal. Watson and I will depart for now and we shall return later...discreetly, I might add. Certainly there is a servants' entrance in the rear."

Olivia's face flushed with relief.

"Thank you, Mr. Holmes, most sincerely."

"Oh, one more thing before we go, ma'am."

"Yes?"

Holmes smiled for a moment as he considered his words carefully. "Have you any photographs of your husband that I might see." Olivia paused, clearly disturbed by the request.

"Yes, of course. I'll get them. I won't be a moment."

When she returned, she set a large dust-covered picture book before us. Holmes turned the heavy pages and studied the photographs closely. Seated across the table from him, I glanced at the faded sepia prints wrong side up. I always found picture books rather unsettling. It is a bit like looking through other people's stolen memories. Holmes was engrossed in the images and appeared to be studying them with great care.

"You certainly enjoyed quite a few holidays together."

"Yes, we were very fortunate in that respect. Alfred was very frugal, but we shared a passion for travel."

"Yes," I added, "Mary was always quite envious."

"And now it is I who envies her," Olivia added forlornly.

I exchanged a glance with Holmes. He nodded almost imperceptibly.

"Well, I think we will be going now, Olivia. Brave heart... we will return soon."

As we stepped outside, Holmes took me by the arm and steered me in the direction of the nearest cab. Climbing into the back seat, he barked an unfamiliar London address to the driver.

"Do you have business in the City, Holmes?" I asked.

"I have business with a solicitor, one Basil Carruthers. I need to see his files on the late Mr. Habersham, specifically his last will and testament."

"That is a most irregular request, Holmes."

"Isn't it? It is also crucial that Mr. Carruthers comply with the request immediately. We haven't the time to spare."

It was extremely rare for Holmes to use his brother's name and position within the government for influence, but in this instance he felt justified in doing so. His request was quickly granted, and a private office afforded us in which to pour through Alfred's files. Several hours later, he closed the last of the large stack of folders and rose from the table with a sigh.

"It is ten minutes to five o'clock, Watson. We must make haste."

"Is there an appointment I have forgotten?"

"The Habersham residence, of course!"

"So soon?"

"We should have left already!"

"But what about the files?"

"I have finished with them."

"You haven't told me what you were looking for."

"Correct, Watson, I haven't. Now come along or I shall be forced to leave you behind."

Holmes would not be drawn into conversation for the duration of our cab ride back to Praed Street. The rain fell in a light drizzle that left smearing wet circles on the windows of our cab. I stared through these blurred portals to the world outside while the horses' hooves clattered against the crumbling road beneath their feet. When we arrived at our destination, Holmes had the driver pull round to the back so that we could enter through the rear entrance, as he had promised Olivia we would do just a few hours earlier. I felt a sense of disquiet, as if the old house were staring at us in resentment as we made our way inside through the servants' entrance. Holmes's eyes darted furtively round the darkened corridor as we entered by the backstairs. Not a sound disturbed the silence to give any indication that our entrance had been noted. Holmes placed a finger to his lips to indicate we should do our utmost to maintain our silence.

Presently, he stepped with great caution to the rear of the staircase. A small cubbyhole was visible beneath the stairs. He indicated that I should crouch and enter the cramped space. As I stepped inside, cobwebs pulled against my face. A sense of revulsion washed over me as I watched a thick brown spider with crimson stripes on its back scurry up its web to escape through the opening between the steps above my head.

Holmes ducked into the cubbyhole to join me and smiled sympathetically in recognition that our lodging for the night was to be an unpleasant one. Soon my eyes adjusted to the gloom. We stood there crouched down and silent for what seemed like several hours until we heard it. The door to the servants' entrance had opened.

My heart raced, but I quickly regained my composure.

There was no reason to fear this unknown arrival. Admittedly, it was likely far too late to be a cleaning woman. I reached for my pocket watch to check the hour when Holmes's hand shot out and touched my wrist. He shook his head slowly to insure that I did nothing to give away our position.

Presently, the new arrival began to quietly climb the stairs unsteadily, one step at a time. At first I feared my movement had been overheard, but I resolved it was likely only an elderly person struggling to ascend the staircase. I looked up as each step creaked beneath the weight of their shuffling step. I could make out shoes and dark pant legs in the dim light that shone between the cracks in the stairs, but nothing else. Holmes's face strained as he listened intently, but what he was expecting to hear I could not imagine.

The footfalls quietly moved down the second floor hallway above us. A door creaked open somewhere in the distance. I had no sense where Olivia's flat was located from the back of the building, but Holmes suddenly appeared electrified as if he'd received an unexpected jolt. He pushed his way out of the cubby hole and, before I could react, he was bounding up the stairs two steps at a time.

Excitement gripped me and I hurried to race after him. When at last I reached the top of the stairs, I found myself frozen to the spot. The disturbing sound of someone snoring unnaturally loud filled the air. I had heard it before, but I could not recall where at the moment. It frightened me for some reason. My subconscious seemed to associate the sound with terror, though I was unable to recollect the particulars of the memory.

All thought flooded from my mind as a mighty crash sounded and a man came hurtling through a doorway on the right hand side of the corridor. He smashed into the wall and slid to the floor. Holmes was upon him before he could pick himself up. My friend was not, by nature, a violent man, which made the scene before my eyes difficult to reconcile. Holmes grasped the man by the lapels with both hands and threw him forward several feet where he landed hard upon his back. Along the corridor, several doors were opening and faces of tenants were peeking out at us in concern.

"In the name of God, Holmes, what are you doing?"

"She's dead, Watson."

His chest was rising and falling from the exertion. "Who is dead? Make sense, man!"

"Olivia Habersham is dead. He killed her."

He gestured toward the cowering figure on the floor before him. "Olivia is dead? How did this happen?"

"He frightened her to death. Meet the unrepentant Alfred Habersham."

My mind reeled from this revelation. It could not be, but as I stared down at the face in the dark of the hallway, I recognized my old friend's features.

"Good Lord, Alfred, how could you?"

It was only then that I had moved close enough to my old friend to be startled by what I saw. The man before me was indeed Alfred Habersham, but as he must have looked 30 years ago!

Holmes and I found ourselves ensconced a short time later at the Metropolitan Police Department. Inspector Jones was somewhat less than welcoming to find that we were already involved in a matter that had just been called to his attention.

"So let me see if I understand this correctly, Doctor Watson. The deceased was a friend of your wife whose late husband was also your patient. The deceased confided in your missus that her late husband's ghost was paying her nightly visits. You took it upon yourself to contact Mr. Consulting Detective here to sort the matter out and, in short order, your friend ends up dead while our Consulting Detective assaults the man he claims scared her to death. A man you believe, incidentally, to be the deceased's late husband as he appeared 30 years ago. Is there anything I have missed?"

I sighed with frustration. There was no way this was going to be a simple task.

"Yes, Inspector, that is correct."

"I'm finished. I'm finished with the lot of you," the Inspector said, slamming his fist down upon the top of his desk.

"Wonderful. Then perhaps you might let Mr. Consulting Detective speak for himself for a change."

"Do you have anything to add, Mr. Holmes?" the Inspector sneered with mock politeness.

"As it happens, Inspector Jones, I have some considerable information to impart. The man you are holding is not Olivia Habersham's late husband."

"But, Holmes," I cried, "you said so yourself!"

"I did no such thing, Watson. I said the gentleman in question was Alfred Habersham. That is an entirely different matter in this instance."

"Is Alfred Habersham not the name of the deceased's late husband?" the Inspector hissed through gritted teeth.

"It is," Holmes replied.

"Then what, by God, are you talking about?"

"Alfred Habersham is also the name of his son." My head was reeling.

"Holmes, you're mistaken. Alfred and Olivia had no children."

"That is true, Watson. Alfred and Olivia Habersham had no children."

Inspector Jones slapped his forehead and muttered an oath beneath his breath.

"The young man being held for Olivia's murder," Holmes continued, "is the son of Alfred Habersham and a woman whose surname I presume is Clovis."

I sputtered for a moment as I followed his meaning.

"Alfred...Clovis...you mean you believe that man is Alfred Habersham's ward?"

"I certainly am not entertaining any doubt about the

matter."

"No, no, no. A thousand times, no. Alfred Clovis was a distant relation that Alfred took as his ward because the boy had no father and would otherwise have suffered a life of destitution. We reviewed the paperwork in Basil Carruthers' office only yesterday."

"Yes, we did. Tell me, did Master Clovis ever live with the Habershams?"

I paused a moment.

"No, he did not. As I've said, Olivia was unable to have children and, if you must know, she told Mary she objected to the idea of taking the boy in. I suppose because they were an older couple at the time. I never questioned her on the matter, but I knew it was a sensitive one, of course. When the boy was made Alfred's ward, it was agreed that Alfred would pay for his education. His school holidays were spent with his mother, I presume. To the best of my knowledge, he never once visited his benefactor."

"Yes, quite. And one more question, Watson. Did Master Clovis benefit financially from Alfred's will?"

"Well you read the will yourself, Holmes, you must certainly be aware of the answer. He did not. Alfred left everything, that is to say, the apartment building he owned, as well as his considerable savings, to Olivia."

"And what arrangements did he make were something to happen to Olivia?"

"Well in that event...."

I paused as a terrible recollection of what I had read only yesterday in the will returned to me.

"By Jove, Holmes, you're right."

"Thank you, Watson."

"Don't tell me," the Inspector covered his eyes and winced.

"In the event of Olivia's death, his entire estate passes to his ward, Alfred Clovis. Alfred Clovis is the spitting image of his father. Alfred Clovis is Alfred Habersham's illegitimate son!"

I would like to say that ended the matter conclusively, but sadly it did not turn out quite so well. Whilst it was true that Alfred Clovis was indeed my old friend's son, he denied any wrongdoing in Olivia's death. He claimed he had recently made an effort to establish a relationship with his father's widow for the purpose of better understanding the man who had sired him. He had no idea that Olivia was suffering from nightmares of being visited by his late father's ghost and claimed that he had only just let himself into the apartment with a key Olivia had personally given him when he discovered his stepmother dead. When Holmes set upon him, he erroneously believed my friend to have been Olivia's murderer.

There was little we could say to counter his claims. He did indeed possess a key to Olivia's apartment. Propriety alone would have precluded her from telling Mary about the boy. It was all entirely plausible, except for the fact that I did not believe his innocence. I was convinced he had indeed posed as his father to frighten his stepmother to death in order to get at the inheritance. The question was how to prove his guilt.

"Oh, for heaven's sake, Watson," Holmes complained bitterly one evening in his study when I paid him an unexpected visit to run through the facts with him yet again. "This is real life, not some penny dreadful. What do you expect me to do, dress up as a ghost myself to trick the murderer into confessing his wrongdoing? We accomplished our task. We solved the case, but we cannot prove his guilt. He was the cleverer of us and he's gotten away with the crime. End of story. There is nothing more to be done with it."

"Holmes, I cannot believe you are willing to accept defeat so easily."

"I am a rational man, Watson. That's why I knew there were no ghosts involved, no matter how convinced Olivia was to the contrary. I was certain that the only rational explanation for Alfred Habersham to appear from the grave seemingly decades younger was for a close relative, such as an unknown son, to be masquerading as him. That made sense, and the mysterious unseen ward fit the puzzle perfectly. There ends the matter. There is no logical way to prove our suspicions are correct. One must accept that he has earned his earthly reward by foul means and, if one believes in a Christian heaven, perhaps justice will be done there. For the present, there is nothing more to do."

"Won't you even speak with him?"

"For what purpose, Watson, to give him further cause to bring charges of harassment against us? We were very fortunate he chose to be understanding, considering the circumstances of his arrest. His level- headedness would only sway the court in his favor. I certainly would command no respect. Inspector Jones is certainly not inclined to look with favor upon our theory that Alfred Clovis killed his stepmother. Again, I beseech you to see reason. There is nothing more to be done."

"Very well, Holmes, you leave me no choice but to follow your example with Basil Carruthers. First thing tomorrow morning I shall refer the matter to your brother."

"You can't be serious," he scoffed. "Do you honestly believe my brother will lift a finger to help in this matter? I gave you credit for greater intelligence than that, Watson."

"I'm happy to hear it, Holmes. I do not intend to enlist your brother's aid. I merely wish to inform him of how badly you bungled the matter and how quick you were to admit you have been bested by a common swindler."

Holmes's features froze as he stared at me aghast. "You wouldn't dare!"

"I trust you know better than to doubt me."

"That isn't cricket, Watson."

"No, it isn't, but then nothing about this case has been. Now...how do you propose to proceed from here?"

Holmes stared at me in something resembling admiration for the first time.

"Do you know, Watson, you have a distinct touch of the blackmailer about you?"

"Don't be vulgar, Holmes. When one heals the ill for a living, one must learn to be persuasive. Blackmail is for the uncouth layman. In any event, there is still the vexing issue of under what pretense we are to approach Mr. Habersham. His story is a reasonable one. His stepmother gave him the key with which he entered the apartment to speak to her when he found her dead.... "Found her dead," I repeated my own words, startled by a sudden thought. "He couldn't have."

"Why is that? The inquest revealed nothing to suggest otherwise."

"We don't need the coroner's report, Holmes; we need only to use our own senses."

"I'm afraid I don't follow you, Watson."

"Do you recall the specific details when you entered Olivia's apartment?"

My old friend paused a moment. His face appeared conflicted.

"No, I cannot recall precisely the sequence of events. Normally I'm very observant about any such matters, as you well know, but I was so preoccupied with what was happening that I rushed blindly forward in the dark."

"That explains your confusion, Holmes, but I know for a fact that Olivia was not yet dead when Alfred entered the apartment. I should have realized it sooner."

"Explain yourself."

"I know because my first recollection was of hearing a terrible sound emanating from the apartment...a sound I now recognize as Olivia swallowing her tongue during the throes of a seizure. I mistook it for an unnatural snoring at the time. I have heard that same awful sound many times before a patient died. I first heard it as a boy the night my mother died. It...it has haunted me ever since. Recurrence has done nothing to accustom me to its terror. Do you recall hearing it now?"

Holmes paused a moment and shook his head.

"I cannot be certain. You may be right, but I could not swear to it. I will trust your recollection better than my own in this instance. The trouble again remains there is no proof, of course. It is simply your word against his. This is no basis for confronting him with his actions."

"Surely, you will think of something?"

"I can but try, Watson. Leave me to my thoughts."

The next morning, I eagerly rang Holmes shortly after breakfast, but there was no answer. I tried several more times to no avail. Frustrated, I took a cab to Baker Street, but was surprised to find Mrs. Turner did not answer the door.

"He's not in."

I spun and saw the bundled form of an old woman walking an ugly little dog.

"He's in the hospital."

"Who is in the hospital?"

"The detective...who else would it be? You're standing on his doorstep."

"What happened to him? When was this?"

She shrugged her shoulders and pulled on the lead to move her little beast along. Without wasting another moment, I hurried to the corner and hailed a cab. My heart was racing when we reached St. John's Wood and I rushed inside the hospital. I found Mrs. Turner in the corridor outside Holmes's room.

"Oh, Doctor Watson...I should have rung you, sir, I am sorry."

"What happened, Mrs. Turner? What is wrong with him?"

"Brain fever, sir, like his mother before him, I fear."

I felt my legs start to give way beneath me. "What...what has the doctor said?"

Mrs. Turner shrugged.

"There is nothing to be done except to watch over him. It is the terrible sleep he may never wake from."

I saw the toll this ordeal had taken on the poor woman. Mrs. Turner cared for Holmes in spite of the frustration he caused her. She was exhausted. I kept vigil with her for several hours, but eventually insisted she go home and get some rest. I had already rung Mary to tell her I would be staying the night. After several hours, I leaned my head forward and rested my chin on my chest and fell into a fitful sleep.

I dreamed the queerest thing as I slept slumped outside of Holmes's hospital room. I saw my old friend appear out of nothingness on a street outside a grand estate. I did not recognize the location, but I knew it could not be England. Tropical trees filled with ripe fruit of a kind I did not recognize grew tall in the forecourt. Dust blew up from the street and mingled in the air around Holmes as he approached the large iron gates. Rather than stopping at them, he simply passed through them as if his body were immaterial. My mind's eye followed him as he approached the grand estate and passed through its walls as easily as he had the gate.

Inside those walls, it became clear the estate was actually a castle. Alfred Habersham, or rather Alfred Clovis, for I now knew it was not my late friend, sat upon a throne at the back of the cold, expansive, stone- tiled room. His face rested in his right hand as he sat in decadent boredom before us.

"What business do you have here, detective?"

Holmes continued to walk, or rather float, toward the throne. He came to a stop, hovering just before that great chair. Young Master Clovis appeared unmoved by this extraordinary visitation.

"My business, as you say, is justice," my friend answered. "You shall find you are still answerable to a Higher Authority than your own cunning."

Alfred Clovis snorted in amusement, but his posture

remained unchanged.

"Oh, am I now? And what authority would that be, pray tell?"

"That which none can deny when facing their Judgement. I speak of the Truth, of course. It is not a game from which the clever trickster can hide forever."

"You have no proof," Clovis sneered at Holmes. "These meaningless accusations are mere trifles without proof to substantiate them, and you have none to offer. Go ho me, detective. You are as unwanted here. Tend to your own business and leave your betters to themselves."

"You speak of proof," Holmes replied. "Will this suffice?"

My friend held up his right arm and a mirror seemed to appear beneath it framed by some ethereal tapestry. Upon the mirror played a series of images that I saw as if I were now staring through the eyes of Alfred Clovis. As I watched these images coalesce and recede, I obtained an understanding of what they signified.

I saw Alfred Habersham, my old friend, in his younger years looking uncannily like Alfred Clovis. I saw a young woman graced with a terrible beauty. I saw Alfred succumb to her charms. I saw my old friend, hardened with the bitterness of his falling, faced with the child that resulted from this adulterous union. I saw Olivia covered in a stony silence to mask the pain of Alfred's betrayal. I saw Alfred Clovis grow up a privileged young man with no parents to love him, no family to nurture him, no identity to anchor him from the wayward path he chose. I saw Clovis and Olivia, but my comprehension now began to fade. I read torture upon Olivia's face, but I could perceive nothing to indicate the nature of her interaction with Clovis. Did she know him? Was she being blackmailed or was he deceiving her into believing she was being haunted by his father's ghost as she maintained?

The mirror went dark, and Holmes pointed a bony finger at Clovis upon his throne, "You know that for which you are condemned. Face your sins, Alfred Clovis. Accept the Judgement your actions warrant."

Clovis' face contorted in pain. His only response was to scream in vain like a guilty man going to the gallows.

I awoke with a start, realizing someone was shaking me. "What is it, Sister?"

"The doctor says you may go in now," the matron replied. "Your friend's fever broke overnight. He is on the road to recovery."

I was elated at the news. Holmes was extremely weak and his face was covered in sweat, but he expressed some relief at seeing me at his side. I was not allowed long to stay in the room with him, but those precious few minutes meant more than the many hours of boredom I endured as their price.

It was with the greatest pleasure that I found myself present to witness Mrs. Turner's joy when she returned and discovered her sister's famous tenant on the mend. Exhausted, I managed to find a cab to take me home just a few minutes before noon. Mary greeted me with enthusiasm and listened patiently to the good news about Holmes's miraculous recovery.

"Before you go off to bed, John," she said, patting my arm with affection, "I should let you know that Inspector Jones rang you up this morning."

"Oh no, what did he want?"

"Now, now, don't be ill-tempered. He only rang to tell you of the tragedy that had befallen that awful Alfred Clovis boy."

"What tragedy? What are you talking about, Mary?"

"It seems his heart burst from shock in the middle of the night. He was asleep in his bed at the time. When the cleaning woman found him this morning, she said he looked as if he'd seen a ghost. The Inspector said to tell you that word for word. It is the queerest thing. I half- wondered whether he only wanted to make sure that Mr. Holmes and you had played no part in the matter. You know how he is about him."

"Of course I do," I replied, as if dreaming. "The Inspector needn't worry. Holmes couldn't possibly have been involved while he was in hospital suffering from brain fever...could he?"

I climbed the stairs, pulled the blinds, undressed and retired into my soft, warm bed. Sleep soon claimed me, and I lay slumbering through the afternoon, undisturbed by dreams and feeling numb to the tragic end of a child born of sin who would not break the fateful chains that bound him to this world.

The Verse of Death

by Matthew Booth

hose members of the public who have taken such an interest in this series of accounts of my association with Sherlock Holmes will recall that the dark affair of the Agra treasure and the revenge of Jonathan Small resulted in my own marriage to the lady who brought the case to Holmes's notice. The natural result of my union with Mary Morstan was an inevitable yet unwelcome disassociation with Holmes. My own happiness and the domestic responsibilities with which I became endowed were sufficient to absorb all my attention but, as often as was practicable, I endeavoured to make every effort to remain in contact with him. My correspondence was seldom reciprocated, unless it was in that austere and terse manner which was peculiar to him, but when it was possible for me to visit him in his rooms in Baker Street, I think that my presence was welcome. It was on one such visit that the story of Edmund Wyke, and the sinister mystery of the verse of death, came to our attention.

It was late one afternoon towards the end of September of 1890, I have reason to recall. As we had done so often before, Holmes and I were sitting beside the fire in the familiar rooms, the smell of tobacco and close friendship hovering in the air between us. Holmes was regaling me with the details of some of his most recent exploits, the circumstances of which made me long to have been by his side. He had only that moment completed his explanation of how he had solved the riddle of the Seventh Serpent when Mrs. Hudson showed in our old comrade Inspector Lestrade, of Scotland Yard.

I had not seen the sallow official for some time and I confess it was a pleasure to shake his hand and see him sitting once again on the settee before us. Whilst my domestic happiness was not to be questioned, there was something about this familiar triumvirate in these particular circumstances and surroundings which both thrilled and comforted me.

"Well, Lestrade," said Holmes, "what brings you to our door? I trust you have been busy since we saw you last during that little affair of the McCarthy murder at the Boscombe Pool?"

Lestrade shook his head. "A bad business that was, Mr. Holmes, I can't deny it, but it was nothing compared to the investigation upon which I am currently engaged."

Holmes's eyes glistened in anticipation. "Having a little difficulty, eh?"

"It is a queer business, sir, and no mistake. You may perhaps have heard of the retired financier, Edmund Wyke?"

"The name recalls nothing to my mind."

"He is a man of considerable wealth, known both for his ruthless sense of business and also his philanthropic endeavours. He is patron of a number of charitable foundations but, conversely, he is responsible for the ruin of many a competitor. He resides in an isolated house called Cawthorne Towers, down in Kent. When I say isolated, you may take it I am not exaggerating. It stands in its own extensive grounds, protected by any outside influence by a high stone wall. Any guest to the house is, I gather, permitted only by express invitation and after careful consideration. I hesitate to say that you could find any property or household so self-contained or cut off from outside influences."

"This man, Wyke, is a man who craves his privacy, it seems," remarked Holmes.

"You may say so."

"And what has befallen him?"

"He is dead, Mr. Holmes. He was found last night, in his bed chamber, stabbed through the heart."

Holmes considered his fingernails. "There does not seem to be very much in the way of interest for me, Lestrade. Despite our friendly rivalry, you are an able and efficient officer. Is a case of simple murder not within your own province?"

"In normal circumstances, I should not dream of disturbing you, Mr. Holmes. But, you see, the man was dead in the room and there was no trace of any disturbance, nor any means by which any human agency could have entered the room."

"No forced entry?"

"None."

"The doors and windows?"

"All locked. A rat could not have entered the place."

Holmes yawned. "I have yet to investigate any crime committed by a flying creature. A locked room mystery always has an explanation. You recall the Speckled Band case, Watson? That, too, was presented as an impossible mystery, but the solution was only too evident once the facts were considered."

Lestrade shifted in his seat and, from his pocket, produced some folded papers. "I did not think to entice you with the sealed room alone, Mr. Holmes, although that in itself is enough to beat me. But, I thought you might be intrigued by these."

Holmes took the papers from the inspector. "What are they?"

"Mr. Wyke received them over the course of the week prior to his death. They are little poems, Mr. Holmes. But, if I am not much mistaken, they warn the man of his own impending death."

I confess that at these words a shudder passed through me, but Holmes remained as impassive and controlled as ever. His eyes betrayed that glimmer which told me that, despite his austere exterior, he was inwardly excited by Lestrade's news. I moved behind Holmes and leaned over his shoulder to examine with him these strange portents of death. They were written in printed capitals and there was nothing distinctive about either the ink or the paper.

The first ran as follows:

In hatred and shame you die.

Of guilt must be made your coffin. Lay down your head and perish.

For it comes for you as it came for me, A death which none can deny,

Not least those souls who are innocent.

The second ran thus:

The maiden of vengeance must serve As my cruel replevin.

Centuries of wrong will she avenge; And to our deaths will she lead us.

Her lips will touch us both and carry on them The kiss of the guilty.

For some moments, Sherlock Holmes read the curious verses over and over again, his brows furrowed and his eyes squinting against the tobacco fumes of his pipe. For our part, Lestrade and I remained silent, both of us more than aware that in such moments of concentration, Holmes's greatest ally was silence.

"What do you make of them?" Holmes asked suddenly. Lestrade shrugged.

"I can make nothing of them."

Holmes gave a quick smile. "I fancy that the author of these fascinating verses gives Shelley and his comrades no reason to fear for their reputations. But there is something very serious behind this, if I am not mistaken. Who alerted you to these messages?"

"It was Mrs. Agatha Wyke, the dead man's wife. A stern and proud woman."

"She knew of their existence?"

"Mrs. Wyke says she and her husband had no secrets."

Holmes lowered his gaze momentarily. "Every man has his secrets. Who else knew of these curious threats?"

"Mrs. Wyke insists that she was the only one aware of them."

Holmes gave a curt nod. "Now, tell me, Lestrade, who are the other members of the Wyke household?"

Lestrade aided his memory with the use of his official notebook. "There is the dead man's wife, as I have told you, and there is their son, Sebastian, a somewhat wayward young man if I am any judge, Mr. Holmes. There is a small staff, led by the butler, Jacobs."

"Is that all?"

"No, there is a friend of the family who is staying with them for the weekend. His name is Dr. James Lomax."

"I have heard of him," said I. "He wrote a splendid article in the *Lancet* not so long ago on the hereditary nature of disease."

"He is a level-headed man, fiercely practical from what I have seen of him," advised the inspector. "He it was who took charge of the situation when the body was discovered."

Holmes leaned forward in his chair. "Pray, give us the precise sequence of events."

"I had better start with the previous night, that is to say two nights ago. The household, including Dr. Lomax, had assembled for dinner and the evening had been pleasant enough. Over the post prandial brandy, however, Wyke and Sebastian exchanged heated words which resulted in a somewhat fraught quarrel. It culminated with Sebastian asking Dr. Lomax for the hour, as he wished to retire and he could stand the company of his father no more. He wished Wyke would go to the Devil, and that if he would it would cleanse the very air they breathed."

"Violent words which he must surely regret now," I observed.

"Just so, Doctor, and words which you might expect me to interpret with some suspicion in light of subsequent events. But, Mr. Holmes, if I have learned one thing only from my association with you, it is to keep an open mind."

"Very wise," murmured Holmes with a sardonic twist to his voice. "Well, after Sebastian had stormed out of the room, Lomax strove to convince Wyke to make it up with his son at once. He said it did no one any good to go to sleep without resolving an argument, but Wyke was defiant. 'If the lad wishes to make up before sleep, he may do so,' said he, 'but I see no reason to do so. Let him calm down before I make any attempt to speak to him.' This approach is, I believe, typical of the man."

"What was this quarrel about?" asked Holmes.

Lestrade shrugged. "What are quarrels between father and son ever about? Love or money, in my experience. In this case, it was money. Sebastian is an errant youth, as I have said, Mr. Holmes, and he is in deep with the wrong crowd."

"The gaming tables?"

"Precisely so. His father has been too generous with him before over money matters, and he now refuses to come to his aid. Sebastian has viewed the refusal as some form of betrayal." Lestrade looked back to Sherlock Holmes. "Now, Mr. Holmes, we get to the core of the matter. The following morning, Mr. Wyke did not appear for breakfast. It was his custom to rise early and take a stroll in the grounds, so he was usually the first to rise. The fact he was not up and about when the rest of the house rose was sufficient to cause concern. Lomax, Sebastian, and Mrs. Wyke all went to Wyke's bedroom, accompanied by the faithful Jacobs, and they found that his door was locked. Sebastian knocked but could get no response. Lomax made his own attempt but got the same reply. He kneeled to the lock and found that he could not see into the room, which showed that the key was in the lock. Thus, together, the three men threw themselves against the door and broke into the room.

"Once inside, they found Wyke lying on the floor. He was on his back and, in his heart, there was one of his own ceremonial daggers which was known to be one of a pair which hung on the wall of his study. The alarm was raised and the local police called in. I was summoned almost at once, and I have spent the morning making my enquiries. As soon as I heard about the threatening poems, I thought of you, Mr. Holmes, and I came straight round to see you."

Holmes had been sitting with his fingertips together and his eyes closed, but now he rose from his chair and stood before the fire. "You did wisely, Lestrade. Now, tell me. Has anything in that bedroom been touched?"

"Nothing. I have a constable on guard by the door."

"Excellent. Now, I have one or two other matters to attend to today. Would it be convenient if I came down to this house early tomorrow morning, Lestrade?"

"Certainly," replied the little professional.

"Capital. Watson, you are not averse to accompanying me? I trust the redoubtable Mrs. Watson and your long suffering patients can spare you for one day?"

Having heard the prelude to this strange story, I felt unable to deny myself the opportunity of witnessing its conclusion. "I would not miss it for the world, Holmes, and my practice is never very absorbing."

"Splendid, my faithful Watson. Be back here for seven o'clock and we shall breakfast together before catching the train. Farewell, Lestrade, and we shall be with you tomorrow morning to continue our investigation into what promises to be a most fascinating case."

I have stated elsewhere that Sherlock Holmes had the remarkable power of detaching his mind at will. When I met him on that following morning, it was as though the whole story surrounding the inexplicable murder of Edmund Wyke had never come to his attention. For myself, I confess that the previous evening had found me distracted by the whole business, and I fear I had been poor company for my wife. She had retired early, but I had stayed up beyond a reasonable hour, trying to discover some clue in the sequence of events which Lestrade had set out. My researches, I confess, were in vain. However, when I met with Sherlock Holmes for breakfast, he was full of energy, and I had that familiar sensation that already he had seized upon some clue which remained far beyond my grasp. Not one word would he utter of the whole business, though, until we had arrived at the railway station and been greeted by Lestrade.

"Well, Mr. Holmes, have you had chance to consider the matter?" asked the detective.

"Certainly. There are particular features of interest to the student of crime which make the matter of specific interest."

Lestrade glowed with a triumphant arrogance. "I have not been idle myself, although I confess I ought to have spared your time. With the exception of a few loose threads, the matter is at an end."

"You do not mean that you have solved it?"

"I have my man, although he has yet to confess."

A glance at my companion's face showed that his anxiety had risen. To me, who knew his manner so well, his composure seemed shaken and the pale tone of his gaunt features seemed to intensify. His eyes remained as keen as ever but it was evident that he was disturbed by the inspector's confidence.

"You have made an arrest?"

"Just so." Lestrade reached into his pocket and produced a small envelope. From it, he dropped a ruby encrusted watch charm into his hand. "A further examination of the body has revealed that this was found in the dead man's hand. He must have wrenched it from the culprit's watch as he slumped to the floor."

Holmes had clutched at the charm between his thin fingers and he had begun to examine it with his lens. "There is no sign of damage."

"What of it?"

"Perhaps nothing," said Holmes, with a shrug. "To whom does this belong?"

Lestrade was unable to keep the chime of victory out of his voice. "I have identified it as belonging to Sebastian Wyke."

"The son with the gambling debts?" I recalled.

"The same, Dr. Watson, and a man whose need for money has now brought him into more troubled waters than he could have foreseen."

Holmes handed the watch charm back to Lestrade. "You consider the murder to be the natural sequel to the quarrel of which you told us."

"Do you not agree?"

Holmes shrugged. "Possibly, but I prefer to reserve my position until such time as I have had the opportunity of seeing for myself all that there is to see."

Lestrade chuckled. "You will have your little ways, Mr. Holmes, and no mistake. If you will come this way, I have a dog cart waiting, for it is a fair drive along this country track to the house."

Despite the invigorating briskness of the breeze which assaulted our faces, the weather was not inclement and there was a shadow of the summer sun still in the sky. The surrounding countryside and its rolling green hills was a treat for the eye, and were it not for the memory of the dark crusade upon which we were engaged, I would have admired it with the fond eye of a man who is proud of his country. And yet, the track along which we rattled was sombre and uninteresting. Lestrade was not guilty of exaggeration, for the narrow lane leading to Cawthorne Towers seemed to me to make the journey seem interminable.

Lestrade had spoken of its isolation but I had not been

prepared for the extent of it. The high wall of which we had heard was sufficient to discourage visitors, so forbidding was it, and the huge iron gates which formed the entrance to the fortress itself were no less relentless in their obstruction. Beyond these imposing fortifications, the Jacobean manor house glared at us from its incongruously beautiful lawns. The windows were like malevolent eyes peering at us maliciously, as though daring us to approach. It was as though the house had shunned any form of social activity, and as though no external influences were desired or to be permitted, save the passing of time which had left its mark in the lichen and faded colours of the bricks.

We drove up the winding path to the house, and we were ushered inside by a lean, cadaverous old man whom it was impossible not to identify with Jacobs the butler, of whom we had heard. Holmes exchanged a few words with him, but nothing of any further importance could be added to the account which Lestrade had given us in Baker Street, and we made our way upstairs to the bedroom which had been the scene of the tragedy. We were halfway up the stairs when a man's voice called out to Lestrade and halted us in our tracks. Looking to the foot of the stairs, I saw a man of rather more than 40 racing up towards us. He was a handsome man, with hair as black as the most fearful twilight, and eyes which betrayed a keen intelligence.

"Is this Mr. Sherlock Holmes, of whom you spoke?" he asked of our official companion.

It was Holmes who spoke. "That is my name, Dr. Lomax." The man stared. "How do you know my name, sir?"

"The inspector here advised me that there was a man by the name of Dr. James Lomax in the house, and your watch chain bears the initials "J.L". If any doubt remained, it is not difficult to discern a doctor from the trace of iodine on his left forefinger."

The doctor let out a wry chuckle. "For a moment, I thought you had done something extraordinary, Mr. Holmes, but I see that it is nothing more than a conjuring trick."

"Just so. Now, gentlemen, perhaps we can continue to the bed chamber."

The room in question was along a dark, oak panelled corridor on the second floor of the house. It was furnished opulently, if in a somewhat old fashioned style. A large four poster bed with delicate veils tied to each post was the central, imposing figure of the room, and the dark crimson stain next to it, which was so familiar a sight to us in our dark investigations, showed where the man Wyke had fallen down dead. The body had been removed, but the mark on the carpet at our feet gave the unmistakable impression that it still lay before us, its horror displayed for us all to see.

"May I examine the weapon?" asked Holmes.

"Yes, I have it here," replied Lestrade, handing over the blade. "It is of a rather ornate design, as you can see."

It was a beautiful object, although its present purpose had diminished its splendour. The handle was carved ivory, decorated with a number of emeralds of the most vivid green. The guard was carved into two claws of advancing menace, and the blade itself curved slightly to its deadly point. There was still the trace of the dead man's blood smeared across the blade.

"A fascinating object," said Holmes. "And it is one of a pair, I believe."

"That is correct."

"It was no secret that they were kept in the study, as I understand it?"

"No, they were displayed on the wall."

"It is certainly a dramatic choice of weapon," remarked Holmes. "It is of course a ceremonial dagger, used by a certain ancient cult of assassins for specific forms of executions."

Lomax nodded his appreciation. "It is a dagger of the El-Khalikan Cult of ancient Egyptian assassins. They used it to execute those members who had transcended the code of conduct."

"In particular, those assassins who knowingly murdered innocent people who were not political targets, if my memory serves me well."

"It serves you perfectly well. You are well read, Mr. Holmes."

"I have been told that I am an omnivorous reader with an immense knowledge of sensational literature. You, sir, are not so far behind, it seems."

Lomax blushed at the compliment. "I have listened to Edmund talk about the ancient history of Egypt many times. It was one of his passions."

Holmes handed the knife back to Lestrade and walked over to the door of the room. He bent to his knees and, with his lens, examined the lock and the hinges. Finally, with his lens close to his eye, he picked up the key from the carpet and examined it in minute detail.

"This key fell to the floor when the door was forced, no doubt," said he.

"I suppose it must have done," said the doctor.

Holmes rose to his feet. "I believe, Doctor, that you attempted to look through the key hole but were unable to see into the room."

"The key was in the lock. We had tried the door several times."

"Quite so. Did anybody else look through the hole?"

"No, I decided it was best to get the door down as soon as possible."

"You acted wisely," said Holmes. "When you rushed into the room, did you ascertain at once that Mr. Wyke was dead?"

"It was perfectly obvious in any event," said Lomax. "Sebastian said, 'My God, he is dead,' and I went over to confirm it."

"You had remained by the door until that moment?"

"Yes."

"Thank you, that is very clear."

"It is a terrible thing, a son murdering his father in this fashion," said Lomax with some sadness.

"You are sure of the young man's guilt?"

Lomax looked at my companion with the expression of a confused man. "Do I take it you are not?"

"I form no biased judgment, Dr. Lomax. I walk where the facts lead me and draw only those conclusions which the facts allow. Now, Lestrade, perhaps I might be permitted to speak to the widow."

In spite of her obvious grief, Agatha Wyke was a stoic and proud woman of perhaps 60 years of age. At Holmes's request, he and I interviewed her alone. Lestrade offered no objection, for he had already spoken with the lady and he had other matters to which he had to attend. When we entered the drawing room, Mrs. Wyke greeted us with dignity and a demure elegance which only seemed to increase my empathy for her. Her features were blanched with sadness, but they retained a delicacy of expression which must once have been captivating, but which the passing of time had slowly sought to eradicate. She took my friend's hand in hers and spoke to him in a voice which was soured by tragedy.

"Can any woman say she has suffered more than me, Mr. Holmes," said she, "to discover that my husband is dead and my son thought to be responsible for it?"

"Might I ask whether you believe that he is truly guilty?"

A flash of colour rose to her sallow cheeks. "Bless you for giving me hope! Do I take it from that question that you believe in his innocence?"

"I have reason to believe so."

"Might I enquire what those reasons are?"

Holmes shook his head. "If I am to be of service to you, you must possess your soul in patience and allow me to act as I see fit, including permitting me to disclose my thoughts when I consider it appropriate."

"I am at your service, Mr. Holmes. I wish only to have justice for my husband and vindication for my son."

"I hope I shall be able to bring you both, madam. You have told Inspector Lestrade of these strange verses which you husband received. I believe they mean nothing to you?"

"I cannot explain them."

"Were they delivered by hand?"

"No; they came through the post."

"Did your husband keep the envelopes?"

"I am sorry, he did not."

"That is unfortunate. An envelope can tell many secrets to the trained observer." Holmes paused for a moment. "I believe no one else knew about these verses."

"No one."

"Not your son?"

"Certainly not. Edmund was at pains to keep them secret from Sebastian."

"How long has your husband known Dr. Lomax?" The lady thought for a moment. "Perhaps five years."

"How did they meet?"

"A mutual friend introduced them. Alas, I am not aware of the details."

Holmes nodded and sat for a moment in serious thought. "I have one final question, Mrs. Wyke, and then I may leave you in peace. Did your husband ever mention a woman by the name of Violet Usher to you?"

The question took the lady by surprise and for a moment she could find no words of response. Finally, with her hand to her cheek in surprise, she gave her answer. "Do you suggest that there was another woman in my husband's life, Mr. Holmes? How did you come by this information?"

Holmes held out a hand of calming gentleness. "Have no fear, madam, I am suggesting no infidelity of that nature."

"Then who is this woman of whom you speak?"

"A woman of great sadness, like you, madam."

"I have never heard the name."

"The fact that you have not may well have kept you alive, Mrs. Wyke," said Sherlock Holmes. With those cryptic words, he ushered me out of the room and we left the lady to her sorrow.

"Come, my dear Watson," said he in hushed tones when we were in the hallway once more. "Let us find a quiet corner and consider the position."

We spent half an hour in each other's company, strolling around the beautiful stretches of lawn which surrounded the house in which these dark deeds had occurred. Holmes walked in silence, and I did not dare to break it for I knew that his mind was turning over all the facts of this strange business into which we had walked. Instead, I allowed the soothing song of the birds and the gentle balm of the breeze to seep into my soul. So peaceful did those gardens seem when contrasted with the dark mystery inside the house that I was startled when Holmes's voice invaded my reverie.

"Your gift of silence is invaluable to me, Watson," said he, "and your presence by my side is always a comfort as well as an aid."

"I did not like to interrupt your thoughts."

"It is well you did not. My mind is now quite made up on the matter."

"You have solved it?"

"The identity of the murderer was never in question. It was the verses which piqued my interest, for in their solution we hold the key to this crime and a serious error of justice."

"I am afraid I do not follow you."

"That is understandable, my dear fellow, and no cause for shame. Come, we must find Lestrade at once. It is time to bring this matter to a close."

We made our way back to the house. Holmes sent at once for Jacobs and requested that the butler find Dr. Lomax and bring him to the study. The request made, Holmes made his way to that very room, where we found Lestrade, collating his reports of his investigation. Holmes sat on the corner of the desk and peered at his professional colleague. "I wonder, Lestrade, whether you may wish to amend those reports in due course. I must advise you that Sebastian Wyke is innocent."

"Why do you say so, Mr. Holmes?"

"The watch charm is a clear indication of his innocence." Lestrade scoffed. "It is the clearest indication of his guilt!"

Holmes shook his head. "And yet, you gave me the proof that the charm cleared the son yourself."

"How so?"

"In your statement to us in Baker Street, you said that Sebastian Wyke asked Dr. Lomax for the hour as he wished to go to bed. Now, why should he need to ask the time if he was wearing his own watch with the very same ruby watch charm attached to it? Furthermore, is it not inconceivable that he would put his watch on before he stepped out to murder his father? Why on earth should he do such a thing?"

"But the charm was found in the dead man's grasp," protested Lestrade.

Holmes waved aside the objection with an impatient gesture. "Then it was placed there. That much is also evident by the lack of damage to it. If it had been wrenched off, as you claim, the link attaching it to the watch chain would surely be bent out of shape. No, Lestrade, the charm was removed from the chain and purposefully put in the dead man's hand. "

"But who could have placed it there?"

"Someone who wished to implicate Sebastian Wyke, naturally. Someone who saw in the argument between father and son a possible motive for murder and a means of diverting suspicion."

"But the only other person present during that argument was...."

There was a knock at the door at that instant and Holmes leapt to his feet to answer it. He threw open the door with a flourish and ushered in the visitor. "Come in, Dr. Lomax. We should very much value your assistance."

"If I can be of service, Mr. Holmes, I am eager to help."

"Pray, sit in this chair before the inspector, then." Holmes indicated one of the chairs at the desk and guided Lomax into it. "Now, the best way for you to assist us, Dr. Lomax, is to explain to us why it was that you murdered Edmund Wyke."

The doctor made a move to rise from the chair in protest but Holmes had his grip on the man's shoulder and any attempt to move from the chair was futile. "Do not be noisy, Dr. Lomax. You have no chance at all."

For a moment or two, Lomax considered his options, but he must have seen that the three of us were not about to allow him to escape. The snared rat glowered at my companion. "What right do you have to accuse me?"

"I suspected you from the first, my dear doctor," declared Sherlock Holmes. "I stated at the outset of this case that any apparently impossible crime has a solution somewhere. It is my experience that the solutions to such mysteries are invariably very simple. The answer to this particular problem lay in your own statement of your conduct, Doctor. You told us that when the door was broken down, Sebastian ran to his father and stated that he had been murdered."

"Yes, I recall saying that."

"Very good. Then you will also remember saying that it was at that moment that you walked over to the body."

"I see no importance in either remark."

"Very likely not. But the significance of those comments struck me at once. I was forced to ask myself why you remained at the bedroom door when you had previously appointed yourself commander of the situation outside. What was the reason behind your sudden passivity? It was surely natural that you would approach the body with Sebastian, especially in your capacity as a medical man."

The sneer on the man's face intensified. "And what conclusion did you draw, Mr. Holmes?"

My friend smiled but there was no humour in it. "All in good time. My next consideration was the key in the door.

You had stated that you, and only you, looked through the key hole before the door was forced."

"So I did."

"And do you maintain that position?" Lomax nodded. "I do."

"And there is the point. The fact that only you looked through the keyhole means that we only have your word for it that the key was in the lock at all. In fact, it was not, because it was in your pocket. You were admitted to the bedroom by Wyke, where you murdered him, took the key from the door, and locked it behind you. The following morning, when the alarm was raised, you made sure that you were the man who was in control of the situation. It was imperative that it be you who checked the lock and no one else. You declared that the key was in the lock and no one had any reason to doubt your word. When the door was forced, everybody but you rushed into the room and attention was focused on Wyke's body. Thus, no one noticed you drop the key on the inner side of the door at the approximate place it would have fallen, had it been in the lock when the door was broken down. You had to remain close by the door in order to drop the key, of course, which is why you held back whilst everyone else entered the chamber and why you did not approach the corpse immediately."

Lestrade had listened to this exchange with increasing interest. Now, he leaned forward and clasped his hands on the desk. "Is this true, Dr. Lomax? I should warn you that what you say may be used against you."

"I see no reason to deny it," replied the prisoner. "Perhaps Mr. Holmes can explain why I did what I did."

Sherlock Holmes reached into his pocket and drew out the two threatening verses which had been the commencement of this dark investigation. "I would not have known your motive were it not for these. You wanted Wyke to know that vengeance had come upon him. Whether he knew from where or whether he interpreted these messages as you intended, we shall never know."

"I will always know. The look on his face showed he had glimpsed the truth behind those poems," said Lomax.

"What is the truth?" asked Lestrade.

Holmes pointed to the verses. "There is a hidden message in those two poems of death. In the first, you will note that the end of the second line and the beginning of the third line form a name. So too do the end of the fourth line and the beginning of the fifth line. The same pattern in the second verse also spells a name. The message is completed by the final word of each poem. Read concurrently, you will see amid these verses the messages 'Finlay Meade innocent' and 'Vincent Usher guilty'."

Lomax raved in the air. "And guilty he was, the villain!"

Holmes turned to me. "You will recall, Watson, that I asked Mrs. Wyke whether she had ever heard the name of Violet Usher. Mrs. Usher was the wife of Vincent Usher, a cruel and violent blackguard. When he discovered that his wife was seeing a man by the name of Finlay Meade behind his back, Usher went berserk. In a violent rage fuelled by jealousy, he beat the woman to death. He escaped justice by placing the blame on her lover, Meade. After the trial, Usher disappeared and was never heard of again. No doubt fearful that his crime would overtake him, he changed his name to Wyke, as we now know, and began a new life as a different person. "

Lestrade nodded his comprehension. "I remember the case, Mr. Holmes. The evidence against Meade was conclusive. There was never any suspicion that it was fabricated and the verdict was obvious."

Holmes's cold eyes were on Lomax. "It was a cruel miscarriage of justice. It must have struck you as a poetic justice when Sebastian and his father argued, Lomax. What more fitting revenge than to kill the villain and put the blame on his son, just as Wyke had done to Meade."

Lomax nodded sombrely. "It was a temptation I could

not resist. My mother's maiden name was Meade. Finlay was her brother. I never knew my parents, Mr. Holmes, but my uncle was a great influence in my life. His death was a crushing blow to me and I could never believe the charges against him. For years, I dreamed of seeking out the truth about what really happened. My researches led me nowhere, however, and my frustrations began to pollute my mind.

"I had not known Usher, but his name was with me every day of my life. When I met Edmund Wyke in Egypt, I could have no way of knowing that the man who had taken my dear uncle from me was gradually becoming one of my best friends. The irony punishes me even now. Naturally, Wyke was unaware of my identity, and there was no reason for either of us to think what a cruel twist of fate our friendship was.

"One day, I met an old family acquaintance quite by chance. I had not seen him for many years and I barely recognized him at first, but as he spoke I began to remember him as a friend of both Usher and my uncle. His name was Harry Coombes, and what he told me shook me to my core. He said that he had witnessed the attack on Violet Usher and he knew that Finlay was innocent. Naturally, I asked him why he had not gone to the police at the time, but he had set sail for the new world soon after the murder and was not in the country for the trial. Besides, he said, he knew what Vincent Usher was capable of and he dared not cross him, even to save another's life.

"This was shattering news to me, as you can imagine, but Coombes had still more to tell me. He had seen me in Wyke's company on a number of occasions, and he had assumed I was unaware of who my friend was. He could not understand why I would be in close company with a man who had so wronged me otherwise. You can appreciate what a devastating blow it was to me to learn that my dear friend was my sworn enemy. It was only when he showed me a likeness of Usher that I was forced to accept it. My soul cried out for justice and my mind raged at the cruelty of truth.

"I urged Coombes to come with me to the police but he refused. At last, I convinced him but, again, fate was against me for the old man died that very night. It is easy to suspect foul play in those circumstances, but it was not. His life had been long and his heart gave out, unburdened at last from the weight it had borne all those years.

"Of course, now I had no proof of Usher's guilt and Finlay's innocence, but my thirst for justice had not been quenched either. I cannot say what made me do it. Perhaps it was the years of frustration and anger poisoning my mind, or perhaps it was that my faith in justice had long ago evaporated. Whatever the cause, I would have vengeance for Finlay Meade, but the law would only fail him again whereas my own breed of revenge surely would not. I wanted him to know that death was upon him. I did not want to be a dagger in the shadows. I wanted to be cruel justice revealed, shining brightly in the sun. Those messages were my advertisement of death. If Wyke, or Usher as he was, saw through them, then he would know why his end was close. If he did not, I cared little, for I would know what those portents of death represented, but I know that he did see through them."

Holmes had listened to this statement with a keen interest. Now, he paced around the room with a troubled expression on his gaunt face.

"I have been known to empathize with criminals before now," said he. "There are times when I have battled with my conscience at the conclusion of a case. I fear I cannot do so now. Your vision is blurred so much by this private retribution of yours that you fail to see that your plan to murder the guilty and incriminate the innocent makes you no better and no different to Usher himself. That is why I cannot show you any mercy."

Lomax looked up at his with eyes of granite. "I ask for

none of your mercy, Mr. Sherlock Holmes. I neither want nor need it. I go to my death with my own conscience salved. I am ready, inspector, for whatever punishment your frail system of justice sees fit to bestow upon me."

It is not necessary to prolong my narrative by telling how we explained the true facts of her husband's death to Mrs. Wyke. Nor do I need to dwell on the details of the release of Sebastian Wyke and his reconciliation with his mother. How we told them of Edmund Wyke's dark past is a matter which I feel must remain private, for I cannot help but think that mother and son have suffered enough for the old man's sins. Justice did not fail them, however, and Dr. James Lomax was sent to his death in accordance with his crime. When I read the announcement in the newspaper to Sherlock Holmes, he turned his face towards the fire and shook his head.

"Our system of justice is a fair and honourable one, my dear Watson," said he. "But it is not infallible. If it were, it would not be the law of mere men such as us. Instead, it would be the unfailing Court of a far greater power than ours."

Lord Garnett's Skulls

by J.R. Campbell

![drop cap A] t the urgent command of the cab's occupant, the horse skidded to a stop in the busy London street. A familiar voice called my name in an impatient tone I had learned to endure. My morning walk interrupted, I turned to see my good friend, Sherlock Holmes, holding the cab door open and beckoning me to join him. It was, as Holmes correctly anticipated, an invitation my somewhat latent sense of adventure compelled me to accept. My well-intentioned schedule for the day forgotten, I leapt aboard the cab and fell into my seat as the driver urged his horse onwards.

"Holmes?"

Recognising the intent of my barely uttered question, Holmes explained the urgency of our trip. "We are bound for Lord Garnett's."

"Young Cambers' case?" I asked, remembering the youthful, thin- faced Detective Constable who had visited Baker Street last evening. Cambers had struck me as rather slight for the rough and tumble of police work, and every thought, every emotion, experienced by the earnest young detective seemed to parade across the thin, handsome features of his open face. Perhaps it was simply the contrast to Holmes's aquiline but often stoic face which misinformed my first impression of the Detective Constable, for it soon emerged that young Cambers had already made quite a name for himself. He'd solved a difficult and gruesome matter in Bedford and, as a result, Scotland Yard offered him an opportunity to practise his trade in London. Having caught the attention of his superiors, the young man was anxious to advance his career – however, a difficult theft blocked his upward path. Having heard his new colleagues at the Yard speaking of the Baker Street consulting detective, Cambers ventured forth to request Holmes's insight into a rather macabre theft from Lord Garnett's London stately home.

"Apparently there has been a new and disturbing development," Holmes informed me. "How much of Cambers' investigation do you recall?"

"To be honest Holmes, I did not consider the matter important," I admitted. "Certainly the nature of the theft was unusual but, really, it seemed of no great consequence. I understand Cambers' desire to impress his Lordship – he is an ambitious young man – but I'm surprised to see you in such a hurry over so trifling a matter."

Holmes, amused by some private thought, looked out the window.

Turning to me, he said, "Indulge me."

"Very well." I proceeded to recite the facts of the case. Lord Garnett had recently returned from an inspection of his North Borneo holdings and, fancying himself a man of science, hosted a dinner party to which several prominent patrons and scientists had been invited. The highlight of the evening was the unveiling of artifacts Lord Garnett had brought back from the steamy, far-off jungle. Specifically, a net containing four smoke-blackened skulls collected from a Borneo long-house, trophies of that distant land's savage headhunters. Apparently, Lord Garnett intended to author a paper concerning the display and could not resist the opportunity to announce his upcoming publication to those who would envy such an achievement. The following day, Lord Garnett locked the drawing room containing the bones, assuring the grisly artifacts were safe from those who might covet his gruesome souvenirs. When Lord Garnett returned four days later and unlocked the drawing room, he discovered his net of skulls missing.

"According to Cambers, the room had not been tampered with," I completed my recitation. "The doors had been locked and the windows securely fastened from the inside."

"Quite true," Holmes agreed. "It was, after all, for that very reason Cambers sought my assistance."

"Yes," I admitted. "So why are we rushing to Lord Garnett's? You provided Cambers a written list of questions to ask, and you seemed quite confident it was all the detective would need to solve the matter."

"This morning I received a message from Cambers," Holmes explained. "It seems another of the skulls in Lord Garnett's possession was taken."

"Another one? Good heavens! How many skulls did Lord Garnett bring back from the jungle?"

"It's worse than you know, Watson," Holmes assured me. "This particular skull was still in use by Lord Garnett's son."

"What?" I exclaimed. "You mean the boy was kidnapped?"

"It is too early to make that assessment," Holmes insisted. "All we know for certain is that the boy disappeared sometime last night. Cambers returned to Lord Garnett's residence early this morning with the intention of putting answers to my list of questions. He was present when the child's absence was discovered."

"Well, Cambers seems a talented detective," I offered my opinion.

"You think so?" Holmes asked.

"You said he'd done well with that matter back in? Where was it? Bedford?" I reminded Holmes. "He seems quite an ambitious fellow."

"In my experience, the mere presence of ambition is not

indicative of talent," Holmes argued. "I should also point out that crimes occurring in Bedford are markedly different than the crimes of London."

"Surely crime is crime, wherever it happens," I suggested, earning a long-suffering look from my friend.

"Not so, Watson," Holmes argued. "Regrettably, we do not have time to debate the point. There is Lord Garnett's. Ah, and here comes your rising star." Holmes leaned forward and, in a conspiratorial whisper, added, "I will admit this detective shows some promise."

"Oh?" I said, somewhat surprised.

"He knows enough to call for me," Holmes explained.

Cambers waited anxiously as the cabbie brought his horse to a stop. Detective Cambers' open face was twisted into an expression of calamity. His eyes darted to and fro, reminding me of a frightened rabbit. Holmes dismissed the cabbie and turned to the Scotland Yard man.

"You've completed a search of the grounds?"

"I have Mr. Holmes," Cambers answered. "We've found nothing, nothing at all. I was just on my way in to inform Lord Garnett."

"How many constables are with you?" Holmes asked.

"Four," Cambers reported. "They're good men."

"And my list?" Holmes asked pointedly. "Have you managed to gain the answers I instructed you to seek?"

Cambers looked surprised by the question, but, seeing Holmes's unfaltering expression, the young man grimaced and confessed, "I'd just begun, Mr. Holmes, when the kidnapping – "

"Kidnapping?" Holmes interrupted the Scotland Yard detective. "Has that been determined?"

"Well," Cambers prevaricated. "The boy is only seven years of age.

It seems unlikely he'd just wander off alone in the night."

"Seems unlikely?" Holmes shook his head. "I trust we're able to do better than that, Mr. Cambers."

The young detective's expression rearranged itself into a guarded look. "Of course, Mr. Holmes, any help you can provide will be appreciated."

Holmes nodded, indifferent to whether his assistance would be appreciated or not. "How many of my questions were you able to answer before abandoning them?"

"I'd been speaking to the chief cook, Mr. Holmes," Cambers explained. "She'd just completed the questions on your list when the alarm went up. As you might imagine, Lady Garnett is hysterical. Her physician has visited, and I believe her Ladyship has been sedated."

"Have you the cook's answers?" Holmes asked.

Cambers dug in his pocket and removed the sheet of questions Holmes had written out for him the previous evening, and another sheet of paper, presumably from the chief cook.

"Very well." Holmes examined the cook's list. "And the other question you were to ask her?"

"She says she had no idea as to the nature of his Lordship's stolen foreign treasure," Cambers said.

"Was that the phrase she used?" Holmes asked. "Foreign treasure?"

"I think it was, yes," Cambers answered. Shuffling his feet impatiently, he added, "I should really report to Lord Garnett. He's most insistent that he be kept informed."

"You must proceed as you think best," Holmes declared. "Watson and I shall make some inquiries of our own. I assume the head butler waits inside?"

"I believe so," Cambers said without conviction.

"Then we shall gather answers for your neglected list." Holmes gestured for the Detective Constable to lead the way into the house.

"If you discover anything – "

"I will keep you informed," Holmes assured the detective. We hurried up the stairs and into Lord Garnett's grand house. Detective Cambers, anxious to make his report, waved us towards the kitchens where the household staff might be found before hurrying away in search of Lord Garnett. In short order, Holmes was questioning the head butler, a white-haired elderly gentleman with a timid but impeccable appearance.

"I wish you to write a list naming everyone who visited this house during the two days before Lord Garnett's dinner party," Holmes requested.

"Of course, sir," the butler replied. "Anything to assist the young master's return."

"You are aware of the other matter?" Holmes asked the butler.

"The theft?" The butler shook his head. "I'm afraid his Lordship has not seen fit to inform me of it."

"Even so, you know of it. Surely the police spoke to you? Asked you if you'd seen anything suspicious?"

"No, sir, they did not." The butler's formal demeanour and neutral expression still managed to quietly express his disapproval.

Holmes scowled in a manner that, to my eyes, seemed somewhat theatrical. The detective complained, "I was hoping you could tell me what was stolen."

"Well, sir." The butler looked left and right before leaning forward and conspiratorially lowering his voice. "I believe it was some object he brought back from his Borneo holdings. Although I don't know the item's exact nature, I did see the trunk in which it arrived. If you care to examine the trunk, I believe it is still in the drawing room."

"Indeed," Holmes said. "The drawing room is down this hallway?"

"By the stairs, sir," the butler agreed.

"Once you've completed your list, please bring it to us there."

The drawing room fitted Cambers' description perfectly. A large, elegant space filled with an assortment of seats scattered around a small fireplace. Two doors opened to the interior of the room and four large windows looked outside. Holmes inspected the lock on the door through which we entered.

"Well, Watson," Holmes mused as he examined the door. "Does it seem strange to you that neither the chief cook nor the butler are aware of the nature of Lord Garnett's stolen items?"

"It is a large home," I reasoned. "Likely the kitchen staff does not normally have access to the drawing room."

"And the butler?" Holmes asked, shifting his attention to the first of the windows.

Frowning, I considered the problem. "No doubt a busy man –"

"No doubt," Holmes agreed, moving to the next window. "However, that explains nothing. If the head of staff was not aware of the skulls' presence, it follows that none of the staff knew of them."

"Can you be certain of that?" I asked.

"Gossip, Watson, is as much a force of nature as sunlight or sea tides," Holmes explained. "If any of the staff had seen the skulls, they would have spoken of it and, once uttered, word surely would have reached the ears of one of the household chiefs. Imagine if I placed a skull on my mantle in Baker Street. How long do you think it would be before Mrs. Hudson informed you of the addition?"

Chuckling, I conceded the point. "But what does it mean, Holmes?"

"Only that Detective Cambers has been shockingly misled as to the nature of the thefts. He believes a net of skulls has been taken, when in fact a mysterious foreign treasure has gone missing."

Holmes finished his examination of the last window and turned his attention to the remaining door. I moved to follow when something outside the window caught my eye. A branch of one of the rose bushes had been recently broken, a few dark threads were tangled in its thorns, and at the edge of the garden a partial footprint was visible in the soft soil.

"Well-spotted, Watson," Holmes commented as he examined the door. I continued to look out the window.

"You saw it too." It wasn't a question, I knew Holmes's methods too well to believe he had missed such evidence. "Why didn't you tell me?"

"Because it is meaningless," Holmes declared. "It has nothing to do with the theft of the skulls or the missing child. As I'm sure you'll agree, the matter of the missing boy is too urgent to allow us to loiter over such trivia. However else he was misled, Cambers was correct when he stated the doors and windows had not been tampered with. Meaning the thief had a key or found another way in and out this room."

Turning his attention upward, Holmes surveyed the high ceilings. "Now Watson, never having visited a Borneo long-house, I must confess to a degree of uncertainty regarding how best to display a net full of skulls. However I suspect that hook in the ceiling would serve, don't you agree?"

"It seems secure enough," I answered.

"And it is a recent addition. You can see a hand print where the workman braced himself as he put it in. And yet – " Holmes turned around, his eager eyes searching for something by the fireplace. "Ah! There it is!" Striding over to the small fireplace, Holmes recovered a long, slender pole with a metal catch on the end. Holding the pole aloft, he retraced his steps to the ceiling hook. The pole easily reached the hook, leaving no doubt it had been constructed for just that purpose.

"And here is the trunk the butler mentioned," Holmes observed, resting the pole between the mantle and a green trunk lying open on the floor. Holmes bent to examine the trunk with his lens. For a moment Holmes was silent. Then he stood suddenly upright with an alarmed expression on his normally reserved features.

Holmes turned to me, putting away his lens, and began to speak. "Watson, I fear – "

Fate deemed I would have to wait to discover what had wrought so sudden a change in my friend's demeanour, as the butler chose that moment to enter the room. He announced his presence with a deferential, "Sir?"

"Quickly man, quickly!" Holmes exclaimed, rushing towards the servant. "You have the list?"

"Yes, sir," the butler replied, holding a folded sheet of paper in his gloved hand. "I only just completed it. I thought, perhaps, you – "

But Holmes snatched the list from the servant's hand and unfolded it quickly. As he did so, I saw Detective Cambers approaching, no doubt reacting to the urgency in Holmes's loud voice.

Behind Cambers came another figure. From the stout man's harried expression, I knew it must be Lord Garnett. The strain of his situation showed clearly on the strong features of his face. Beneath dark brows, his Lordship's brown eyes seemed wary, as if cringing in anticipation of the morning's next blow. Yet even in the midst of these troubles, a ghost of the old adventurer remained. Thick, dark hair and a moustache he had not yet attended to, a tan darkening his face and the back of his strong hands. There was doggedness to his movements, as if his every step was an act of determination, and anyone who dared hamper his way had best be prepared to pay a steep cost for their insolence. Yet, even as he approached, my reaction towards his Lordship was not one of intimidation or respect, but was, rather, one of sympathy. It was plain to my senses Lord Garnett was very close to being overwhelmed by the unexplained disappearance of his son.

Such were my impressions of Lord Garnett. Holmes seemed to take no notice of his Lordship's approach. Holmes's formidable powers of concentration were focussed on the butler's list and, in his other hand, the chief cook's list he'd pulled from his pocket.

Detective Cambers and Lord Garnett entered the room together. His Lordship, seeing his butler waiting, raised his hand and started to give instructions to his servant. "Ah, I wonder if you might see to – "

"I have not yet finished with this man." Holmes interrupted firmly, though he did not look up from the lists he was examining.

"I beg your pardon?" Lord Garnett asked, blinking in surprise. Apparently his Lordship was not accustomed to being interrupted while addressing his servants.

"I have further need of this man," Holmes insisted.

Turning to acknowledge his employer, the butler seemed intent on ignoring Holmes and letting the matter drop. Whatever else he had endured, it seemed Lord Garnett was not willing to suffer impertinence such as Holmes was displaying.

"And who, sir, are you?" Lord Garnett asked, his voice a threatening rumble.

"My name is Sherlock Holmes." Pulling the butler's coat until the man was forced to turn and acknowledge him, Holmes pointed to a name on the list. "I require an address for this man."

"I regret, sir, that I do not know the address offhand."

"Then find someone who does!" Holmes demanded forcefully. "And hurry!"

Shocked by Holmes's insistence, the butler turned pleadingly to Lord Garnett. His Lordship seemed quite taken aback by Holmes's manner and was about to voice his displeasure when Holmes spoke first.

"Lord Garnett, your son's life may depend on the speedy resolution of your butler's errand. If you value your child's life, I suggest you give him leave to go."

"Of course," Lord Garnett nodded to his servant, who promptly left the room at a pace seeming, for one so dignified, a run. "Now then, Mr. Holmes, is it? I fail to – "

But Holmes had turned his attention to Detective Constable Cambers. "I will require two of your uniformed officers, those you judge to be most capable, and I require them now."

Cambers, his face clouded with displeasure at being addressed so in front of his Lordship, frowned. "Now see here, Mr. Holmes – "

"Now!" Holmes repeated. "We must act quickly if we are to capture this villain."

Cambers opened his mouth to argue, but snapped it shut when he noticed Lord Garnett's formidable attention on him. With an uncertain shrug, Cambers hurried from the room, much as the butler had before him.

"Now then, Mr. Holmes," Lord Garnett started, but, to the surprise of both his Lordship and myself, Holmes set off down the hallway at a quick run. For a moment Lord Garnett seemed at a complete loss. I had the impression it had been quite a long time since his Lordship had met anyone as insolent as Holmes. His Lordship watched Holmes's slender figure disappear beyond the doorway, and then he turned to me in a manner reminiscent of heavy artillery.

"And you are?" Lord Garnett asked me.

"Doctor John Watson," I said, offering my hand. Lord Garnett shook it firmly, apparently relieved to be dealing with someone familiar with the concept of courtesy.

"Are you with the police?"

"No," I answered, somewhat embarrassed. "I'm here with Sherlock Holmes."

"Ah," Lord Garnett nodded. "Then perhaps you can tell me: Who is this Sherlock Holmes? Is he a policeman?"

"No," I admitted. "He is a detective, a consulting detective. Cambers came to seek his advice last evening and sent word this morning of your misfortune. Naturally, we came to offer what assistance we could."

"Assistance?" Lord Garnett repeated in surprise. "Is that what he was doing?"

"I assure you, Lord Garnett, my friend's methods may seem odd but he is a remarkable detective." Yet I had barely finished uttering these words of confidence when Holmes rushed back into the room bearing a large basin of water. Ignoring both Lord Garnett and myself, Holmes hurried to the fireplace and, upturning the heavy basin, doused the burning coals. An enormous plume of smoke and steam spilled from the fireplace and when it cleared Holmes was standing surprisingly close to Lord Garnett.

"Lord Garnett," Holmes addressed the missing child's father directly for the first time. "Can you tell me when this room was last cleaned?"

"Have you lost your mind?" Lord Garnett sputtered, waving away the last of the steam.

"It was cleaned before you locked the room, was it not?" Holmes asked, refusing to be distracted by Lord Garnett's outrage.

"Of course," Lord Garnett answered.

"Naturally." Holmes turned to me and explained. "It would make little sense to lock the servants out of the drawing room if it had not already been tidied. And as the staff was unaware of the nature of his Lordship's souvenirs, it follows the skulls were closed up in that trunk. Correct?"

Lord Garnett's complexion changed to an unhealthy ruddy colour as he replied to Holmes. "Who the devil do you think you are, coming into my house and – "

"Oh, I am sorry," Holmes apologised, much to Lord Garnett's surprise. "I thought I had introduced myself. My name is Sherlock Holmes, and your son's life depends on me."

Holmes's reply had a profound effect on Lord Garnett. The man's bluster seemed to disappear, his ruddy complexion paled in horror, and he reached for a nearby chair to steady himself.

"The skulls were closed up in that trunk, correct?" Holmes repeated his question.

"Yes," Lord Garnett answered meekly.

"I see no evidence of the trunk having been locked," Holmes mused. "Yet it seems likely the skulls were not simply laid inside. There must have been something more."

"There was," Lord Garnett agreed. "A bag, I purchased it from a sailor. It was – "

"Forgive me, your Lordship," Holmes interrupted Lord Garnett dismissively. "I hear your man approaching."

Just as Holmes predicted, the butler appeared in the room, a slip of paper in his hand.

"You have the address I requested?" Holmes asked. "I do, sir."

Detective Cambers, with two of his constables in tow, followed on the butler's heels. The expression on Cambers' open face made it clear he intended to regain control of the situation. Holmes, however, completely ignored the detective.

"Give the address to the constables here," Holmes instructed the butler. "Gentlemen, you are to go to this address and search the premises for Lord Garnett's missing skulls. Take note of all you see there, with a special eye towards any children you might observe. Find the man and ask to see his certificate. I doubt he has one, despite the law concerning his trade. Regardless of what excuse he provides, take him to Scotland Yard for questioning. If he has the temerity to ask what he is to be charged with, inform him the charge is murder."

"Murder?" Lord Garnett whispered, his face paling even more. His Lordship staggered against a seat and fell into it.

"Courage, Lord Garnett," Holmes instructed the missing child's father. "There is still hope. You were about to describe the bag you purchased from the sailor, the one you used to store your net of skulls. If you would be so kind as to share your description with the constables?"

"What?" For a moment Lord Garnett looked confused, and I feared the events of the dreadful day had overtaken his reason. After a moment however, sensing the rapt attention of the constables, Lord Garnett managed to speak in a curiously disconnected, uncharacteristically soft voice.

"The bag? Oh yes, I purchased it from a sailor. It fit quite neatly into the trunk and was made of sealskin. Waterproof, you see, very handy. It opened at one end and I threaded a chain through the grommets so I could lock it with a padlock. I didn't want anyone to look inside. It could give someone quite a fright and I was planning to write a paper. I didn't want to give any of my rivals a chance to examine them. Of course, I lined the inside of the bag with wool. You cannot allow the skulls to get cold, you know, or else the souls of their owners will come back and haunt you."

Lord Garnett's eyes had grown quite wide as he uttered the last part of this speech, weaving a macabre spell which held the constables, Cambers, the butler, and myself captivated.

Breaking the spell, Holmes proved himself immune to the fascination gripping us. "How charming. Constables, you know your duty. See to it!"

The constables started off, completely oblivious to the hand Detective Constable Cambers' raised to stop them. Or perhaps the constables merely reacted to the more forceful nature of Holmes's authority.

Cambers was, by this time, glaring at Holmes, and I feared a confrontation between the two men was imminent. Holmes must have sensed the Detective Constable's hostility as he suddenly spoke. "Watson, why don't you show the Detective Constable what you discovered at the window?"

Suddenly I found myself the focus of Cambers and Lord Garnett. "Of course, Holmes," I replied, remembering how Holmes had dismissed the apparent clues as trivial. "I was over here when I noticed – "

"A footprint!" Cambers exclaimed.

"Yes," I agreed. "And you see there, some dark threads tangled among the rose bushes.

"They certainly weren't there yesterday," Cambers proclaimed. "Obviously, the footprint was made by the kidnappers."

"Whoever made the footprint didn't gain entrance into the drawing room," I observed. "The windows were still secure, and there's no trace of mud in here."

"Likely they tried the windows and found some other way in," Cambers judged. "We'll need a closer look."

Cambers left the room, presumably to go out to the garden and examine the footprint. I turned and was surprised to discover I was once again alone in the room with Lord Garnett. Holmes and the butler had disappeared while I was distracted by Cambers.

"They've gone upstairs," Lord Garnett informed me. "Your friend said he urgently needed to examine the roof."

"Whatever for?" I asked.

Lord Garnett simply shrugged. He seemed utterly drained by the experiences of the day. I suspected Holmes's use of the word murder had deeply frightened the man. Wishing I had some comfort to offer, I stood and said simply, "I think I'll join them."

"Yes," Lord Garnett agreed. "Perhaps I'll come as well."

"It might be best if you were to rest." It was, I reflected, not a very helpful suggestion, but the urge to prescribe rest is deeply ingrained in all physicians.

Lord Garnett shook his head. "I know you mean well," he said, "but I couldn't rest. What if they found something and I was asleep? No, it would be best if I went somewhere in case I was needed."

"Then perhaps, before we go, you'll join me for a brandy?" It was all I could think to offer.

"Yes," Lord Garnett agreed. He stood and went to fetch the drinks from one of the cabinets along the wall. Returning, he passed me a glass with a generous measure of amber liquid in it.

"And to think yesterday my most pressing concern

was the missing skulls." Lord Garnett shook his head and grimaced. "And now your friend seems to think he has found them."

"Likely he has," I said. "As I said, he is an extraordinary detective."

"Do you believe he can find my son?" Lord Garnett asked, unable to look me in the eye as he voiced his deepest wish.

"He will find him," I assured the man. "Of that I have no doubt." Lord Garnett nodded sadly, hearing the unspoken fear in my voice.

In truth I had no doubt at all regarding Holmes's ability to locate the child but there was no way of knowing what condition in which we would find the boy.

"Henry is often a difficult child," Lord Garnett confessed. "Headstrong and quite independent, despite his young age. We've often quarrelled, but I am extremely proud of him. Do you think I will have the chance to tell him so?"

"Honestly, I don't know," I admitted. "But if anyone can find the boy, it's Sherlock Holmes."

Nodding, Lord Garnett drained his brandy and set the empty glass on a nearby table. Though I had barely tasted mine, I set my glass next to his. The brandy had done Lord Garnett a world of good, returning some colour to his complexion and easing some of the strain in his determined features.

"Let's find Holmes, shall we?" I suggested.

"Yes," Lord Garnett agreed, leading the way out of the room. I caught a glimpse of Cambers and his remaining constables through the windows as we passed.

Apparently Lord Garnett saw them as well. "Your friend tricked them. He saw Cambers was spoiling for a fight so he had you point out the footprint in the garden. He only did it to keep them out of his way, didn't he?"

"I believe so," I admitted, following Lord Garnett up the stairs. "When I first noticed the footprint in the garden,

Holmes told me it meant nothing. He seems to be in a dreadful hurry, but I don't understand why."

"Well," Lord Garnett said, "I suppose that's a hopeful sign."

We found the butler on the uppermost floor of the house, standing on a small balcony and clutching a precariously perched ladder which Holmes climbed down with a fearlessness that bordered on the reckless.

"Watson! I trust Cambers is occupied in the garden?" "He is," I agreed. "But Holmes, why – "

"Sorry Watson, time is short," Holmes forestalled my question. "Lord Garnett, could you show me to your son's room?"

"Of course," Lord Garnett nodded. "This way."

"Lord Garnett," Holmes asked as he followed his Lordship out to the stairs. "Your son came to see you late last night."

"How on Earth did you know that?" Lord Garnett asked.

"He must have had some complaint," Holmes observed. "What did he say?"

Lord Garnett led the way down the flight of stairs. "It sounded so childish at the time, but it chills me to think of it now. He claimed he'd heard a ghost Mr. Holmes, a ghost moaning in agony."

"You did not believe him?" Holmes asked with perfect sincerity.

"No, I didn't," Lord Garnett admitted.

"That is your son's room there?" Holmes asked, not waiting for Lord Garnett's direction.

"It is," Lord Garnett confirmed, again startled by Holmes seemingly supernatural abilities.

Holmes turned and addressed Lord Garnett and the butler, who had followed us downstairs.

"Go to the garden shed." Holmes instructed them. "Bring me a pick, a pry bar, a lantern, some rope, whatever you can lay hands on. Quickly! Bring them to me here!"

To my surprise, both the butler and Lord Garnett hurried away to fulfil Holmes's command. Holmes turned and looked at me with weary eyes. "I will say this for the headhunters of Borneo, they are honest enough to display their sins in plain view. It is an example we could learn from."

"Holmes, whatever do you mean?" I asked.

"Bones, Watson," Holmes admitted, walking into the missing child's room and pulling out a pocketknife. "My knowledge of the subject is not as extensive as Lord Garnett's, but it is enough to confirm my observation. Headhunters display the fruits of their savagery proudly, rather than hiding them inside walls. You didn't, by any chance, bring your stethoscope with you?"

"No." Holmes had stopped me on the street, between home and my Paddington practice, before I'd reached the tools of my profession.

"Pity," Holmes observed as he unfolded his pocketknife and inserted the blade into the wall.

"Holmes?" I asked, watching in mute horror as Holmes dragged the blade through the wall. He was making a dreadful mess but, after carving a gouge more than two feet long in the wall, he seemed to find what he was searching for. He withdrew the blade, folded it and put it back in his pocket.

From outside came the sounds of men running up the stairs. Lord Garnett rushed into the room, a large pick in his hand. The butler had found a pry-bar, a hammer and a lantern, which he dropped onto the child's unmade bed with obvious relief.

"Some water would not go amiss," Holmes observed as he took hold of the pick Lord Garnett had brought. The butler, his refinement stretched somewhat thin, observed Holmes with a cool look but left to fulfil the detective's request.

"This must be done with some care," Holmes told me

as I picked up the pry bar. "The trick is to pull the bricks outward, not to let them fall inside."

"Bricks?" I asked.

In answer, Holmes swung his pick into the wall and, in a shower of lath and plaster, uncovered a section of chimney. Such destruction caused me a measure of surprise, but Lord Garnett, sitting on the edge of his son's bed, simply watched without expression.

"Hurry, Watson," Holmes swung the axe again, knocking one of the chimney bricks inward at an angle. Hurrying to help, though not at all certain the purpose behind this extravagant destruction, I reached in with my pry bar and attempted to pull the brick outwards.

"Back in the hallway, you were going to ask about Cambers and the footprint in the garden," Holmes explained as I worked. When the brick fell out, he swung the pick once more, loosening more bricks. "No doubt by now you've reached the obvious conclusion. The footprint and remnant of cloth were left by one of the police constables as they searched the grounds this morning."

Hearing this, Lord Garnett was unable to contain a bleak chuckle. "Can you be certain of that?" I asked.

"Of course," Holmes said as he swung the pick again. "You saw the footprint, the distinctive pattern of a hobnail boot. And the colour of the threads match the police constable's uniform precisely. While I do not wish to mention the constable's name, I have matched the evidence to the subject. If his name was mentioned, I fear the poor man would suffer Cambers' displeasure. It is a peculiar conceit of Scotland Yard investigators, they seem convinced all the footprints in the world belong to someone else."

"And the skulls?" I asked. "What makes you believe you know where they are?"

"Believe?" Holmes swung the pick again. "Watson, your lack of confidence is astounding. The man whose address the butler found is the chimneysweep who finished tending to Lord Garnett's chimneys the morning of the party."

"A chimneysweep?" I shook my head. "Holmes, there's
no possible way a grown man could fit down that chimney."

"No?" Holmes asked. "It would, of course, depend upon
the man, but you are most likely correct. Unfortunately, and
to our nation's great shame, chimneysweeps discovered a
method of overcoming such obstacles centuries ago. There
are laws against the practise now, a system of certification
designed specifically to bring an end to the dreadful practise.
Surely you see it now, Watson? Lord Garnett?"

At that moment I was prying out bricks, enlarging the
hole Holmes had knocked in the chimney.

"Lord Garnett, if you would be so kind as to light that
lamp," Holmes asked. "The boy's complaint of spirits
moaning in the night, that must clarify matters? This is,
after all, the same chimney we saw in the drawing room,
one floor beneath us."

"Are you suggesting something is trapped in the
chimney?" I asked.

"Something?" Holmes shook his head. "No, Watson,
someone. The evidence is clear, although the crime itself
is obviously based on a series of misunderstandings and
random chance. Start with the assumption the chimneysweep
is a villain. He comes to Lord Garnett's to practise his
trade and hears the servants talking about their Master's
return, and the strange trunk he has taken such care to bring
back with him. Surely, the servants gossip, it must contain
a great treasure! The chimneysweep, being a villain, listens
carefully and constructs a plan. He apologises for not being
able to complete his work that day, but promises to return
early the next morning to finish."

The hole in the chimney was now large enough I could
insert my head through it but Holmes urged me to continue
widening it. "Early next morning, the sweep returns,
carrying the brushes of his trade with him. Hidden in among
his tools is the means by which he hopes to accomplish his

theft. A climbing boy."

"A climbing boy?" I stopped my task.

"Not so long ago the city was teeming with them," Holmes explained as he gestured for me to continue my efforts. "It is entirely likely this sweep was once a wretched boy earning his living as a sweep's apprentice. The legislation forbidding the use of climbing boys is quite recent, but the sweep, having survived his apprenticeship, feels the law unjust. After all, what is his crime? Teaching children a trade? And if nine of his ten young apprentices perish, well, London is filled with orphans, after all. A child trapped within a chimney brings no harm to anyone, even saving his master the cost of a burial. And those that fall to the fumes or the diseases arising from breathing smoke and eating soot can easily and inexpensively be disposed of."

"Holmes?" I asked.

"Slightly wider, Watson," Holmes said, taking the lit lantern from Lord Garnett. "My fears were first stirred in the drawing room when I discovered a smudge of soot on the lid of the empty chest. They were confirmed when I saw the sweep's name and occupation on the list of visitors the butler prepared. You recall my next action?"

"You fetched water to put out the fire in the grate," Lord Garnett recalled.

"Then proceeded to the roof, hoping to find the boys up near the opening of the chimney," Holmes explained. "Unfortunately, all I found there was a trail of blood."

"Boys?" Lord Garnett asked. "How does my son's disappearance figure into this?"

"The role of the climbing boy was quite straightforward," Holmes explained. "He was to wait in the chimney, enduring the smoke and fumes of the fire below, until nightfall. Then, putting out the fire with water brought for that purpose, he was to climb down, remove the exotic treasure from its case, and bring it to the roof where the sweep waited. Unfortunately for the boy, the sweep betrayed him. Rather than take the child and the treasure, the sweep opted to take only the treasure. He struck the boy, leaving a trail of blood inside of the chimney. The climbing boy fell, becoming entangled in the flue. Whatever his injuries, he still had the water he'd brought to douse the fire. Somehow he clung to life until your return."

"The ghost Lord Garnett's son complained of?" I asked.

"The climbing boy," Holmes agreed. "Finding no one willing to believe his night-time tale, your son acted on his own. Quite bravely too, if I may be permitted to observe. He crawled up the chimney himself. Unfortunately, it appears he also became entangled in the dark. There, Watson, that should be large enough."

Holmes hurried in, sticking his arm with the lantern and his head into the opening we had made. He quickly pulled his head out again. I couldn't help but notice the soot staining his cheek.

"They are there!" Holmes announced. Holmes took off his coat and tied a large loop in the thin rope from the garden shed. Lord Garnett was up and running to the stairs, yelling in commanding tones for assistance.

"Are they – " I couldn't bring myself to finish the sentence.

"They're not moving," Holmes observed. "And they are black as night. Beyond that, I cannot say."

Lord Garnett returned with Cambers and the constables in tow. The butler reappeared, bearing a full glass of water in each hand. It was a tight fit, but Holmes was able to reach into the darkness and loop the rope around the trapped boys. He pulled out the first blackened form, then the other. The two small children were indistinguishable under the soot they wore.

One of the boys coughed and gratefully accepted water from the butler. As the child's face was cleaned I witnessed the joyful reunion of Lord Garnett and his son. The climbing boy was, I am saddened to say, already dead when we pulled his small, broken form from the darkness.

"He'll hang for this," Detective Constable Cambers vowed as Holmes explained the nature of the crime. When the two constables returned from their errand, they reported finding everything as Holmes predicted. A sealskin bag containing the darkened skulls, its lock broken, was found in the sweeps' home, as was evidence of several orphans. The sweep had no certificate and had been practising his trade with no license.

As we took a cab from Lord Garnett's, his Lordship's profuse thanks still ringing in our ears, Holmes expounded on the point he'd been trying to make when we arrived at the manor. "As a rule, the crimes of the countryside are crimes of honest malice, acts of base motive, and Cambers is well-suited to such offences. London, on the other hand, offers its denizens crimes of opportunity. Misdeeds requiring little or no planning, acts of indifference, and Cambers is ill-prepared for such random villainy. I would also point out that it is not enough for a detective to simply ask the correct question. After all, Cambers did ask Lord Garnett for a list of everyone who visited the manor the day of the theft. Yet how was his Lordship to know which trades-people had visited? No, a detective must match the right question to the right person, a lesson young Cambers has yet to learn."

Larceny in the Sky with Diamonds

by Robert V. Stapleton

collected a glass of champagne from the waiter's tray, and looked around the room. A string-quartet was playing, elegant young couples were dancing, and I was in search of a victim.

It was the early spring of 1891, and I'd been invited to this society gathering a few miles outside London. For some reason, the hostess regarded me as a philanthropist, and I didn't like to disillusion her on that matter. Organised crime was flourishing, and my greatest adversary was on the run, but I was bored. I needed something to lift the gloom. Sherlock Holmes might resort to cocaine, but I needed a fresh hands-on criminal project to engage my attention. I knew the sort of person I was looking for. He or she would be alone, vulnerable, and brooding. I've discovered that there's always at least one such person to be found at every social event.

I spotted her at the far side of the room. The young woman was standing on her own, not touching her drink, and with her eyes fixed on the unfocused distance. Her mind was clearly on matters far away from this place.

"Her name is Lady Jacinta Pulmorton," the waiter told me. He was one of our men, and he'd noticed my interest in the woman.

"Of Oakenby Hall?"

"The same."

We retreated to an alcove where we could talk freely without being overheard.

"Ah, yes," I told him. "I remember we blackmailed her last year over some personal matter."

"We had some letters she wanted kept hidden from her husband."

"Indeed, a most unfortunate business, but we gave most of those letters back to her in the end."

"That's how I remember it, Professor."

"And my name never came into the affair."

"I believe not."

"Good. That's just as it should be. So, out of a sense of guilt, this lady will now be even more devoted to her husband than ever before. She can't still be worried about those letters. I wonder what's troubling her now."

Through the crowd of guests, I noticed Grimdale's mop of chestnut hair. He was lurking quietly beside the fireplace. He's a good man to have around: a first-rate dodger. He had also seen the young woman, and was watching her like a predacious cat eyeing a doomed mouse. Grimdale turned his hooded eyes towards me. I nodded, and we converged on her from our different directions.

"Good evening," I began. "It's Lady Pulmorton, isn't it?"

She looked up, startled by my interruption to her thoughts. "That's right." Her periwinkle blue eyes were enchanting, but they were clouded by sadness.

"We haven't been introduced," I told her, "but my name is Moriarty. Most people just know me as The Professor."

"Good evening, Professor," she replied. She'd obviously never heard of me before.

"And this is my colleague, Harold Grimdale," I said, indicating my companion.

She gave us each a melancholy smile.

"The evening's going well," I said, trying to break the ice with small-talk.

"Is it?" she said, looking down at her still-full glass of wine. "I hadn't noticed."

I decided to jump straight in. "Forgive me for approaching you like this, your ladyship," I said, "but I was concerned. You appear to be rather unhappy."

She looked up at me. "Is it that obvious?"

"I'm afraid so." I gave her a smile that I hoped would convey deep sympathy. It didn't matter if it was sincere or not, just so long as she thought it was. There was a mystery here that needed to be investigated.

Lady Pulmorton looked as if she was holding back from saying something important. I needed to gain her confidence.

"I can assure you, your ladyship," I told her, "we are both completely trustworthy." I can lie most convincingly when I want to. I gave her another warm smile.

She began to thaw. "It's about my husband," she began.

Grimdale and I exchanged glances. The signs of a profit here were already looking good.

"Is he making you unhappy?"

"Oh, we've had our ups and downs," she admitted, "but we have been extremely happy together. Until recently."

"Recently?"

"You see, Professor, over the last three years, my husband has developed an absurd interest in flying."

"Indeed? Flying?"

"It's become an obsession. He began by building a glider, and then testing it himself."

"That sounds a dangerous pastime."

"So it turned out. He crashed the thing on its very first flight. He was lucky to escape with nothing worse than a broken leg and a dislocated shoulder."

"All part and parcel of the adventure, I believe."

"Then he became obsessed with building a powered flying machine."

"People all over the world are experimenting with powered flight," I told her. "But to build a machine capable of taking a man into the air and then keeping him aloft, now that really is the aeronautical Holy Grail."

"Well, my husband has done just that," she said. There was a hint of pride in her voice. "He's built one."

"Really? You mean to say he's actually got the thing to fly?" I began to imagine the enormous income we might gain from this business.

"Oh, yes. It took off all right. Then it crashed, just like last time.

He's been injured yet again."

"I'm sorry to hear that."

"That was nearly two months ago now."

"And has it put your husband off flying?"

"Not a bit of it. He can't wait to have another go."

"And how's his recovery going?"

"He's up and about again, but he still walks with a limp."

Tears welled up in Lady Pulmorton's eyes that would have melted any other man's heart. Pah! I almost felt sorry for the woman.

"I can see how that would upset you," I told her.

"That's not the only problem, Professor," she continued.

Out of the corner of my eye, I noticed our hostess bearing down on us. I was afraid she might make Lady Pulmorton clam up altogether. I needed to hear what more she had to tell me, so I sent Grimdale to occupy our hostess in some engrossing conversation. As a cockney born and bred, that's where his real talents lie.

Meanwhile, I put down my glass and took Lady Pulmorton out onto the terrace. We stood together, looking out over the greening fields of the Thames valley. The cool air was still, loaded with the sweet aroma of new life and fresh growth. The evening was delightful: if you like that sort of thing.

"You see, Professor," she continued, "the engineer who was working with my husband has gone missing. What's even worse is that he seems to have taken my husband's design blueprints with him."

I hesitated for a moment. Then I asked, "Have you informed the police?"

"No. My husband believes it's much more serious than that. He thinks the man might try to sell those papers to some foreign power, possibly to be used against this country. He is extremely upset."

"Naturally. So, it's becoming a matter of national security?"

She nodded. "With my husband confined to the house and grounds, I decided to consult Mr. Sherlock Holmes myself. But they tell me he's away from London at the moment."

"Yes, I believe he's somewhere on the Continent." I tried to keep the bitterness I felt for the man out of my voice. Holmes had been making life very difficult for me recently, and I was glad he was making himself scarce.

"I don't know who else to turn to." Her face clouded over again.

"As it happens," I told her, "I, too, am interested in crime and the criminal classes. Perhaps I could find this scoundrel for you." A criminal operating outside my sphere of influence was a personal matter for me. The man had to be dealt with.

A look of hope filled her ladyship's charming eyes. "That would be wonderful," she said. "Thank you, Professor."

"As time is clearly of the essence," I told her, "we'll come down to Oakenby Hall by the first train tomorrow."

"Moriarty?" said Sir Henry Pulmorton when we arrived at Oakenby Hall on the following morning. "I don't think I know the name."

"I am well known for my academic and charitable work," I told him.

Well, at least that was half true.

"In that case, welcome to my home, Professor."

Sir Henry was in the Morning Room, sitting beside a

window that looked out over the parkland in front of the house. He was a man of medium height, with dark hair, a pointed nose, and piercing brown eyes.

"Your wife has told me something of your problem," I began. "You think your engineer might have stolen the blueprints to your flying machine."

"Oh, there's no doubt about it," he replied. "I discovered yesterday morning that my safe had been opened and that those papers were missing. He's the only person with anything to gain from taking them. Now the rascal himself has disappeared."

An enterprising fellow, I thought to myself. "What's the man's name?"

"Jeremiah Silt," he replied, in a tone that implied utter contempt. "Physical description?"

"He's a short, mousy sort of fellow, with grey hair framing a balding head. His most distinctive feature has to be his long sideburns."

"Your wife thinks he might try to sell those plans to some foreign power."

"That is highly likely," said Pulmorton. "He often talked about how useful flying machines might be in times of war. If he can steal from me, then he might well be capable of betraying his country."

"Will you allow us to investigate the matter for you, Sir Henry?" I asked.

"I can't do it myself," he replied, pointing to his ash walking stick, "So yes, please do whatever you can, Professor. Get those documents back for me, and I'll pay you well for your time and effort."

I bowed graciously. I'd willingly have done the job for nothing. "But first," I told him, "I'd like to see your machine."

"Certainly. Come with me."

Obviously still in considerable pain, Sir Henry picked up his stick, hobbled out through the front door and led us round to the far side of the house. There we approached a vast wooden tithe-barn. From the front of this building, a pathway of hard-packed earth led off across the garden.

When I stepped inside the barn, I was utterly amazed. The flying machine almost filled the place. It was a monoplane, shaped like some gigantic bat, with a wingspan of over 40 feet. The bone-like structure of the wings was covered with a black silk-like fabric. The fuselage consisted of an open carriage on wheels, with a wooden seat at the back.

"The carriage would normally be enclosed," Sir Henry explained, "but we've been concentrating on repairing the wing mechanisms first."

"Even so," I told him, "it's a magnificent machine."

"It's based on a French design."

"By Clément Ader?"

"You've heard of him, Professor?"

"Indeed."

"Silt got the plans for me. The machinery is complicated and expensive to make, so I was glad of his engineering skills and know-how. He even made a few improvements of his own. Flight is controlled by adjusting the wings. You can alter the flow of air over the front edge of the wings, change their total area, or flex the end-sections."

"And the engine?"

"We're using a steam-powered engine," said Sir Henry. "It's situated just in front of the aviator, and powers a single propeller at the front. The engine is cooled by a radiator directly above. It's a light-weight apparatus, fuelled by alcohol-spirits. We store the alcohol in barrels at the back of the barn."

"Amazing!"

"Again, it's based on Ader's own revolutionary design."
"Did Silt get that for you as well?"

"Yes, but he refused to tell me how."

"In test-flights last year, Ader's machine proved to be underpowered."

"Perhaps, but this one isn't."

"You mean to say it really flies?"

"Oh, yes. It crashes spectacularly as well. While I've been recovering from my injuries, I've been busy putting the machine back together again. As I said, the damage was mostly to the wings. That's now been fixed, so I'm hoping to fly it again very soon."

"Tell me, Sir Henry," I said, "how do you operate the engine?"

"Put simply, you open the tap on the fuel-reservoir, light the boiler jets and wait for the water to boil. Then you allow high-pressure steam into the engine. This drives the cylinders, which turn the propeller."

"Just like boiling a kettle."

"Pretty much. Then hang on for the ride of your life."

Before Grimdale and I left for London, Lady Pulmorton stopped us. "We have yet another problem, Professor."

"Can I help?"

She looked flustered. "In two days' time, an important visitor will be coming to stay with us. A lady from Russia. The Countess of Felixburg."

My eyes lit up. "Isn't she one of the richest women in Europe?"

"I believe she is," said Lady Pulmorton. "It means that we're going to need some extra security here." She turned her heart-melting eyes onto me. "Could I possibly impose on you to take this extra duty on for us, Professor?"

I felt like an alcoholic who's just been asked to take charge of a brewery. "I would be delighted," I told her. "I have some business to attend to first, but I shall return the day after tomorrow."

In the train back to Waterloo, I sat alone with Grimdale in a First Class compartment. We had bribed the guard, locked the door, and drawn down the blinds, so there was little danger of anyone interrupting us.

"Are you really going to help this man?" Grimdale asked me.

"I don't see why not," I told him. "Especially now that the Countess is coming to stay at Oakenby Hall."

"As you say, she is reputed to be extremely rich."

"Indeed, but I'm going to need more details," I told him. "Contact our colleagues in the European criminal underworld and ask them for a description of her jewellery. Somebody will know."

"I'll get onto it the moment we reach the Smoke," said Grimdale.

I tore a sheet of paper from my pocket notebook, wrote a few brief words on it and handed it to my companion. "But first, I want you to deliver this message."

His eyes opened wide when he saw the address. "Are you sure, Professor?"

"Completely."

The message was simple: "Meet me in the Calcutta Room of the Century Hotel, Mayfair, at seven tonight. Come alone. Moriarty."

Sherlock Holmes and I have much in common. We are both chameleons: cold and calculating, whilst at the same time being masters of deception and disguise. He is a worthy but deadly opponent. But it was not Sherlock I'd asked to meet me that evening, it was his brother, Mycroft.

For this meeting, I adopted my persona as a cold fish. I stood at the far end of the room, placed my gloves and top-hat on the table beside me, and leaned on my silver-topped cane.

When he arrived, Mycroft remained near the door. It amused me to think that he didn't want to come any closer.

"I take great exception to being summoned like this," he told me.

"Regrettable, but necessary," I replied.

"I have important state business to attend to."

"No doubt, but I need to consult you on a matter of national security."

Mycroft raised one eyebrow in surprise. He can

sometimes appear as unemotional as his brother.

"You may have heard about Sir Henry Pulmorton's obsession with flying-machines."

"He has made no secret of it."

"But what you might not know is that he has now succeeded in building one."

"Have you seen it?"

"Indeed."

"Have you seen it fly?"

"Not yet."

"Then it's a purely academic matter."

"But his assistant believes it can fly. So much so that he has stolen the blueprints. He may try to sell those documents to some foreign power."

In the fading light, I saw Mycroft's eyes sparkle. Now he was interested.

"The man's name is Jeremiah Silt," I told him.

"Someone of that name did make an initial approach to our government," Mycroft admitted, "but we didn't think it was a matter worth pursuing."

"So he may wish to try his luck elsewhere." "He might."

"You know the diplomatic scene better than anyone," I continued. "Who is there in London who might be willing to pay good money for those papers?"

"What's your interest in this?"

"You may be under the impression that I have criminal tendencies, Mr. Holmes," I told him. "The truth is that I am an intensely patriotic man. I wish, as much as any other true-blooded Englishman, to see to all enemies of our Queen and country vanquished." I was putting on a very convincing show. I could easily persuade myself that all this claptrap really was true.

Mycroft looked pensively out of the window at the darkening sky. "The German Ambassador is expecting a visitor from Berlin," he said. "A man with direct access to the Kaiser himself. I believe he has a particular interest in flying machines."

"That has to be more than a coincidence."

"But whether the Kaiser is also interested is another matter entirely. However, if this fellow Silt is hoping to sell those plans to some foreign power, he might begin by taking them to the German Embassy."

"When?"

"Their visitor arrives tomorrow morning."

"Another foreign visitor!" I exclaimed. "It must be a sign of spring. But the cuckoos are a little early this year. In that case, I shall have my men keep a constant watch on the place until our man shows up."

"He might not."

"But there's a good chance that he will."

From first light, my men kept a discreet vigil outside the Embassy of the Imperial German Government. I'm pretty sure that Mycroft had his own people watching the street as well. I'd have been disappointed if he hadn't.

Later that morning, a young lad, who works for us as a runner, reported to me that the German official had now arrived.

"A posh toff, with a beard as long as Methuselah's," he said. "Came from the station in a carriage as if 'e was the King of Prussia 'isself."

I took a hansom to Belgravia and stopped across the road from the Embassy. Grimdale gave me his succinct report. "He's definitely in there, Professor."

"Then all we have to do is wait for Silt to arrive," I told him. "Are your men in position?"

"We've got a newspaper-seller, a road sweeper and some men pretending to work on repairing the road," he replied.

"He mustn't be allowed to reach the front door."

"Don't worry, Professor. The moment Silt turns up, we'll have him."

"Very well," I told him. "I'll wait here."

I made no secret of the fact that I was watching the place.

Leaning on my swordstick cane, I stood with my eyes fixed on the front door of the Embassy. All afternoon, diplomats came and went, but I never for one moment took my eyes off that door.

The lamplighter was already doing his rounds by the time Silt arrived. The engineer's sideburns were almost undetectable in the fading light, but I can recognise a guilty man when I see one. There was no mistaking the furtive way he shuffled along the street towards the Embassy building.

The front door of the Embassy opened, and a tall man with an impressive white beard stood in the entrance. But it was too late. Before he could come within 20 feet of the place, my men took Silt in hand.

I crossed the road towards him. "Jeremiah Silt, I believe."

"How dare you treat me like this!" he snapped.

"Because I know all about you."

A look of concern crossed his face. "What do you mean?"

"We both know that you stole those blueprints to Sir Henry Pulmorton's flying machine."

"Stole? I was the one who got them for him in the first place," said Silt. "If I stole anything from anyone, then it was from the Frenchman. I adapted his designs. I added more power to the engine. I was the one who made the thing fly. I am a genius!"

"No doubt," I replied coldly, "but we also know that you came here hoping to sell those blueprints to the German government. You're a traitor to your country, Silt."

"I tried to interest our government in my machine," Silt sneered, "but they didn't want to know. I wanted to develop the design further, but for that I needed money, more than Sir Henry could give me. This country ought to celebrate me as a hero, not condemn me as a traitor."

"Sir Henry wants his documents back," I told him. "Hand them over to me immediately."

He thrust his hand beneath his coat, drew out a bundle of papers and handed them to me, muttering darkly to himself.

Mycroft Holmes now arrived in his own cab. He was looking very pleased with himself.

"At least now those plans won't be used against this country," he said.

"You regard the Germans as potential enemies?" I asked him.

"They are a growing threat in Europe," he replied. "One day, Professor, they will become a direct threat to us." That was very interesting.

"Give me those plans," said Mycroft. "I'll make sure they get safely back to Sir Henry Pulmorton."

"Do you still not trust me?" I asked, trying to sound offended. "Not in the slightest," he replied.

I handed over the plans. "I'll keep Silt," I told him.

"This isn't a police matter," Mycroft told me, "so I'm sure I can safely leave him in your hands."

Oakenby Hall was in turmoil when we arrived there on the following afternoon.

"The Countess has arrived from Russia," said the butler. He sounded exasperated. "Together with her entire household."

"I was hoping to speak with Sir Henry," I told him.

"He's extremely busy, sir," the butler replied. "But he is expecting you. He hopes you will both join him at dinner this evening."

"As members of the security staff," I replied, "we shall certainly both be there."

"There are two bedrooms prepared for you and your companion in the south wing of the house," the butler added. "I hope you will find the arrangements to your satisfaction."

"I'm sure we will," I replied. "But where will the countess be staying?"

"In the Blue Room, sir. On the first floor at the front of the house."

After we'd settled into our rooms, Grimdale joined me to discuss our next step.

"What have you learnt about the Countess?" I asked him.

"Following the death of her husband last year, she now owns a great deal of land in her native country," said Grimdale.

"Her income is more than enough to keep herself and her entire household very comfortable indeed."

"And her jewellery?"

"She never goes anywhere without it."

"That's what I like to hear," I replied. "It gives us a realistic chance of taking it from her. Do you have any details?"

"There are several pieces large enough to attract attention if sold on the open market."

"Then we must concentrate on the smaller ones."

Grimdale laid the complete list of jewellery on the table in front of me. "There's one piece that looks particularly interesting," he told me. "It's described as a necklace made up of three strands of diamonds."

"I have no doubt she'll be wearing it tonight," I said. "So we must find out what happens to it after the meal."

"Sir Henry might lock it away in his safe."

"Perhaps."

Our luggage was light, suitable only for a flying visit, but we both managed to turn up to dinner that evening looking suitably turned out.

"Ah, Professor," said Sir Henry, when we met just before the meal, "it's good to see you again."

"And you, Sir Henry," I replied. "I trust you received your papers."

"Indeed. They came by special delivery from Whitehall this morning."

"That's just as it should be," I told him. I added modestly, "I have my contacts there."

Grimdale raised an eyebrow in surprise at such a pretentious statement.

I ignored him.

"I hope those blueprints are back where they belong."

"They are now once again locked away in the safe in my study."

"That's good to hear." It was indeed very good to hear. If some grubby little engineer could open that safe, then a criminal mastermind like myself should have no difficulty with it.

At dinner, I was seated opposite the Guest of Honour, the Countess herself. At first, we talked of unimportant things, but my attention was fastened on her necklace. It was just as my informants had described it. There were three strands of diamonds, no single stone remarkable on its own, but together undoubtedly worth a fortune.

"That's a magnificent necklace, madam," I told her.

"My late husband gave it to me," she explained. "The stones came from the private treasury of the Tsar himself."

"Indeed? They must be worth a great deal."

"Several millions of roubles, I believe."

"Then, as the man in charge of security here, I must caution you to be on your guard, Countess." I shook my head sadly. "There are thieves active in this country. Are you sure the necklace will be safe during your stay here?"

"I am quite sure it will be," she replied.

"Of course," I continued. "Sir Henry has a heavy-duty safe in his study."

She laughed, then fixed me with her steel-grey eyes. "It will not be in his safe, Professor," she said. "I insist on keeping this particular necklace close to me at all times."

"That is a very wise decision, madam," I assured her, "very wise indeed."

I had to get my hands on those jewels. But how? As I watched the wine waiter serving out the hock, the germ of a plan began to form in my mind.

I noticed that the lower button on the man's jacket was hanging loose. As he leaned over me, with the bottle in his hand, I grasped hold of the button and gave it a sharp jerk. It came away so easily that the man failed to notice that anything was wrong.

By the time the meal was over, my plan was complete in every detail. The below-stairs staff would be key to its success.

When nobody was watching, I left the dining room and descended to the servants' hall. There my eyes fell on a charming young chamber maid.

"Excuse me, my dear," I began. "Yes, sir?"

"Would you like to earn a sovereign?"

She gave me a suspicious look. "What do I have to do?"

"Oh, nothing much." I took out a glass vial and held it in front of her. It's amazing the things a master criminal keeps concealed in his pockets. "All you have to do is to pour the contents of this vial into the Countess's last drink of the day."

"But why?"

"The Countess has had a long journey," I explained. "She needs a good night's sleep."

"Don't we all?"

"You must also make sure that her bedroom door is left unlocked tonight."

"It's the job of her lady's maid to secure the door."

"But not this time," I told the girl. "Tonight, her maid will have her mind on other things."

"What if someone sees me? Are you sure I won't get into trouble over this?"

"Quite sure," I replied. "If anyone does question you, just tell them that you saw the wine waiter loitering in the corridor outside her room. That should leave you completely in the clear."

I gave Grimdale the job of keeping the Countess's lady's maid occupied that night. He seemed pleased with the assignment.

"But first," I told him, "I want you to have a word with our coachman."

"Are we leaving tomorrow?"

"Most certainly. At first light."

"What do you want him to do, Professor?"

"Just make sure that our bags are on the brougham and that he's waiting for us at first light down by the old packhorse bridge."

"The stone bridge across the river?"

"That's the one. Then I want you to go to the barn and make sure the flying machine is fuelled-up and ready to go."

"Are we going to fly out?"

"If necessary. As you know, every good burglar prepares an alternative way of escape."

Grimdale nodded.

"Then, first thing in the morning, go back to the barn and light the boiler. Until then, the night and the girl are yours."

Shortly after midnight, I tried the door of the Countess's bedroom. The handle turned easily and without a sound. Inside, the air was infused with the smell of expensive cologne. The Countess was alone, lying on her back; a well-upholstered woman in a well-upholstered bed. She was snoring like a pig. The sleeping potion had obviously worked. It ought to have done. There was enough in that vial to put an elephant out for the count.

Now I had to find the necklace. But where would she have put it? The Countess had boasted about keeping it close to herself at all times. The idea of searching her person didn't appeal to me in the slightest, so I began with the bedside cabinet. I had a lantern with hinged shutters on all four sides. This was the only light I had to work with. In addition, I would have to rely on the well-honed sensitivity of my fingertips.

The top drawer contained only personal documents. I slipped these into my coat pocket. Then I tried the middle drawer. Nothing. Then a stroke of luck. I found the jewels in the bottom drawer. They were in an ordinary jewellery-case, hidden beneath a large fur hat. I took the jewels, returned the case and closed the drawer.

On my way out, I dropped the wine waiter's button onto

the floor beside the bed. That would see his goose nicely cooked.

It was still dark when I reached Sir Henry's study early the next morning. The safe stood in its usual place, against the wall directly opposite the door. I lit my lantern and knelt down to examine the lock. It was a simple combination affair. I tried the number we'd extracted from Jeremiah Silt just before he died. It was no use. Pulmorton had obviously changed the combination number. I'd certainly have done the same in his shoes.

It didn't really matter. I had it open within five minutes anyway.

I was now glad that I was wearing my voluminous coat with the cavernous pockets. It might look an ungainly garment, but it is extremely practical for a burglar. Faced with a pile of jewellery-cases, and with no time to examine their contents, I transferred them all to the pockets of my coat.

At the back of the safe, I found what I was looking for. The bundle of papers we'd taken from Silt outside the German Embassy. I took them out of the safe and locked it again. Then I stood up and turned towards the study door.

There, in the gloom, I saw Sir Henry Pulmorton. He was standing in the doorway, holding a double-barrelled shotgun, and pointing it directly at me.

"Moriarty!" he exclaimed. "I've had a message from Whitehall warning me not to trust you. Now I see the truth of it. I've sent a telegram to Scotland Yard, asking what they know about you. I expect a reply imminently."

I'd anticipated something like this. That's the trouble with honest people; you just can't trust them. But it was too late now to protest my innocence.

"Damn you, Mycroft!" I hissed. "And damn you too, Pulmorton!"

"No, you're the one who'll be damned, Moriarty," he growled. "Put those things back in my safe, or I'll shoot you as an intruder."

Was he bluffing? Did he have the nerve to pull the trigger? In this world, I consider myself the measure of all things. If the hereafter brings judgement, then I shall have to face it in due time. But I had no wish to be sent to my doom by Sir Henry Pulmorton. Nor, on the other hand, did I wish to return my ill-gotten gains to his safe. The result was a tense stand-off.

It was now that Grimdale appeared. And just in time, as well. He opened the front door and called out, "Everything's ready, Professor."

Instinctively, Sir Henry turned his attention away from me and looked out into the entrance hall.

I am no gymnast, but today I had to act quickly. In the blink of an eyelid, I kicked out at the shotgun in Sir Henry's hands.

The gun went off, peppering the ceiling above us with the contents of both barrels, and bringing down a shower of plaster. The noise was loud enough to waken the dead. The fact that it would rouse the rest of the household was bad enough. Time was now extremely short.

When Sir Henry turned to face me again, I pressed the point of my swordstick blade tightly against his throat.

"Drop the gun, Sir Henry," I told him. He dropped it onto the floor beside him. "Now step away from it."

He shuffled to one side.

Without repeating Sir Henry's mistake of taking my eyes off my opponent, I spoke to Grimdale. "We have to get away from here quickly," I told him. "Go back to the barn and open the doors."

When my companion had left, Sir Henry turned his blazing eyes fully onto me. "You'll never be able to fly that machine, Moriarty," he growled. "It took me 12 months to learn, and then I crashed the thing."

"I'm a fast learner," I replied.

"Very well. Take the thing, and break your neck."

I could hear footsteps hurrying along the corridor. It was time to leave. I sheathed the blade, picked up the shotgun and rushed outside. There I dropped the weapon into the herbaceous border. I hoped that might give me enough time to get clear of the grounds.

When I reached the barn, I found that Grimdale had the flying machine ready for me. It was an impressive sight. The boiler was bubbling nicely, steam was bursting out through gaps in the machine's boiler-jacket, and the sweet smell of industrial alcohol was hanging in the morning air.

I climbed onto the seat and jammed the blueprints safely behind a couple of struts. Then I pushed my cane into a space beside the seat and pulled my hat firmly down on my head.

Pulmorton had been right about the controls. They were fiendishly complicated. I was now faced with a confusing array of valves, cranks, dials and foot-pedals.

I tried to remember what Sir Henry had told me on my previous visit. I cautiously opened a valve. High-pressure steam hissed into the engine cylinders. One of the dials indicated an increase in steam- pressure. The four-bladed propeller started to turn. The flying machine emerged under its own power and began to move slowly along the pathway. The wheels rattled noisily on the hard-packed earth.

Then I heard angry shouts coming from somewhere nearby. I needed to make a quick exit. I opened the steam valve still further. The pressure in the engine now increased rapidly, the propeller began to turn more quickly, and the machine shot forward, giving me a violent kick in the rear.

A gunshot rang out. Trust Sir Henry to have another 12-bore. I was spared a direct hit as shotgun pellets peppered the structures around me. One of them hit the fuel cylinder, and alcohol-spirits began to spray out through the hole. I was lucky the entire thing hadn't exploded there and then.

As the flying machine picked up speed, a gust of wind caught the wings and made it swerve off the pathway. Fortunately, the wheelbase was wide enough to keep it upright when it landed on the lawn. On the other hand, it was now out of control, and careered across the front lawn like a demented chicken. Its wheels gouged unsightly ruts in the carefully manicured turf. I didn't know how to control the thing, let alone how to make it take off. All I could do was to hang on tightly.

The machine soon reached the end of the lawn, where it bounced against the raised edge of the gravel footpath and hopped across the ha- ha. No longer having any solid ground beneath it, the machine began to fall. Desperate to avoid a crash, I opened the steam-valve as far as it would go. The contraption immediately picked up speed, and just about managed to keep clear of the ground. I was flying!

I had no idea how to control the direction of travel. I was having to learn the basics of flying as I went along. At the same time, my mathematical brain was devising possible improvements to the design.

Using a mixture of cold logic and blind panic, I fiddled with the controls until the wings opened to their fullest extent. Then I managed to alter the camber of the leading edge of the wings. These, together with the early morning breeze and increased airspeed, made the flying machine slowly gain height.

But something was wrong. I sensed that the machine was overbalanced at the front. I looked down and saw Grimdale hanging onto the wheel struts for dear life.

"What are you doing there?" I shouted.

"I wasn't going to stay and have that maniac shoot at me," he hollered back.

At that moment, the morning sun rose from behind a nearby hill and bathed the countryside in its bright warming glow.

In its light, the harsh shadow of the bat-shaped flying machine swept rapidly and menacingly across the landscape beneath us. Seen from below, the spectacle must have been utterly bizarre. Black against the clear blue sky, a tall man in a top-hat and flapping coat-tails was riding a gigantic bat, whilst another man was desperately clinging on underneath. The effect it had on the estate workers, who were coming out to begin their daily work in the fields, was startling. When they saw us coming, many of them ran away screaming. Others simply stood still, gazing into the sky, with eyes and mouths wide open in terror.

Superstitious minds might have thought that we were a vampire fleeing the light of the new day, and coming to suck their blood. Scaring people witless always gives me a great thrill.

The land was now sloping downhill. As I'd intended, we were flying towards the river in the bottom of the valley. More alarmingly, we were heading directly towards a line of trees on the far bank of the river. With the additional weight on board, we were flying so low that we risked going straight into them.

I knew I had to jettison something. I now had a choice. Either I choose to throw away the boxes in my pockets, together with the treasures they undoubtedly contained, or else I elect to drop Grimdale off as soon as possible.

It was no contest.

I noticed a willow tree on the nearside bank of the river and decided to direct the machine towards it. I flexed the ends of the wings and leaned over to my left. The machine began to turn. My colleague's extra weight helped, and we were soon making our way directly towards the willow. We flew so close to the treetop that Grimdale became entangled in the upper branches. He released his grip on the undercarriage and fell ten feet into the water below.

Now free from its destabilising load, the machine quickly gained height. Indeed, it rose so steeply that it rapidly lost airspeed. With the fuel also running low, the propeller lost power, and the flying machine plummeted towards the ground.

I struggled frantically with the wings, trying to direct the falling machine towards the far bank of the river. I had no intension of getting wet like Grimdale, but I didn't want to kill myself either, so I looked desperately for somewhere soft to land.

Then I spotted it. Along one edge of the riverside meadow, just in front of the trees, stood a large haystack. My only hope now was to I reach this without hitting the trees. I flexed the wings, held tightly onto my hat, and prepared to hit the ground.

The flying machine landed in the haystack with a tremendous crash. It immediately broke up. The impact threw me out of my seat and into a pile of soft grass. Some might think I didn't deserve such an easy landing, but they can keep their opinions to themselves. I admit I was shaken, but I was also relieved that I was able to walk away from the wreckage.

Which was just as well. A few seconds later, the remains of the flying machine burst into flames. The pall of black smoke drifted across the fields, turning the sweet morning air acrid with the smell of burning hay and scorched textile fabric. The heat was so intense that it forced me to back away. At least I still had my hat and cane with me.

The estate workers, having overcome their initial shock, now came running. They used anything they could lay their hands on to try to beat out the flames and save what was left of the haystack.

As arranged beforehand, our carriage was standing beside the old stone bridge. The coachman now opened the door and helped me climb aboard. Once inside, I sat down and heaved a sigh of relief.

A moment later, Grimdale joined me there. He was soaked to the skin. I had no time for sympathy; my mind was already on other things.

"To the German Embassy," I announced. "Let's hope their government official still wants to buy the plans to Sir Henry's flying machine."

It was only as I looked around for the blueprints that I realised where they were. For safety, I'd pushed them behind some struts on the machine. They were still there, already burnt to ashes.

I roundly cursed my bad luck.

"All that work for nothing," said Grimdale.

I felt like throwing the man back into the river. "Drive on," I told the coachman.

As we rumbled out of the estate, I took off my hat and pulled something out from beneath the lining. It was the diamond necklace belonging to the Countess.

The sight of the jewels cheered us both up as nothing else could have done at that moment.

Grimdale gave a low whistle. "It must be worth a king's ransom," he gasped.

Then I took out the jewellery boxes I'd removed from Sir Henry's safe. We opened them one by one and took out their contents.

"You must have got every piece of jewellery the Countess owns," said Grimdale.

"She is indeed a very rich lady," I replied.

"Or at least, she used to be," added my companion.

"Scotland Yard are already making plans to arrest me," I said. "This is going to stir them up like a nest of hornets."

"They'll scour the entire country looking for us," Grimdale told me.

"In that case," I replied, "we're going to need a vacation. Somewhere abroad, I think. Possibly Switzerland."

The Glennon Falls

by Sam Wiebe

May 3, 1891
Meiringen, Switzerland

The Colonel has found the ideal spot. Far enough up the trail to prevent witnesses, yet scenic enough for a plunge to seem like the wayward footfall of an overeager tourist. One crooked step and my most recent antagonist bows out of my affairs permanently, joining a long line of others.

I am well-practiced in removing such nuisances. Since sleep has forsaken me, I have taken pen in hand to document my earliest foray into the world of crime. Yet I must admit to a certain hesitation. While the run-of-the-mill criminal values nothing save his own neck, and cares only about his "get-away," we professionals strive for anonymity. To perpetrate fraud or robbery is a confluence of luck and skill; to convince others no crime has been committed demands a rather Napoleonic genius.

There is no vanity as that of an anonymous man, and I find myself desiring a record of this, my first and by some measure, most perfect crime.

was from childhood something of a scapegrace, a blight on the Moriarty coat of arms. Mrs. Glennon, my former governess, informed me of my inherent wickedness before I reached my 11th year.

"James," she scolded on more than one occasion, "you were born ready for the gallows."

Whether Mrs. Glennon was prescient remains to be discovered, but there was no misleading her. Stout and eagle-beaked, she bestrode my childhood, handing down sanctimony and punishment like a wrathful deity. While later in life I would find other antagonists, at that age she was my chief foil and mortal enemy. I loathed her.

I know little of her childhood or upbringing, only that her parents had been liberal-minded and had seen fit to grant her an education. She had some Greek and High German, was familiar with Virgil and the Caesars, and grasped enough of mathematics to make sense of Newton.

To hear her speak of this patchwork education was to hear a beggar flaunt her rags.

The Glennon woman had married a dull-witted dogs-body who'd ended up in my father's employ. The wife's services were far from optimal, but my father, a skinflint at heart, granted her employment as well. Their shared living expenses more than made up for the deficiencies in her pedagogy.

I confess that in my early years I displayed no interest or aptitude in studies, and was accounted a dilettante. An accelerated intellect such as mine might find purchase in following its own curriculum, yet not show itself to advantage when corralled with lesser lights. While my father could have provided me with tutors, the miserly soul employed only the Glennon woman, believing her adequate. What impertinence and lack of foresight on both their parts!

Early on in this arrangement, Mrs. Glennon challenged me in one or two trivial details – a Latin declension or two, the difference between Thucydides and Heraclitus.

Emboldened by these minor victories, the oat-fed knave saw fit to intrude on larger matters. She became an expert on everything, from Locke's philosophy to the arrangement of coprimes in Euclid's orchard. Even diction – and her unable to conquer her scullery maid's burr. Utter absurdity, and untenable, to say the least.

I resolved to be done with her, and sued my father to end her employment. With an asinine judgment matched only by his miserly nature, he sided with the Glennon woman against his own son.

"The dressing gown cord."

"I have explained that," I replied.

Holmes shook his head. "Not at all, my friend. Consider this. How could I have got up from my bed, crossed the room, and taken the cord from my dressing gown without waking you? Remember, you were sitting against that door and my dressing gown, with tables at both sides blocking my approach. It would have been impossible to reach without moving either a table or yourself, and what is it that I try to impress upon you? When you have eliminated the impossible, whatever remains, however improbable, must be the truth. Don't you agree, Watson?"

For those readers whose senses are dull and slovenly – I assume this to be the majority of you, frankly – it may seem childish petulance for an adolescent to resent such a hovering, harping figure to such extent that he would consider transgressing the law to be rid of her. You may never understand what a great intellect feels when stifled by overbearing idiocy. Imagine a child caged at birth, straining to grow, yet bound by the narrow confines of dull iron bars. Now magnify this discomfort considerably, and you may begin to grasp my yearning for a more self- determined existence.

My plan was a perfect engine of such intricate craftsmanship that its memory still causes its author to smile nostalgically. My father possessed nothing so valuable as his collection of rare manuscripts. Religious tomes inscribed on vellum, first editions of Johnson and De Foe – even several Shakespearean quartos, a rough draft of *Lear* lacking Nahum Tate's civilizing amendments. My father fancied himself educated by virtue of possessing such works. I would make better use of them later.

Of particular value was an illuminated Celtic version of the Gospels, something akin to the *Book of Kells* which one can visit nowadays in the Irish colony. The artifice and detail of this work raised it to the forefront of his collection. I doubt the fool read the words of the apostles in the vulgate, let alone parsed through this Latinate version. Yet its ownership caused him great pleasure, and I had little hardship in including this volume in my plan, as a double punishment.

My father had encased the volume beneath a thick pane of glass and the sturdiest hinges and lock available. Heaven forbid he read the book. It was sufficient to gaze at two of its pages through glass, and to acknowledge it was in his possession.

Among my father's acquaintances was the painter Yarborough, a celebrated landscapist of the pastoral school. My father had commissioned him to paint my portrait, with my young self-dressed as a shepherd boy. While degrading to stand amidst our yard in such peasant garb, clutching a crook while a tenant farmer's ewe nudged my ankles, I struck up a friendship with Yarborough, and presented myself as enamored with his skill and desirous of instruction. In this, I will admit to severe exaggeration – his paintings are held in high esteem by those who ought not to be.

In any case, won over by my interest, or perhaps anticipating further commissions, Yarborough and I began correspondence. While his advice on painting went ignored, it wasn't long before Yarborough furnished me with intelligence I could use.

Some months prior, Yarborough had taken on an apprentice, who had since fallen into disrepute. This young man had shown considerable promise, which went unfulfilled due to a fondness for drink and extravagant living. Yarborough soon terminated their arrangement. This young man, whose name was Cutler, appealed several times to re- establish his tutelage. Yarborough demurred.

Cutler, then, had applied his skills to forgery, a trade he found more suited to his talents. Yarborough became aware of his pupil's new trade when a critic congratulated him on a recent canvas of the Lake District – a picture he had not painted. (The critic had pronounced it a necessary and not unwelcome progression from his previous works – if he but knew!)

Yarborough wrote to me of this, only after much prodding on my part. He seemed to wish to unburden himself of the guilt. If he'd only accepted Cutler back; if he'd only been more tractable. I reassured him there was little fault to be found in his decision, and in fact Cutler's actions bore out Yarborough's judgment. At the same time, though, I made note of Mr. Cutler's address and particulars.

My own tribulations under the Scotch witch continued. Mrs. Glennon criticized, prodded, corrected. Her intent was to remedy my weakest skills, namely history and Latin. Every criticism was a lash from a whip held by the most dim-witted of slave masters. Was I not excelling in mathematics, far beyond others my age? Was that not enough? Was mastery of a select few fields truly less praiseworthy than well-rounded mediocrity?

I vowed not to spend my 12th birthday under the same servitude as my 11th. I vowed my terrorizer would be removed.

Some months later, upon my father's return from a week's sojourn in Manchester, he found his case empty, his precious Gospels nowhere to be found. The case was locked, the dust atop it undisturbed.

Flabbergasted, he mustered the entire household. A search was conducted of the house and grounds, led by the Glennons, with my father studying them as much as appraising himself on the progress of the search. Finally the volume was located beneath the bed of the Glennons themselves, found by Mr. Glennon, presented to my father, to the astonishment and bewilderment of all three.

Unleashing a monolog of self-serving rhetoric befitting her countrywoman Lady MacBeth, Mrs. Glennon explained to my father how I had taken umbrage at her corrections, and had attempted petty vengeance by somehow unlocking the case and salting the book beneath her bed, to pin the blame upon her. She entreated him to see through my ploy and deal fairly with her, and with myself. She reminded him that kindness to the wicked is cruelty to the righteous.

My father found it easier to accept that fate had cursed him with a disloyal son, than that his own bad judgment had led him to hire shoddy menials. I protested my innocence, which of course went ignored. I was punished, cloistered in my room, my jail now also made physical.

I refused to admit to the crime, or explain how I had unlocked the display case. My father was of a choleric nature but weak-willed, happy to hand down a sentence but happier still to allow someone else its administration. The churlish Mrs. Glennon was allowed to whip me for my bad behavior. I accepted it; I pleaded only that I was not responsible.

For a month I was confined, receiving no visitors, sending nor accepting no letters. The month passed gradually. I returned to the bosom of my loving family a meek exemplar of the benefits of the corporal punishment of children.

"We'll speak no more of this matter," my father said. "I've no idea how you unlocked the case, but the book is restored and the locks have been changed and doubled. Let us resume as we have been, with mercy and forgiveness all around. A new start."

And it *was* a new start, for a scant few days after my re-admittance to the household, the book again disappeared.

While the case had been picked the first time, the second found the glass smashed. No one had heard the sound; a bundle of thick linen was found near the remnants, indicating that it had been used to muffle the shattering glass.

I was naturally accused and thrashed again, twice as severely, and unceremoniously marched back to my small room. Again a search was undertaken; again Mrs. Glennon was at hand to pour wormwood into my father's ear, and twist father against son.

The book was not found in the house. It was not in my chambers, nor Mrs. Glennon's. Neither was it hidden among the other volumes in my father's overstuffed library. I was questioned, and hit, and hit, and questioned. Then the blows ceased, and a rare burst of logic overtook my father. The book was not on the grounds; I hadn't left the grounds; no packages had been mailed, nothing unusual found in the ashes of the furnace. I was, at least, not the sole instigator.

After much hesitation the constabulary was called for. I've always had a certain disdain for the police, especially the supercilious clew-sniffers and alibi-rattlers whose education seems to be the over-reading of Vidocq's memoirs and certain salacious stories of the American author Poe. This inspector, Collins, was such a martinet. Obviously fancying himself a "great detective," he began his investigation by repeating the same searches and interrogations began by my imbecilic father. Collins reached the same conclusions.

When the search had finished, this Collins turned to me, reigned in his puffed-up demeanor, and attempted a kindly disposition. "Young master James," he said, "I am not accusing you. But since you've filched the book on a previous occasion, I have reason to think you know more than you're telling."

At this I glanced at Mrs. Glennon, then lowered my head and made no reply. Observing my body language, Collins said, "Perhaps a private chat, the two of us, if that is all right with Mr. Moriarty."

"Whatever restores to me what's mine," came my father's reply. Returning to my chambers, Collins and I resumed our conversation.

"Was there something you felt unable to tell me in their company?" Collins asked, going so far as to take a knee and grasp my shoulders.

"Someone I should look at more closely? Don't fear them; be forthright, young master."

"Mrs. Glennon is a good woman," I said. "A very good woman. She'd never do anything."

The lummox's line of questioning turned to my governess. Was she violent? Well, I admitted, she had struck me several times. Prone to peculiar behavior? Covetous of objects in the household? I admitted she had been taught to read, and regarded herself an expert and somewhat of a scholarrette.

"She's a good woman," was the invariable conclusion of my every reply.

I've no idea what Collins inferred from this, my answers being whole cloth truth. He soon nodded and we returned to the hallway and the company of my father and the Glennons. All three were questioned, though the Scotswoman received more scrutiny than the other two did, and was invited to a private *tête-à-tête*.

I noticed a softening to Mr. Glennon's features, the longer his wife was absent from the room. He began glancing frequently at the clock and busying herself with needless stoking of the fire.

When they returned, Mrs. Glennon's face was wan. Inspector Collins found pretense to repeat the search, asking permission to include the Glennons' private chambers. Since he had already acceded to such a request, several times, Glennon agreed.

Mrs. Glennon pawed at the grubby coat sleeve of her husband, leaning on his slight frame. She would not meet my eyes. When Collins had started for the domestics' quarters, I whispered to her in a tone I tried to make as reassuring as possible, "Don't worry, I didn't tell him anything."

Collins's heavy bootsteps stopped. He called out to ask if perhaps the Glennons would join him for this leg of the search.

His inspection did not turn up the missing tome, but it evidently turned up something, for I was yet again sent to my chambers, and the four adults remained in conference for the better part of the afternoon. Then suddenly a coach was sent for, and the cook informed me that I'd be dining in my room, alone, while my father and the Glennons accompanied Collins to the East End.

"Something about a note found in the missus's cabinet," the cook told me in his guttural drawl. "Something about a rented room, and a Mr. Cutter or Cutler or some-such, and a great deal of money."

Apparently the Inspector had found a scrap of paper in Mrs. Glennon's vanity, a rough note in a hand unlike that of her or her husband. The note supplied an address, an assurance that "the job" would be done "beyond the most expert scrutiny", and reiterated an agreed- upon sum. What the transaction entailed lay beyond the Inspector's knowledge, but his interest was piqued. Mrs. Glennon swore that she'd never seen the note before.

Collins, accompanied by the Glennons and my father, were conveyed to the address mentioned in the note. There was no answer at the door, and the landlady was sent for. She confessed she'd let a suite to a Mr. Cutler, who had insisted on having a separate entrance. She had only met this man twice, and was unaware of his goings or companions. Collins mentioned his police credentials, and the landlady permitted them entrance into Cutler's quarters.

Collins, no doubt believing himself a keen bloodhound, took in the contents and state of the room and deduced the story in full. My father identified various trinkets as belonging to my departed mother – ivory handbrushes, minor bits of jewelry, along with a pawnbrokers' ticket for several other familiar items. Collins inferred them as payment; unobtrusive items which could easily be stored, say in one's skirt or bags.

Among the various paintings and supplies were a series of preliminary sketches of a scandalous nature, featuring the rough outline of a woman of advancing years. Glennon looked at these, then removed himself from the room. His wife stood mute, her face drawn and bloodless, no doubt assembling some cunning justification.

Near the window, Collins identified my father's prized book, and next to it, a painstakingly accurate facsimile of several of the pages, one only half-complete. Inks, leathers, dyes, magnifying glass – materials were on hand, enough to produce several ersatz tomes. Collins also turned up a wax copy of a skeleton key, which my father identified as a match to the display case's original lock.

Mrs. Glennon began to enumerate her own beliefs regarding the scene, but she was hushed quite violently by the good inspector. Collins had them open the door to the adjoining room. Himself being speechless, he wished this state imposed on the others until he processed what he saw.

It was a bedroom, in filthy state, with men's and women's hygienics arranged on the drawing board near the mattresses. Amongst the disarray Collins noted a not insignificant quantity of laudanum, along with several political tracts and a few novels of a lurid nature.

Collins assembled these facts into a story of lust and avarice befitting the reading materials of the flat's inhabitants. It was clear Cutler had attempted to procure the volume from Mrs. Glennon, and that the pair obviously shared much more than a passing acquaintance. Not only had she cast a key to help remove the volume, she had filched enough of the bereaved family's own keepsakes to capitalize this venture. Worst of all, though, she had incriminated her student and charge – then dealt the punishment to the child herself!

Returning to our house, and ignoring Mrs. Glennon's protestations, Collins and my father once again interrogated me. When I attempted to say that Mrs. Glennon was a good woman, my father said he'd have no more lies from me.

I said I'd never seen her commit any wickedness. In the hours I was under her tutelage, I would see her come and go at admittedly odd intervals, but assured them her actions seemed benevolent. On the contrary, her brief separations seemed to reinvigorate her, and she returned to our studies with an improved demeanor, if less than full concentration and sobriety.

I told them, if I'd withheld this information from them, it was only because Mrs. Glennon had so insisted on pain of further lashings.

Inspector Collins had his constables roust Cutler from a local tavern and account for himself. He protested innocence, even agreeing to furnish samples of his handwriting. These would be identified as a match to the note found in the Glennons' living quarters.

Mr. Glennon admitted several of the products found in the flat were similar to those used by his wife. The pawnbroker produced a brooch belonging to my mother, an anniversary gift. The broker said a man roughly matching Cutler's description had pawned the bauble, well below its value, but the broker admitted he had trouble differentiating the specific facial features of gentiles.

Cutler accepted his sentence to hard labor, no doubt grateful he wasn't born a few years earlier, when forgery was a hanging offense. Mrs. Glennon was remanded to a women's' institute. While the scandal-mongerers presented them as desperate lovers, and Mrs. Glennon especially as a modern-day Black-Eyed Sue or Sweet Poll, to my knowledge they never exchanged so much as salutations.

I happily finished out my studies with the self-determination I so craved. What joy to set the chart and rudder of one's own voyage! Such freedom is priceless, desperately priceless, and all too rare.

When I began lecturing at the university several years later, I received a letter from Mrs. Glennon informing me that she'd been released. She'd found work in a hotel kitchen, and cheap lodging in a boarding-house in Southwark. She wrote that since the divorce, she'd entertained few visitors in her admittedly-shabby accommodations. Nevertheless, if I could tear myself away from my lectures for a fraction of an afternoon, I'd find myself welcome to join her for tea.

I've since made a rule never to consort with a known criminal, and never, for any reason, in that person's private quarters. Youthful arrogance! I sent her a reply indicating my pleasure to call on her.

The former Mrs. Glennon had aged severely, thinned out and grown sickly. We sat on a pair of carefully repaired cushionless chairs. Mrs. Glennon's unsteady hands poured out black tea from a battered service. No keepsakes of her prior life adorned her small apartment. Her quarters had the charm of a Dickensian orphan, and I informed her of such. She accepted the compliment graciously.

"I think you'll find," she said, "I've quite reformed. I practice nothing of the sort of activities I was accused of."

"A profitable way," I agreed, "to ensure one's happiness and liberty."

"Yes, one should confront what one has done, for by making peace with oneself, one makes peace with the world." I agreed with the sentiment for decorum's sake – who would wish to make peace with the world? Mrs. Glennon asked if I recognized the maxim's author.

"Cicero, I believe."

She shook her head but did not correct me. "Coleridge? Swift, then."

"Margaret Ann Glennon," she said. "Something I made up just now. I was always quite gifted at coinings."

"An impressive trick," I said, "most useful for amusing a husband – beg your pardon."

"He saw education the same way," she said. "A parlor game, a diversion. I'm often glad my parents didn't share his sentiment. They valued *qua* knowledge, being devotees of Mrs. Wollstonecraft's inestimable volume. Knowledge is a lonely blessing, isn't it, James?"

I said nothing.

"I will admit, James, your infinite superiority in cunning and cleverness. I needed a year to deduce the authorship of your plot. Who could hold such a grudge against me, and to what end?" Her smile was not ironic. Sensing my hesitation, she added, "We're alone, I assure you, and I'm past the desire for retribution. But I would like to hear your reasons, as well as exactly how you accomplished my ruin." I indulged her – another weakness I have since attempted to correct.

She'd believed, erroneously, that I'd employed Cutler only to double-cross him. I explained that my accomplices numbered only two, and Cutler had not been among them. Rather, he had been part of the price for my partners' complicity.

"Yarborough," she exclaimed, speaking to herself as if validating a private theory.

"Indeed. The master felt a certain guilt for his apprentice's crimes, but nothing touching the infernal rage and humiliation of having his own works forged – and bettered, according to one cretinous critic."

I went on. "Yarborough himself forged the book; he did so twice, or more accurately, one and a half times. The volume first found in your room was a forgery – the best he could do without close scrutiny of the book. Luckily such scrutiny evaded my father as well. It resembled his precious volume enough to assure him of its authenticity."

"The volume which was returned to the case," Mrs. Glennon began. "Stolen and traded with Mr. Yarborough's trusted servant, the forgery placed by your bed – yes, knowing it would be perhaps too spot- on at first, and my father's wrath would be incurred by me. But how much more on *you*, when he realized you'd deceived him, and acted as the instrument for the unfair punishment of his son?"

"A double blind," she marveled.

"Quite so." I was enjoying myself. Mrs. Glennon took the opportunity to refill our cups.

"Yarborough's servant helped me funnel several minor items out of the household. I'd drop them from my window to the garden below, or secret them during a walk. While delivering messages, the servant would retrieve them. Doubtless it was he who pawned the brooch, and arranged the room, resembling as he does Mr. Cutler in a very general way."

"And Cutler's note?"

"Included in Yarborough's correspondence – the old master outdid his pupil at forgery. When the time came, I broke the glass case and slipped the forged book into the garden in much the same way."

"Then the volume recovered from the apartment was the original?"

I smiled. "It is the one father still treasures in its case to this day. He is satisfied, and the profits of others with similar volumes are beyond his care."

"And Yarborough?"

"The old man died satisfied, happy to have outlived Cutler by several months. I understand prison weakens one's constitution – perhaps you could confirm this yourself. In any case, prison aged Mr. Cutler quite horribly."

"As it did me," she said. "Poor Mr. Cutler. Poor Yarborough, for that matter. A great deal of death."

I didn't respond.

"You remember, James, I spoke of the lonely blessing of knowledge? It is clear you have it. It would take the mind of Shakespeare to conceive a plot such as yours."

"Shakespeare nicked most of his plots from the Romans," I said.

But I thanked her for the compliment.

"I apologize to you for my harshness as a governess,"

Mrs. Glennon said.

This I didn't expect. Stunned, I muttered my acceptance of her apology.

"I know well the feeling of being stifled, underestimated, underappreciated. All women know this, James, but my own education made me rather more sensitive to the issue. It is an English-man's world; a woman from the Hebrides has little place in it. I felt so fortunate your father chose me as your governess. How forward-thinking he was, to overlook class and race and gender! How I hoped to inculcate in you that same open-mindedness!"

"Mrs. Glennon," I began, but couldn't quite finish.

"James," she said, "I'm not long for this world, so permit me to play Cassandra to you – she was a prophetess whose words invariably fell on deaf ears."

"I know who she was," I snapped.

"I could have been an ally, James, even better, a friend. But your genius is singular. It brooks no competition, and therefore accepts no one as equal, no one as companion-worthy."

I shook my head, anger rising.

"You are a great man, young Mr. Moriarty – professor, I should say. A great man, and destined to make enemies of all those most able to understand you. If and when you are confronted with a true equal, rather than companionship, I suspect you'll find only mutual destruction. It's a fall from grace, and one your young self has already taken. I wish I could pity you."

She prattled on; I took little heed of her MacBethian pronouncements. The passing years bore out my deafness. My wealth, my successes, my empire, stand in testament to the falsehood of her words.

In her way, Mrs. Glennon was a bright creature, perhaps at one time capable of overcoming the natural inferiority of her sex. To Professor James Moriarty, though, she would always be, merely, a woman.

The Adventure of the Sleeping Cardinal

or

The Doctor's Case

by Jeremy Branton Holstein

y name is Watson, Doctor Watson, and it was my privilege to share the adventures of Sherlock Holmes. Throughout the many years I lived with Holmes in Baker Street, I came to know both his many gifts and his many faults. Chief among those faults was an intolerance of dull routine, an impatience that was often tested in the interim between clients when no new problems were available to challenge his active mind. It was during one such lull, in the summer of 1899, that my story begins.

It was early morning, and I was supping upon one of Mrs. Hudson's excellent breakfasts. Holmes, however, had declined the meal, and was instead pacing back and forth before the mantelpiece in our sitting room. Finally, he threw up his hands and bellowed his frustration at the top of his lungs.

"Bah!" he cried. "This is interminable, Watson! Interminable!"

"What's that, Holmes?" I said, even though I knew the answer.

"This inactivity!" said Holmes. "Has the entire criminal population of London gone on holiday? Give me a case to solve, a problem to unravel! Anything but this endless boredom!"

"Calm down, Holmes," I said. "Something will turn

up soon. Why don't you have some of Mrs. Hudson's breakfast?"

"I don't need food, Watson," said Holmes. "I need clients! I am a thinking machine, and my mind must be fed problems, lest it wither from languor."

"Perhaps there's something in the paper for your mind to chew on." I picked up the morning paper and leafed through the pages. "Ah," I said. "Here's an interesting item. They've found Henry Tuttle alive and in hiding! He'd faked his death to avoid his creditors."

"A cowardly act," said Holmes, "but far from interesting."

"I seem to recall you did much the same a few years back," I said.

"For entirely different reasons, Watson," said Holmes. "You know that."

I did my best to hide my smile. "If you say so." I turned another page, and a new article caught my eye "Ah, here's something. Apparently the Sleeping Cardinal has been put up for auction."

"The Sleeping Cardinal?" said Holmes. "Now that is interesting. I believe you were involved in the painting's recovery a few years back?"

"I played my part, yes," I said.

"Yet you've never told me the full story," said Holmes. "It's never come up before."

"Well then, Doctor," said Holmes, "if the criminals of the present cannot challenge my mind, then perhaps the criminals of the past can. Tell me your tale."

"Are you, Sherlock Holmes, really asking me to tell you one of my stories? You usually dislike my writing in the Strand Magazine."

Holmes fixed me with the gravest of stares. "It's either your stories or the needle, Watson," he said. "I leave the decision to you."

"Very well," I said, and pushed my breakfast aside. "Where to begin?"

"You are the storyteller, Watson," said Holmes. "I place myself in your capable hands."

"I suppose," I began, "that the best place would be the summer of 1892. It had been over a year since your disappearance, Holmes, and some months before your reappearance in London. During the intervening time, I had left the world of criminal investigation behind, choosing instead to focus upon my medical practice and the health of my beloved wife Mary, God rest her soul."

"Indeed," said Holmes. "Pray continue." I gathered my thoughts, and began.

It was a beastly hot summer, as I recall, and my list of clients had swelled as a result. I had just finished treating a patient for heat exhaustion over near Covent Garden when I, quite literally, ran into an old friend. I was walking home and so consumed with thoughts of my wife and her health that I didn't even see the gentleman until I had barreled into him.

"I beg your pardon, sir," I said.

The gentleman, however, did not want to give pardon and began to yell back at me. "Why don't you watch where you're...." he began, but then stopped, his eyes widening in surprise and his mouth spreading into a grin. "Well, if that doesn't beat all," he said. "Is that you, Doctor Watson?"

My heart burst with joy at the sight of the man. "Why, it's Inspector Lestrade!" I said. "My dear fellow. It's good to see you."

"What brings you down to Covent Garden?" said Lestrade.

"Oh, I've just finished up with a patient," I said.

"And you?"

"Business, I'm afraid."

"Ah!" I said. "A case?" I could not help but feel a tingle of the old excitement at the prospect.

"Still investigating crimes, Doctor?" said Lestrade.

"No, of course not. Not since Holmes's death at

Reichenbach."

"Of course."

"I still follow crime in the paper, though," I said. "Try to puzzle them out as Holmes would have done."

Lestrade regarded me with a curious expression. "Actually," he said, "it's funny running into you like this. This robbery I'm looking into. It's exactly the sort of case your Mr. Holmes would have enjoyed."

"Really?" I said.

Lestrade considered me for a moment, and then said, "See here, Doctor, this is a bit irregular, but are you busy? I could use a fresh set of eyes on this one."

I smiled. "For old time's sake?" I said. "Why, Inspector, I'd be honoured."

"Capital," said Lestrade. "Then follow me, and I'll outline the details of the case en-route."

"Lead the way," I said. "I'm your man."

We set off together down St. Martin's Lane, Lestrade talking as we walked.

"It's like this, Doctor," he said. "Last night, one Lady Margaret checks into the Hotel Metropole, carrying with her a very expensive painting, called..." Lestrade pulled a notebook from his pocket, and consulted his notes. "... The Sleeping Cardinal," he finished.

"I'm not familiar with it," I said.

"Neither was I before now," said Lestrade, "but they say it's a masterpiece and worth a king's ransom. Lady Margaret had brought the framed painting into town for an exhibition. Not wanting to leave it in her room, she asks the manager..." Lestrade checked his notebook again. "... one Patrick Pardman, if he'd store it in the hotel safe for the night. Mr. Pardman agrees, and locks the painting up in his office before heading home. You follow me so far?"

"Perfectly," I said.

"Well, Doctor," said Lestrade. "Imagine Pardman's surprise when he arrives the next morning, goes to open the safe, and finds the painting gone!"

"Stolen!" I said.

"One would think so, but there's no evidence of a break-in at all! The safe is stored in Pardman's office, a small room with no windows and only one entrance in or out, a door just behind the main desk of the hotel."

"And the desk was manned all night?" I asked.

Lestrade nodded. "They assure me it was. By one..." He checked his notebook again. "... James Ryder, I believe."

"James Ryder," I said. "I know that name from somewhere."

"Do you now?" said Lestrade. "Well, this Ryder claims no one else entered the office between the time Pardman left for the night and when he returned the next morning. So how did the painting disappear?"

"Was the office locked at night?" I asked. "Could someone have slipped in while Ryder wasn't looking? Or perhaps it could have even been Ryder himself?"

Lestrade shook his head. "Mr. Pardman assures me he locks the door when he leaves at night, and only unlocks it first thing in the morning."

"No sign of tampering, I suppose."

"None."

I thought about the problem as we walked. "This is a bit of a stretch," I said after a time, "but could Pardman himself have taken the painting?"

"Pardman was seen last night leaving the hotel by both Ryder and the porter," said Lestrade. "He wasn't even carrying a bag, let alone a framed painting."

"You're right, Lestrade," I said. "This is exactly the sort of case Holmes would have enjoyed."

"I thought as much," said Lestrade, "As you can imagine, Lady Margaret is quite distraught and demanding the hotel cover the value of her painting in currency. If we can't find the culprit and recover the Sleeping Cardinal, the hotel will find itself in quite a financial bind! Ah, here we are," he said, stopping on the street before the Hotel Metropole. "This way, Doctor," he said.

We entered into an opulent hotel lobby, empty save for a constable guarding three people by the main desk. The woman, who I took to be Lady Margaret, for she was well dressed and ample, stood beside the two gentlemen who could not have looked more different from one another. One, who I soon learned was Patrick Pardman, was a tall, handsome fellow. The other, James Ryder, was short and rat-faced.

Lady Margaret wasted no time in pouncing upon Lestrade. "At last!" she said. "What took you so long?"

Lestrade was ever the professional. "My apologies, Lady Margaret," he said, impassively. "Yard business."

Lady Margaret huffed at this. "I don't understand what could possibly be more important than my compensation."

Lestrade ignored her indignation, and instead introduced me. "This is my colleague, Doctor Watson," he said. "He'll be assisting me with the investigation. Doctor, this is Lady Margaret, Patrick Pardman and James Ryder."

We all mumbled, "How do you do?" to each other.

"Excuse me," said Pardman, "but are you the same Doctor Watson who works with Sherlock Holmes?"

I considered correcting his grammatical tenses, but decided to let it pass. "I am," I said.

Pardman seized me by my hand and began to shake vigorously. "Bless me!" he said. "It's an honour, sir. An honour."

"You've read my stories?" I asked.

Pardman let my hand go, somewhat sheepishly. "Well, not as such, no," he said. "But you're quite popular among the hotel guests. They're always chattering on about your friend's exploits. Is he here with you now? It would be a privilege to meet him."

"I'm afraid not, Mr. Pardman," I said. "Holmes is..." I paused, searching for the right word. "... away," I finished.

"If we can get back to the business at hand, please," said Lestrade, never one to let a sentimental moment remain uninterrupted. He pulled out his notebook yet again, and flipped open to an empty page. "Now, let's review the details for Doctor Watson's benefit. Lady Margaret, you checked in to the hotel last night around seven. Is that correct?"

"Correct," said Lady Margaret.

Lestrade recorded this in his notebook. "And while checking in, you turned the painting over to Mr. Pardman for safe-keeping?"

"Well, of course!" said Lady Margaret. "I couldn't have such a priceless masterpiece of art lying around my room, now could I? You never know who works at these sorts of places."

"Madame," began Pardman, with the greatest indignity. "The Metropole is among the top hotels in London...."

Lady Margaret interrupted him. "The top hotels in thievery, you mean."

"If I can continue?" said Lestrade, waving his notebook about for emphasis. "Now then. Lady Margaret, can you describe the painting in question?"

"Certainly," said Lady Margaret. "It is a particularly lovely piece of impressionistic artistry by the painter Flemming. With sublime brush strokes, Flemming depicting a priest at rest upon an altar...."

Lestrade cut her off. "Just the size of the painting will do."

Lady Margaret looked as if she might explode, but she answered with even precision. "Two by three feet, Inspector, mounted in a mahogany frame."

Lestrade wrote this down in his notebook. "Thank you. Now, Mr. Pardman. You put the painting immediately into your safe, is that correct?"

"Immediately, sir," said Pardman. "Security is a top priority." "And you locked the safe thereafter?" asked Lestrade.

"Of course," said Pardman. "I even double-checked the lock." His lip trembled at this, as some of his professional composure broke. "Oh, Inspector, how could this have happened?" he said. "I'll be out of a job!"

"Have some faith in the force, Mr. Pardman," said Lestrade. "We'll recover the painting, never fear. Now what time did you leave the hotel?"

"Just after eight that night," said Pardman. "Ryder had come on to work the desk shortly before Lady Margaret checked in, and I retired to my office to finish some paperwork. When I was done, I locked the office and bid Ryder good night."

"Ryder," said Lestrade, "can you confirm the time?"

Ryder, who had been very quiet up until now, nodded his head. "Indeed, sir," he said. "Eight o'clock."

"And you're absolutely certain," said Lestrade, "that no one entered the office between eight that evening and when Mr. Pardman arrived for work the next morning?"

"On my honour, sir," said Ryder. "It was a quiet evening, and I never left my post at the desk."

"Excuse me, Mr. Ryder," I asked, "but you look very familiar. Have we met before?"

"I don't believe so, sir," said Ryder, but he never met my eyes. I could tell he was lying.

Lestrade noticed none of this. "What time did Mr. Pardman return?" he asked.

"Around six this morning, I think," said Ryder.

"Six on the dot, sir," said Pardman. "Punctuality is my motto."

"And it was then you discovered the painting missing?" said Lestrade.

"Well," said Pardman, "not immediately. It wasn't until Lady Margaret came down and asked to check on her painting that I opened the safe. But when I did, the painting was gone!"

"No sign of a break-in?" said Lestrade.

Pardman shook his head. "None that I could see, sir."

"And Lady Margaret," said Lestrade. "What time did you come down?"

"Just past 6:30," said Lady Margaret. "I'd had a bad dream, and woke up convinced something had happened to my painting!"

Lestrade rubbed his chin. "A dream, eh?" he said. "That's quite a coincidence."

"Mr. Pardman," I said, "could we have a look at this safe?"

"Of course," said Pardman. "Anything I can do to help. This way, gentlemen."

We left Lady Margaret and Ryder behind in the lobby as Pardman ushered us into a spartan office, devoid of any charm or character. No pictures adorned its windowless walls, and the only furniture was a single desk, two chairs and the large safe pushed into the far corner. The only luxury the room offered was its fireplace; a prize, I was sure, during the cold London winters.

"As you can see, gentlemen," said Pardman, "the door is the only way in or out."

Lestrade studied the safe. "I see no signs of tampering. What about you, Doctor?"

I studied the safe, looking for the scratches and dents that might indicate foul play. "None that I can see," I said at last. "Who knows the combination to the safe?"

"Only myself," said Pardman, "although I do keep it recorded on my desk ledger."

"Isn't that a security risk?" said Lestrade.

"Maybe," said Pardman, "but I've got a terrible memory, so it's better to have it written down than not. Besides, the office is locked at all times when I'm not here."

Lestrade turned away, whispering aside to me so that Pardman could not hear, "Little doubt how the thief got into the safe, is there Doctor?"

"Indeed, Inspector," I whispered back. "But there still

remains the question of how he got into the office in the first place."

Lestrade turned back to Pardman. "Who all has the key to your office?" he asked.

"There's only one key, Inspector," said Pardman. "I keep it with me at all times." From his pocket he withdrew a keyring, singling one out.

"That's a rather unusual looking key, Mr. Pardman," I said.

"A Roman design, Doctor," said Pardman. "A trick for my memory to know which key fits my office lock."

"Now then, this Ryder," said Lestrade. "How long has he been with the hotel?"

"Less than a year," said Pardman, "but he came with references from the Hotel Cosmopolitan. I know the manager over there personally."

"And how long have you been with the Metropole, Mr. Pardman?" I asked.

"It'll be 20 years this January," said Pardman. "I'm second only to the hotel's owner, Mr. Saul."

I knew the name of Zacharias Saul very well. He was reputed to be one of the richest men in London.

I looked around the room, trying to think beyond the obvious, searching for any clues for how the thief might have entered the office. "This fireplace," I said. "Is it possible someone could have entered the office by the chimney?"

Lestrade shook his head. "I thought of that, Doctor," he said, "but if they had entered by the fireplace, they would have left traces in the ashes, and as you can see the ashes are undisturbed."

"Besides, the chimney's only a foot wide," said Pardman. He began to chuckle. "We joke about it around here. Say that it makes it very difficult for Father Christmas."

"What did you say?" I whispered.

"Father Christmas," said Pardman. "He's supposed to come down the chimney...."

Memories rushed into my head. "Ryder!" I said. "James Ryder! Of course!"

I rushed out into the lobby, pointing my finger in accusation. "Constable," I cried. "Seize that man!"

The constable seemed surprised, but did as he was told, seizing Ryder by him arm. Ryder struggled, but soon realized the constable was too much for him and his resistance evaporated into pitiful wails.

"Please, Doctor Watson!" he cried. "I haven't done anything this time! Have mercy!"

"Holmes gave you mercy once, Ryder," I said, "but he's not here to do it again."

Lestrade barged back into the Lobby, followed by Pardman. "Explain yourself, Doctor!" said Lestrade.

"Certainly," I said. "It was several Christmases past that Holmes and I investigated the theft of the Blue Carbuncle from the Hotel Cosmopolitan. Holmes's investigation determined the thief to be this man! James Ryder!"

Lestrade blinked in disbelief. "Ryder stole the Carbuncle?" he said. "And Holmes just let him go?"

"A thief!" cried Pardman with indignation. "A thief working the desk of my hotel!"

"Why'd you do it, Ryder?" I said. "You promised Holmes you'd flee the country and never steal again!"

Ryder stifled back a sob. "I tried to leave, Doctor Watson," he said, "but London's the only home I've ever known! I even tried to stick it out at the Cosmopolitan, but the manager came to suspect me, so I had to leave. I was trying to make a fresh start here at the Metropole. I didn't steal the painting! Honest I didn't!"

"We'll see about that," said Lestrade. "Constable, hold him tight while I search his pockets." Lestrade turned Ryder's pockets out, and searched through their meager contents. Unsatisfied, he looked about the lobby for more. "Where's his coat?"

"I believe I saw it behind the lobby desk, Inspector," said

Pardman.

Lestrade strode around to the back of the lobby desk, seized the coat and raised it aloft like a prize. He thrust his hands deep into the pockets and fished about until he seized upon an object which he pulled out with a flourish of triumph. "Ah-hah!" he said. "What's this, then? Do you recognize this little beauty, Mr. Pardman?"

In Lestrade's hand was a metal key with the same distinctive Roman design we had seen only moments before.

"Of course I do," said Pardman. "That is a duplicate of the key to my office."

"I thought as much," said Lestrade. "James Ryder, you are under arrest for the theft of the Sleeping Cardinal!"

"But that key isn't mine!" said Ryder. "I've never seen it before in my life!"

"That's what they all say," said Lestrade, but then he began to laugh.

"What's so funny, Inspector?" I asked.

"It looks like your Mr. Holmes was finally wrong about something!" said Lestrade. "Letting a criminal go free like that. Mercy, indeed! Just goes to show you; once a thief, always a thief."

Despite Ryder's protests Lestrade led him away, assuring both Pardman and Lady Margaret that he would procure the painting's location during interrogation at the Yard. I watched Lestrade escort Ryder away down the Strand with the nagging suspicion that I had missed something, some detail that would turn this case around, but I couldn't then put my finger on it.

Holmes interrupted me, taking me away from my tale. "Leave the dramatics for your readers at the Strand, Watson," he said. "Please limit yourself to the facts.

"If you'd rather I stopped...." I began.

"Oh, not at all, Doctor!" said Holmes. "While your prose may be overly colorful the problem is to my liking. Pray continue."

The following evening I spent in the manner which had become my custom: working on my memoirs in the company of my beloved wife. Mary was seated by my side reading the evening paper, and cried aloud as she came across something that sparked her interest.

"Did you see that you're in the paper tonight, John?"

"Hm?" I said, putting my pen aside. "No, I didn't. What does it say?"

Mary cleared her throat and began to read. "'Inspector Lestrade of Scotland Yard arrested James Ryder for the theft of the painting, the Sleeping Cardinal, from the Hotel Metropole. Assisting in the investigation was the long-time associate of Sherlock Holmes, Doctor John Watson!' My famous husband." She smiled at me, but that smile crumbled as a fit of coughing overwhelmed her.

I poured Mary some water, which she gratefully accepted. "Mary," I said as she drank, "you should get to bed. You know you aren't well."

"I'll be all right, John," she said, putting the water glass aside. "I'm just so happy for you. There's a sparkle in your eye when you're involved in a mystery. It's just like you used to say about Sherlock Holmes; you're happiest when there's a problem to unravel."

"Perhaps so," I said. "I just can't get this Cardinal business out of my mind. Something doesn't feel right about it."

"But you have the right man, surely!" said Mary. "Ryder's a thief twice over."

"He certainly had ample opportunity," I said. "Although the idea that he thought he'd be able to get away with it strikes me as incredible."

"If Scotland Yard is happy," said Mary, "then you should be too."

"I suppose you're right," I said. "But I'd be even happier if we can get you well again, Mary."

Mary put her arms around me. "I'd like nothing better, John."

I kissed her then, relieved that her coughing had, for the moment, subsided.

In the days following Lestrade was kind enough to keep me informed of his progress, or lack thereof, with the investigation. James Ryder continued to insist he was innocent, but Lestrade assured me it would only be a matter of time before he'd crack and give up the location of the painting. And that would likely have been the end of my involvement in the matter if not for a message that arrived at our doorstep a week later.

I was writing again in my study when I felt Mary's slender hand upon my shoulder. "John?" she said. "A telegram's arrived for you."

I lay down my pen. "Oh? Who's it from?"

"It doesn't say," answered Mary. "Just an initial at the bottom. The letter 'M'."

"M?" I said, excitement building within me, spurred by the possibilities of that initial. "Let me see that."

Mary handed me the telegram and I read it aloud.

> WHERE IS THE PAINTING? CONSULT
> SHERLOCK'S CONTACTS. CONSIDER THE
> ASHES.
>
> – M

I confess to being puzzled. "Consider the ashes...?" I mused. "What does it mean, John?" asked Mary. "Who are Sherlock's contacts?"

"Holmes kept numerous sources among London's criminal class," I said. "They helped him in his investigations."

"And you know these gentlemen?" I could hear the disapproval in her tone.

"A few of them." I saw no reason to scare my wife with the number of miscreants who I had come into acquaintance with during my time in Baker Street.

Mary was not fooled for a moment. "John," she said. "It might be dangerous."

"It might be at that."

Mary sighed. "But there's no stopping you, is there? I know that look in your eye. All right, John. Just be careful."

"I will, Mary," I said. "For your sake."

The telegram had reawakened the case in my mind. What had happened to the Sleeping Cardinal? There seemed two possibilities; either it had been hidden within the hotel prior to Ryder's arrest, or it had been secreted away from the hotel to be sold on the black market. Seeing as the police had conducted a thorough search of the hotel, I decided to pursue the second possibility. To that end, I sought out a man I only knew as 'Jones,' a shady sort I had seen frequently in our rooms at 221B Baker Street. His information had been instrumental in solving the Darlington substitution case several years ago.

I found him drinking in a disreputable pub in the lower-east end of London. I sidled up beside him at the bar.

"Is that you, Jones?" I said.

Jones looked askance at me. "Who wants to know?"

"My name is Doctor Watson. You might remember from the times you visited Sher – "

Jones clamped his hand over my mouth, silencing me mid-name. "Shhh! Shhh!" he said. "Not so loud! You want everyone in the pub to know who you is? Yeah, I remembers you, Doctor." He dropped his tone to a whisper. "Did Mr. H send you? Haven't seen him around lately."

"No," I said. "Mr. H is not in London at this time."

"Pity," said Jones, turning his attentions back to his drink. "He owes me money, he does."

"I'm looking for information," I said. "I was wondering if you can help me."

"Well, guv," said Jones, "help ain't cheap. It'll cost you."

"And just how much will it cost me?" I said.

"Depends on just how helpful you want me to be," said

Jones.

"I'm looking for a painting."

Jones chuckled. "Oh! And not just any paintin'! You be lookin' for the Sleepin' Cardinal that got lifted out of the Metropole last week."

"Why, yes," I said, surprised. "How did you know that?"

"'Cause you ain't the only one," said Jones. "Scotland Yard's been down here lookin' for it too."

I felt a tinge of excitement. "You have it, then?"

"Good lord, no, guv!" said Jones. "You think I'm going to touch somethin' that hot?"

My excitement withered. "Then this has been a wasted journey," I moaned.

"Aw, cheer up, Doctor," said Jones. "I might not be able to help you find the paintin', but I might be able to give you a hint as to who took it." He looked around to make sure no one was listening, and then spoke to me in low tones. "There's this fellow, see?" he said. "Works at the Hotel Metropole, and he's in for some serious money with the local bookies. They say he likes the ponies and isn't the luckiest man in the world."

"Can you describe this fellow?" I said.

Jones smiled. "Course I can," he said. "But not until I see some coin."

"How much?"

Jones rubbed his chin, considering his options. "For information that valuable?" he said. "Well, now. Let me see. Five pounds might loosen my lips."

"Five pounds?" I cried. "That's outrageous!"

Jones shrugged. "Well, you think it over, Doctor," he said. "I'm not going anywhere. Not with it being so blasted hot outside."

I couldn't help but agree. "It certainly is that," I said. "It hasn't been this warm since...." I broke off mid-sentence as something fell into place within my mind. "Good lord!" I said. "I have it!"

"What's that, then?" said Jones, sensing his fish had fallen off its hook.

"The ashes!" I cried. "Consider the ashes! I know who took the Cardinal!"

"Calm down there, Doctor," said Jones. "You're not makin' any sense."

"I have to go to Scotland Yard at once!" I said. I seized Jones by his hand, shaking it vigorously. "Thank you very much, Jones. You've been most helpful." I fished a coin from my pocket. "Here's a crown for your trouble."

Jones snatched the coin from my hand before I could even blink. "Why, thank you, Doctor." I turned to leave, and heard Jones call after me. "You're welcome!" he cried, followed by a mumbled, "I think...?" As I left the disreputable pub behind, my mind buzzed with excitement. I could see it all now, exactly who had taken the painting and how.

"Absolutely scintillating, Watson," said Holmes, who was pacing back and forth again within our sitting room. "You had of course noticed that the ashes...."

I interrupted my friend before he could ruin my tale. "Holmes, please. Let me tell my own story."

"Of course," said Holmes. "Do forgive me, Doctor. Pray continue."

I rushed to Scotland Yard and sought out Lestrade. Together, we then made out way back to Covent Garden and were soon standing before a small set of rooms near the Hotel Metropole. We knocked at the door, and a tall, handsome man answered.

"Yes?" said Patrick Pardman. "Ah, Inspector. And Doctor Watson!

What a surprise."

"May we come in?" asked Lestrade. "Of course, of course," said Pardman.

He stepped aside, and ushered us within.

Pardman's quarters were spartan, devoid of the luxury the Hotel Metropole provided. It was a single room, with a small bed, a dresser and side table. A decanter, some bottles and glasses were perched on top of dresser, and Pardman poured himself a drink.

"May I offer you gentlemen some brandy?" asked Pardman.

Lestrade shook his head. "I'm afraid we're here on business."

"Oh?" said Pardman. "You have news of the Sleeping Cardinal?"

"We do," said Lestrade.

"Well, that is welcome news," said Pardman. "Mrs. Margaret is demanding her compensation by no later than noon tomorrow. Mr. Saul is most unhappy with the situation."

"I can imagine," I said.

"Then don't keep me in suspense, gentlemen," said Pardman. "Have you located the painting?"

"We have information that points us in a direction," said Lestrade.

"Well, that is encouraging!" said Pardman. "And where is the Cardinal presently?"

"That is what we've come to ask you, Mr. Pardman," I said.

Pardman blinked in surprise. "Me?" he said. "But it was Ryder who took the Sleeping Cardinal!"

"No," I said, "but that's what you wanted us to think."

"You knew of Ryder's suspected involvement in the disappearance of the Blue Carbuncle from your discussions with the manager of the Hotel Cosmopolitan," said Lestrade, "and knew he'd make a perfect scapegoat should a robbery ever occur at the Hotel Metropole."

"All you had to do was somehow mention Ryder's involvement with the Blue Carbuncle theft to the proper authorities," I said, "and Ryder's arrest for the new robbery would be almost assured. My appearance at the scene must have seemed an early Christmas to you. Why raise the affair of the Blue Carbuncle to the authorities when a known associate of Sherlock Holmes could do it for you?"

"The spare key was a nice touch in the frame-up," said Lestrade. "Only you made a small slip up there."

"Really," said Pardman.

"You said you never let the key of your sight," I said. "How then could Ryder have made a copy? I suspect if we were to check with locksmiths in the area of the hotel, they'd remember making a copy for you, Mr. Pardman, and not for Mr. Ryder."

"That proves nothing," said Pardman. "I have keys made for the hotel all the time."

"But the rest of the hotel uses standard keys," I said, "while the key to your office is Roman. Something with that unique a design is bound to stick out in a locksmith's mind."

"You slipped the duplicate into Ryder's coat so I could find it," said Lestrade, "which completed your frame-up. A very clever touch, but not clever enough for an officer of the Yard."

Pardman drained his glass, and regarded us calmly. "An entertaining tale, gentlemen," he said, "but you still haven't told me where the painting is."

"The painting's disappearance is really only a mystery if we assume it was ever in the safe to begin with," I said, "and we only have your word for that. If, however, the opposite were true and the painting were never in the safe, then the solution becomes obvious."

"You walked out of the Hotel Metropole that evening with the painting in hand," said Lestrade, "determined to sell it on the black market."

"That's ridiculous!" said Pardman. "How could I walk out with a painting that size and not be seen? The idea's ludicrous!"

"It is ludicrous," I said, "until you remember the ashes in your fireplace."

Pardman blinked at me in surprise. "I beg your pardon?"

he said. "Lestrade noted the ashes in your office as evidence that no one had snuck down the chimney," I said, "but what we should have been asking is why you were burning a fire at all during the hottest summer in recent memory? The answer is that you were burning the frame upon which the Cardinal was mounted!"

"With the frame removed, the painting was much easier to conceal beneath your coat," said Lestrade. "You wrapped the canvas around your body and walked out of the hotel, right in front of both Ryder and the porter, with neither the wiser."

"But this is madness!" cried Pardman. "Why should I do such a thing? I've been loyal to that hotel for 20 years! Ryder's your man! He's a thief, I tell you, a thief!"

"Yes," I said, "I wondered about that too. Why would you steal from your own hotel? But then, I did some checking with Holmes's criminal contacts and discovered a very interesting fact."

"We know about the bookies," said Lestrade. "We know about the gambling, and we know how much you owe them. The game's up Pardman. Why don't you give us the canvas and be done with it?"

Pardman stared back at us in defeat. "Fine," he said at last. "You can have the blasted thing. No one's buying it anyway. They say it's too hot! But you have to protect me, Inspector! If I don't have the money by tomorrow, they'll kill me!"

"Then it's a good thing you're going to the safest place I know," said Lestrade. "A jail cell at the Yard."

Pardman retrieved the Sleeping Cardinal from its hiding place, and Lestrade took him away to an awaiting cell. That evening, with the painting in hand, Lestrade and I visited Lady Margaret to return her property. She seemed oddly cold to the Cardinal's recovery. In fact she hardly even bothered to thank us! But justice had been served, and I felt satisfied.

"And that, Holmes," I said, "is the story of how we recovered the Sleeping Cardinal."

Holmes, who had been smoking as he listened, opened his eyes and laid his calabash pipe on the mantle. "An entertaining tale, Doctor," he said. "I'm sure the readers of the Strand Magazine will enjoy it."

"Oh, I'll never write it up," I said. "It's your adventures they want, not mine."

Holmes smiled. "Ah, but perhaps I had more to do with the case than you realize."

"How do you figure, Holmes?"

"Did you never wonder who sent you the mysterious telegram?"

"Well," I said, "I had always assumed the message came from your brother, Mycroft."

"You are only partly correct," said Holmes. "The telegram was indeed from Mycroft. The message, on the other hand, was from me."

"You?" I said, astonished.

"I had requested that my brother keep tabs on you during my absence," said Holmes, "along with sending me full reports of your progress. When he sent me Lestrade's police report on your involvement with the robbery of the Sleeping Cardinal, I could not help but smile."

I sighed. "At how poorly I performed the investigation?"

"My dear fellow," said Holmes, "you underestimate yourself. You had the tenacity to question the obvious while Lestrade rushed toward the easiest conclusion. I knew if we provided you a small push in the right direction you would find the truth. No, I smiled as, despite my absence, you were still in the game."

"Ah," I said. "Well, thank you, Holmes."

"You did, however, miss one avenue of investigation."

"Oh? And what's that?"

"I find it difficult to believe," said Holmes, "that a woman who has just had her priceless painting stolen would immediately demand compensation rather than the canvas' recovery. I find it very probable that she planned the theft together with Mr. Pardman."

"Now, Holmes, that really is too much!"

"Consider the facts," said Holmes. "Consider that Pardman knew immediately how to smuggle the painting out of the hotel, almost as if he'd had advance warning. Consider that Lady Margaret chose not to store her painting in the gallery where it was to be exhibited, but instead to store it in a hotel safe. Consider also that she chose not to stay in a hotel near the exhibition, but instead a hotel owned by the richest man in London?"

"Good Lord," I said. "I have been blind all these years."

"Ah, but we shall never know for certain," said Holmes. "It was her estate sale you saw in the paper. Lady Margaret died last week. But cheer up, Watson. You did find the thief and recover the Sleeping Cardinal. As good an outcome as could be hoped for."

"Well," I said, "after your telegram provided a thread to follow, the solution was...er...." I hesitated, wondering if I should dare.

"Go ahead and say it, Watson," said Holmes. "You've earned it."

"Why, it was elementary, my dear Holmes," I said. "Elementary."

The Adventure of the
Willow Basket

by Lyndsay Faye

"An artisan of considerable artistic skill," Sherlock Holmes answered in reply to my latest challenge, pulling a thin cigarette from his case. "A glass-blower to be specific, although I nearly fell into the rash error of supposing him a professional musician. Shocking, the way the mind slips into such appalling laxity after a full meal – I'll be forced to fast entirely tomorrow in case my wits should happen to be called upon."

"Dear me, I shall have to stop for tobacco on our – "

"No, I won't have it!" I lightly slapped the white linen tablecloth between us, causing our whiskys to shiver with a sympathetic happy thrill. "Eight in a row is quite too many, Holmes! Even you cannot pretend to clairvoyance."

"You wound me, my boy." He lit the cigarette, suppressing an impish expression. "I have never pretended to clairvoyance in my life, though I have placed 11 such repellent creatures in the dock for swindling the credible out of their hard-earned savings. One, a Mr. Erasmus Drake, defrauded over a dozen widows using only a mirror, a pennywhistle, and a cunning preparation of coloured Chinese gunpowder. He won't be free to roam the streets for another three years, come to think of it."

"Well, well, never mind clairvoyance then, but you have just identified the professions of eight individuals at a single

glance! I shall have to commence approaching complete
strangers and demanding they give us a full report of their
lives and habits in order to corroborate your claims."

"My dear fellow, surely you know by now that you
needn't trouble yourself."

"All right – how do you know he is a glass-blower?"

The detective's eyes glinted as brightly as the silver case
which he returned to his inner coat pocket. We sat at our
preferred table in the front of Simpson's, before the ground-
glass windows where we so often watched the passersby;
but despite the glow bestowed upon London minutes
before by her army of gas-lighters, the illumination beyond
the wavering panes no longer sufficed for even my friend's
keen gaze to pick out those details by which he had built his
reputation, and thus we had shifted in our seats to examine
the restaurant patrons instead. Holmes's turbot and my leg
of mutton had long since been whisked away following our
early repast, and we sat in a small pool of quiet amidst the
throng of hungry journalists and eager young chess players,
their sights fixed upon sliced beef in the dining room or
cigars and chequered boards up the familiar staircase. There
seemed not a man among them my friend could not pin with
the exactitude of a lepidopterist with a butterfly; and, while
his remarkable faculty always gives me as much pleasure
as it does him, on that evening we reposed with the more
luxurious complacency of two intimate companions who
had nothing more pressing to do than to order another set
of whiskys.

"I know he is a professional glass-blower because he
is not a professional trumpet player," Holmes drawled,
gesturing with slight flicks of his index finger. "His clothing
is of excellent quality, only a bit less so than yours or mine,
suggesting he is neither an aristocrat nor a mean labourer,
but rather a respectable chap with a vocation. His cheeks
are sunken, but the musculature of his jaw is strongly
developed, overly so, and there are slight indications of

varicose veins surrounding his lips. His lungs are powerful – I don't know if you heard him cough ten minutes ago, but I feared for the crystal. He has been expelling air from them, with great strength and frequency. At first, I nearly fell into the callow error of supposing him an aficionado with some brass instrument, possibly playing for an orchestra or one of the better music halls, for which failing I blame the exquisite quality of Simpson's seafood preparations. However, when I glimpsed his hands, I instantly corrected my mistake – his finger-ends display no sign of flattening from depressing the valves, but they do evince a number of slight burn scars. Ergo, he is a glass blower, one I would wager ten quid owns a private shop attached to his studio if the cost of his watch chain does not mislead me, and you need not disturb his repast, friend Watson."

I was already softly applauding, shaking with laughter. "My abject apologies. I was a fool to doubt you."

"Skepticism is widely considered healthy," Holmes demurred, but the immediate lift of his narrow lips betrayed his pleasure at the compliment. My friend is nothing if not gratified by honest appreciation of his prodigious talents.

For some 40 minutes and another set of whiskys longer, we lingered, speaking or not speaking as best suited our pleasure, and I admit that I relished the time. My friend was in a rare mood – for, while he is tensely frenetic with work to energise him, he is often brooding and silent without it. The extremities of his nature can be taxing for a fellow lodger and worrying for a friend, though I suspect not more so than they are burdensome for Holmes himself. It was a pleasure to see the great criminologist at his ease for once, neither in motion nor plastered to the settee in silent protest against the dullness of the world around him.

I was just about to suggest that we walk back to Baker Street when we wearied of Simpsons's rather than flag a hansom, for it was mid-June and the spring air yet hung blessedly warm and weightless before the advent of summer's stifling fug, when my friend's face changed. The languid half-lidded eyes focused, and the slack draught he had been taking from his cigarette tightened into a harder purse.

"What is it?" I asked, already half-turning.

"Trouble, friend Watson. Let us hope it is the stimulating and not the unpleasant variety."

It was then I spied our friend Inspector Lestrade casting his dark, glittering eyes around the dining room, turning his neatly brushed bowler anxiously in his hands. His sharp features betrayed no hint of their usual smugness, and his frame, already small, seemed to have shrunk still further within his light duster. When I raised a hand, he darted towards our table with his head down like a terrier on the scent.

"By Jove, there's been a murder done!" Holmes exclaimed, as usual failing to sound entirely displeased by this development. "Lestrade, pull up a chair. There's coffee if you like, and – "

"No time for coffee," Lestrade huffed as he seated himself.

Holmes blinked in urbane surprise, and I could not blame him. I, too, suspected that beneath the inspector's obvious anxiety lurked another irritant – while Lestrade is often officious, he is never curt, and he had not bothered to greet either one of us.

Musing, I took in the regular Yarder's rigid spine and brittle countenance. My examinations drew a blank, save for the obvious conclusion that his nerves had been somehow jangled. I could not imagine what the matter might be, for the year was 1894 and I had not seen the inspector since April and the arrest of Colonel Sebastian Moran, a dramatic event indeed, but one which paled significantly in comparison to the fact of Sherlock Holmes being alive at all. Following my friend's return from his supposed death at the grim plunge of Reichenbach Falls, I had wrestled briefly with powerful conflicting emotions, the pain of abandonment and the joy of an unlooked-for miracle foremost among them – but by June of that year, the occasional haunted, hunted looks in Holmes's eyes, which even he could not conceal, combined with the rueful courtesies he showed me when his natural impatience ought to have driven such considerations clean from his vast mind, had convinced me he could not have done otherwise than he did. Excluding the deep pangs caused by my recent marital heartbreak, I felt as ebullient as any shipwreck survivor, and only wished our old friend Lestrade the same felicity.

"Tell me about the murder," Holmes requested, "since you decline to be distracted by coffee."

"Beg pardon?" Lestrade growled, for he had fallen into a reverie with his fingertips pressing his temples.

"Report to me the facts of the homicide, since you refuse the stimulating effects of the roasted coffee berry."

"I do speak English, Mr. Holmes." Lestrade tugged at his cuffs in fastidious annoyance, recovering himself. "It's a bad business, gentlemen, a very bad business indeed, or I should not have troubled you. I applied at Baker Street, and Mrs. Hudson said you were dining here."

"That much I have deduced by your – "

"Shall we skip the parlour tricks, Mr. Holmes?" Lestrade proposed with unusual asperity.

Holmes's black brows rose to lofty heights indeed, as did mine, but he appeared more curious than offended. As I had not observed the pair interact other than a terse welcome back to London from Lestrade at Camden House in April, followed by some professional discussion of the charges Colonel Moran would face, I sat back against the horsehair-stuffed chair in bemusement which verged upon discomfort.

"It is a murder," Lestrade admitted, clearing his throat. "Mr. John Wiltshire was discovered in his bedroom in Battersea this late morning, stone dead, without a trace of any known poison in his corpse, nor a single wound upon his body to suggest that harm had been done to him."

"Remarkable, in that case, that you claim a murder has been committed."

"He was drained of blood, Mr. Holmes. His body was nearly free of it." Lestrade suppressed a shudder. "It disappeared."

A chill passed down my spine. As it has been elsewhere mentioned in these chaotic memoirs that Holmes rather admires than abhors the macabre, I shall not elaborate upon this quirk of his nature – I must mention, however, that Holmes's entire frame snapped into rapt attention, while Lestrade's bristled in what I can only describe as animosity.

"There's some who would think that horrible, but you're not to be named among them, I suppose." The inspector levelled a challenging stare at Sherlock Holmes.

"I readily admit to thinking it varying degrees of horrible based upon the character of the deceased," Holmes replied with a yawn, reverting to his typical supercilious character. "The facts, if you would be so kind."

"The facts as I have them in hand are these: Mr. John Wiltshire dined with his wife and an old friend on the night of his death, and later Mrs. Helen Wiltshire called for a bath to be drawn for her husband. The housekeeper asserts that the ring occurred, the water was heated, and nothing else of note took place. The upper housemaids all confirm that Mrs. Wiltshire slept in her own room that night, afraid to upset her husband's apparent need for quiet and solitude. Other than the fact a man has apparently been bled to death by magic, you'd not find me disturbing your supper."

"You know very well that we would hasten to come whenever you have need of Holmes," I asserted, only noting in retrospect my grammatical error.

A glass of whisky appeared before the inspector. Nodding subtle thanks to the jacketed waiter, Holmes ordered, "Do have a sip – it seems as though the circumstances merit it."

Lestrade's countenance dissolved into what might – save for his own restraint – have been a sneer even as he tasted the drink. "Another deduction?"

"You have clearly been much taxed," said Holmes, as dismissive as ever. "Pray, what would you have us do? I require an invitation or a client, and presently I have neither. Shall I look up vampires in my commonplace book and wire you upon the subject, or test your patience so far as to accompany you to the crime scene? Has the body been moved?"

"No. I came straight to you," Lestrade retorted, taking another swallow, "whether I liked it or not."

My mouth fell open, and Holmes's deep-set eyes widened fractionally. I fully expected a scathing retort to follow close upon this subtle hint of dismay. To my great surprise, he merely rose, however, nodding at the quaint tobacconist's shop nestled inside the restaurant, and said coldly, "I am at your disposal, Lestrade, after buying more cigarettes. You are giving me the distinct impression I shall have need of them. Watson, settle the bill if you would be so good."

Never will I forget that crime scene, for it occurred after what had been so casually glad a day for me, and the shift into horror was as swift as our cab ride. John Wiltshire lay dead in his tastefully appointed bedchamber, its heavy emerald draperies thrown wide to let in the sunlight and now forgot under the shrouded gaze of invisible stars. He reclined in a bath over which a muslin cloth had been draped, the atmosphere in the room stale with police traffic and tense with revulsion, and a still-damp rubber tarp on the rug nearby informed me he had been examined by the coroner and then returned to his original attitude. Mr. Wiltshire's head and upper torso were visible, his mouth slack and lips white as chalk. The setting and the centerpiece were utterly jarring, with the stately furnishings surrounding a body that appeared horribly – nay, obscenely – withered. Should I have reached out and touched the late Mr. Wiltshire's skin, I could picture it crumbling to dust like paper left to desiccate for centuries. He had in life been a slender man, with deep pouches beneath his eyes and a thin, downturned mouth.

The coroner was finishing his notes wearing a grim expression and, after a gesture from Lestrade, he stepped aside to allow Holmes and myself to view the deceased. My friend whistled appreciatively, which garnered a dark look from Lestrade.

"Skin white as that cloth and utterly parched, vessels drained, form shrunken, as if he had shriveled into a husk," I summarised. "But are we *certain* there were no epidermal wounds inflicted which could have caused this? He was examined on this tarp, I take it."

"Indeed, Doctor. A minute examination was made in this room, but Inspector Lestrade insisted the deceased be replaced lest his original positioning or the water itself provide a clue for Mr. Holmes here," the coroner answered, nodding politely.

"By the Lord," Holmes said mildly, "and here I supposed the circumstances of the killing itself the only miracle which took place today. Admirable, Lestrade."

My friend appeared to be getting a bit of his own back at last, and the official detective ground his teeth as Holmes dipped his torso towards the bath. Avid as the most passionate connoisseur, he lifted the dead man's dripping hand from the water and examined the ivory cuticles, checked the underside of the limb draped over the lip, made a minute study of his dark hair and his unmarked scalp, even lifted the wizened eyelids to reveal his unseeing pupils. I watched, eager to help if I could, but all I beheld seemed the stuff of nightmare and not medicine. Holmes next drew his delicate fingertips along the copper rim of the tub, going so far as to touch the now-tepid water and bring it to his nose.

"For heaven's sake," Lestrade muttered in my ear – but at me there was directed no pique, merely the casual camaraderie of old.

I half-drew a hand over my moustache to hide a smile, but added under my breath, "If Holmes weren't the most thorough investigator the world has ever known, I doubt he would be here."

"More's the pity," Lestrade sighed as my companion pushed upright again.

"I have exceptionally keen hearing, you realise," Holmes mentioned tartly. "Fascinating. As I happen to trust in your thoroughness, coroner – Adams, was it? Yes, Mr. Adams, I suppose you correct in stating that the body lacks superficial wounds. They should have bled into the water if he was killed here, in any event, and this liquid is far too pure to indicate a man's entire life-force could have possibly been drained into it. I can see no trace of blood at all. Testing it for minute traces may prove necessary, and I have that ability, but more urgent matters demand our attention, supposing we can keep this evidence intact? Very good. I detect no more sign of poison than you do, but anyhow poisoning is a medically impossible means of sapping a fellow's blood, unless we are dealing with a substance altogether unknown to science. So here we have a man whose blood was somehow siphoned, and the water is clear. Supposing the corpse had been moved, that would have proven nothing whatsoever, but...."

"But the corpse was not moved," Mr. Adams obliged when Holmes paused expectantly, "because the deep depressions upon the back of his neck and the other on his forearm – there, where it was resting – indicate he was robbed of his blood here somehow, and left to die."

"Capital!" Holmes exclaimed.

"Yes, we worked that one out on our own, Mr. Holmes," Lestrade groused.

Sherlock Holmes did not deign to reply, instead turning his attention to the crime scene as Mr. Adams excused himself, intending to help the constables make arrangements to remove the remains. Holmes made every effort, as he always does, diving into corners and walking with his slender hands hovering before him, seeking any aberration which might bring light where all was dark. After some 15 minutes of studying carpeting, framed photographs, a mahogany bedstead, and every crevice of every object in the room, however, he tapped his fist against his lips and turned back to Lestrade.

"Will you be so good as to deliver me this unfortunate fellow's biography?"

"Readily, Mr. Holmes. Mr. Wiltshire is employed at a banking firm in the City and has been for some six years hence. We've had scant enough time to question anyone, but this afternoon his direct superior sent me a good report of him. The servants seem to think him a somber man, but altogether a satisfactory employer. He has no outstanding debts and no known enemies – he lives in a quiet fashion with his wife, Mrs. Helen – "

Holmes snapped his fingers. "I hadn't forgot the detail, but was admittedly distracted by so very dramatic a corpse. They entertained an old friend last night – the wife, take me to the wife," he commanded, and quit the room.

Lestrade followed, and I matched my stride to the shorter man's. "I cannot help but sense that our presence on this occasion distresses you, Inspector."

He glanced backwards in surprise. "Oh, I could never be distressed by your help, Doctor. It's always a pleasure to see you. It's merely that Mr. Holmes – well, never mind, Mr. Holmes has never cared a fig what I think, and I don't see why he should start now, so I'll say no more. He'll be waiting for us, and he's right to want interviews at this stage. There *was* a visitor, and it was the wife who rang for the bath to be drawn. I've not been able to question Mrs. Wiltshire yet – she fainted dead away at the sight of her husband and only recovered whilst I was fetching you. Never mind Mr. Holmes's quirks when there's a murderer to run to ground, I always tell myself."

Still mystified for multiple reasons, I could do nothing save accompany him downstairs. We waited in a pretty parlour with all the lamps blazing, a room full of light and colourful decorative china, its walls masked by potted greenery. Something about its coziness unnerved me, and the chamber seemed all the more garishly cheerful when my imagination flashed upon the ghastly events doubtless taking place upstairs, as the shrunken rind which had once been a man was taken out the back through the servants' entrance and at last to the morgue.

When Mrs. Helen Wiltshire entered, she naturally appeared greatly disturbed in mind – her comely complexion was ashen with dismay, her full lips a tremble, her green eyes red at the edges, her pale blonde hair disarrayed from clutching it in the extremity of her emotion. She was of an age with her late husband, midway between 30 and 40, and was a lovely woman despite her distress. My friend was up in an instant and led her with easy courtesy to the settee, where she perched as if about to take flight.

Holmes smiled gently as he regained his own chair, displaying the almost mesmeric softness he only ever expends upon the fair sex, and only when he desires information from them; but then, I am not being quite just when I say so. My friend may not seek the company of women, but he genuinely abhors seeing them harmed.

"Are you quite comfortable, madam? Should you like a little refreshment to strengthen you? My friend here is a doctor, and he will be happy to locate something fortifying."

"I...I don't think that would be...." Mrs. Wiltshire shifted, attempting to smile with little success. She was silent for so long that Sherlock Holmes continued, face alive with encouragement.

"You are of Scottish origins, I observe. In the vicinity of Paisley, Renfrewshire, unless my ears deceive me."

A wash of colour infused Mrs. Wiltshire's dulled cheeks. "Aye, Mr. Holmes, though I've lost a good deal of that manner of speaking."

"Yes, it's extremely subtle. You went on a long stroll

this morning, Mrs. Wiltshire? It must be pleasant, living so close to Battersea Park and its walkways, especially at this time of the year – though I discern from your boots that you wandered alongside the Thames on this occasion."

She glanced up, twisting her fingers in her coral skirts. "Why, yes, Mr. Holmes. I was out walking. That is the reason I only learned at around noon that – oh, I can't, I can't," she said upon a small sob. "I very often take long constitutionals. I've never regretted the habit so much as I did this afternoon, when I arrived home and discovered the house was in an uproar and the police had already been summoned over... over..."

"Quite."

"I was most unwell afterward. I've only just found a tiny store of strength – I hope you will forgive my weakness, but...."

Again she trailed off, and again Holmes continued. "Will you please tell me about your caller of last night?"

Helen Wiltshire nodded, more tears forming. "His name is Horatio Swann, an explorer of some note."

"Indeed!" Holmes exclaimed. "Yes, I have heard of him. He has made quite the name for himself in scholarly monographs."

"Yes, that is the man," she agreed with another weak twitch of her lips. "My husband and he were acquainted years ago, but Mr. Swann has been traveling in Siam, studying indigenous wildlife. We passed a most pleasant meal, and afterward John seemed fatigued at having spent so much time over vigourous conversation and plentiful claret. I ordered him a bath and left him to himself. He could grow...melancholy at times, Mr. Holmes. But for such a fate to befall him...."

Mrs. Wiltshire at this point dissolved entirely and ran from the room.

Lestrade exchanged a glance with Holmes, all pique forgotten in the peculiarity of the moment. He leant forward with his elbows on his knees. "She must have been quite devoted to him."

"It would seem so," Holmes replied without inflection.

"The poor woman must be wrought to her highest pitch of nerves over such a ghastly shock. We must seek out this Horatio Swann," I conjectured, "and ascertain whether he has anything to do with the affair."

"As usual, Watson, you have hit upon the obvious with uncanny accuracy," said Holmes dryly. "But I wonder...well, there may be nothing in it after all."

"Nothing in what, Mr. Holmes?" Lestrade questioned, a furrow forming above his narrow nose.

"It's only a whim of mine, perhaps a trivial one at that. But why one should walk along the Thames, noisome as it is, when one could walk through Battersea Park?" Holmes mused, rising and ringing the bell.

A maid appeared within seconds. "Show in the housekeeper, please–what is her name?" Holmes inquired. "Mrs. Stubbs, sir."

"Mrs. Stubbs, then. Thank you."

Lestrade nodded absently, stretching his legs out before him as if in agreement over Holmes's choice of witness, and I dared to hope that whatever mood had plagued him had been a fluke, and that all would henceforth be well again. Mrs. Stubbs, when she entered, proved a broad woman with neatly arranged curls, the flinty spark of extreme practicality in her eyes, and a direct manner. She stood upon the Turkey carpet with her hands clasped placidly before her, the slight slump of her shoulders the only indication she had been sorely tried that day.

"Yes, gentlemen?"

"Mrs. Stubbs." Holmes remained standing, pacing as he questioned. "My name is Sherlock Holmes, this is my friend and colleague, Dr. John Watson, and this is Inspector Lestrade of Scotland Yard. We wonder whether you might help us in clearing this matter up. You have been the housekeeper for how long?"

"Six years, sir. As long as the Wiltshires have lived in Battersea."

"You find the position amenable?"

"I do."

"Would you describe for me the nature of your late employer?"

"John Wiltshire was a good provider, and I hadn't much cause to speak with him. At times, he seemed a bit wistful perhaps, but he never lashed out or gave me the impression such spells were anything more serious than fatigue."

"Then you would say Mr. and Mrs. Wiltshire were happy together?" Holmes pressed, selecting a cigarette.

Mrs. Stubbs sniffed, seeming more impatient than offended. "As happy as anyone, I hope. They never quarreled, and when banking cost him long hours away, she never begrudged him the time."

"Did she not?" Holmes threw the spent Vesta in the fireplace. "Have you any theory as to what happened last night?"

This at last seemed to move her, but she maintained a neutral expression, swallowing. "That'll be for you gentlemen to decide, I'm sure."

"Was there sign of any intruders this morning?" Lestrade put in.

"No, sir. Well, not precisely."

Both Holmes and Lestrade paused at this, tensing. "What do you mean by 'not precisely,' Mrs. Stubbs?" Lestrade urged.

"It's a silly thing, but the new scullery maid has misplaced the marketing basket." Mrs. Stubbs shrugged. "She's more than a bit simple, and everything is so tospy-turvy today – I'm sure it will turn up. Last week she managed to put the cheese wheel in the breadbox after clearing the servants' supper."

Lestrade sagged, disappointed.

"Would you describe this basket, Mrs. Stubbs?" Holmes requested. Our eyes flashed to the detective in disbelief.

"It's a plain split willow basket, about a foot-and-a-half long though not so wide, with a handle for the shoulder, lined with a cotton kitchen towel," Mrs. Stubbs answered readily, though her tone was skeptical.

"Thank you," said Holmes, whirling a bit as he strode in tight loops before the fireplace. "One question more, I beg. What was Mr. Wiltshire's mood like after Mr. Horatio Swann had departed?"

"Morose, sir," the housekeeper replied flatly.

Sherlock Holmes stopped, quirking an agile brow. "The usual affliction?"

"Worse, sir. Perhaps he had a premonition." Mrs. Stubbs set her lips grimly. "To die in such a way...God knows he deserved warning of it. Do call for me if you need aught else, but I've plentiful extra tasks to see to and would fain take my leave," she concluded.

When she had departed, Lestrade slapped his knees and hopped to his feet, his unexplained ire fully returned. "This is a serious investigation, Mr. Holmes!"

Holmes swiveled to face the inspector, his high cheekbones dusted with colour, for the first time visibly vexed at the criticism. "I assure you I am treating it as such."

"Oh, yes, I'm sure the *exact* description of this misplaced potato basket is going to greatly assist us in tracking down the killer! Why don't *you* solve that mystery – question the scullery maid, that'll be a good start – and *I'll* catch a murderer. I need to see whether my men have finished," Lestrade growled, storming out.

"What on earth can be the matter with him?" I wondered, regarding Holmes in amazement.

My friend pulled in smoke with a vengeance before crushing the cigarette in a tray for the purpose and shaking his dark head. "I had six theories at the beginning of the evening. I've eliminated five of them," he confessed, striding in the direction of the outer hallway.

"Then what is wrong?" I repeated as we donned hats and gloves. "A conundrum even I cannot solve."

I opened my lips to protest but found Sherlock Holmes's face as stony as I had ever seen it; he pivoted away from me, thrusting his hands into his pockets as we made to quit the blighted Wiltshire residence.

"But the murder, Holmes! Hadn't you better question more of the ser – "

"That conundrum I *can* solve," Holmes interrupted me. "As a matter of fact, I just did solve it, about five minutes ago. There was never any difficulty in the matter. Come, Watson. We must see what Mr. Horatio Swann has to say."

As circumstances had it, we could not call upon Mr. Horatio Swann until the next morning, as Lestrade had not found us at Simpson's until well past seven after travelling from Battersea and stopping at Baker Street, and Mr. Swann lived some miles distant, in a grand house near to Walthamstow. Lestrade supplied us with a four-wheeler and a pair of constables lest matters take a dark turn, and the journey would have been pleasant enough, passing through the small brick towns with their peacefully crumbling churches and snowlike dusting of white petals from the blooming Hawthorne bushes, had the inspector not been sullen and Holmes coolly silent. I, meanwhile, was abuzz with anticipation, desperately eager to discover what my friend had made of the dreadful affair.

When we three at last stood before the stately structure in question – walled round with charming grey stone, a little lane leading up to a curved set of steps, mullioned windows all sparkling as they reflected the dancing shadows of the white willow branches – Holmes hesitated upon the gravel. Lestrade and I by habit likewise slowed to see whether he would deign to share any of his thoughts.

Then Holmes froze entirely, his spine quivering. We waited, with bated breath, for him to speak – or at least I did.

"Well, what the deuce is the matter?" Lestrade queried, every bit as waspishly annoyed at my friend as previous.

Holmes chuckled, rubbing his hands together. "It's all too perfect. I told you I had heard of Mr. Horatio Swann yesterday, did I not? I have followed a few of his monographs upon the subject of certain freshwater wildlife with particular care."

"And what of it?" Lestrade demanded, exasperated.

"Rather an outlandish residence for a scientist, wouldn't you say?" Holmes replied, winking. "Call for the constables. We'll want them."

Brown eyes widening in astonishment, Lestrade at once did as he was bid, returning a few yards up the lane and gesturing for the Bobbies to follow. By the time they had done so, Holmes had cheerily knocked upon the door and been admitted, I at his heels.

The taciturn butler led us – and, after some persuasion, the Yarders – into Mr. Swann's study. From the instant I entered it, my eyes knew not where to light; the place was a splendidly outfitted gentleman's laboratory, replete with chemical apparatus and walls of gilt-stamped leather books and specimen jars. Of these last, there were dozens upon dozens, lining the shelves like so many petrified soldiers at attention. When my friend saw them, he smiled still wider.

Mr. Swann, surprised, emerged from behind his desk. He was a strongly built man, with a shock of ruddy hair and a ruggedly handsome visage, still wearing a dressing gown and house slippers, as we had begun our journey as early as possible. He appeared merely intrigued at the sight of Holmes and myself – but when he glimpsed the uniformed constables behind Lestrade, his expression shifted to a grimace of pure rage.

"Gentlemen, allow me to introduce Mr. Charles Cutmore, the mastermind behind the infamous Drummonds Bank robbery which so confounded the Scottish authorities, the renowned author of no less than 20 scientific articles of note, and likewise the cunning author of the murder of Mr. John Wiltshire – whose name is actually Michael Crosby, by the by, and who some seven years ago aided this man in making off with six thousand pounds sterling. The pair of them had a female accomplice, to whom you have been introduced under the alias of Mrs. Helen Wiltshire. A pretty little bow to top this strange affair, would you not say so, Lestrade?" Holmes rejoiced.

The inspector stood there stunned for an instant; but a howl of fury and a charge for the door on the part of Mr. Charles Cutmore ceased all rumination. The set of brawny constables hurtled headlong into action, and the pair wrestled their frenzied captive into a set of derbies.

"You've no right!" Charles Cutmore spat at us. "After all o' this time, by God, how d'ye think ye've the *right*?"

"Precisely my question, Mr. Cutmore," said Holmes. "After all of this time safe in Siam with your plunder, why return?"

A steely shutter closed over the bank robber's face even as he renewed his violent efforts to break free. He was dragged, spitting curses at the lot of us, into the adjoining parlour as the men awaited instructions.

"What the devil was that?" Lestrade cried. "A clearer confession I've never heard, but that doesn't explain – "

"No, but this does," Holmes said almost reverently, turning as he lifted one of the glass jars from its shelf.

A miniscule red creature swam within, suspended in pale green- tinged water. It was no bigger than my thumbnail, and the shape of a repulsive maggotlike larvae. I felt my skin tingle with disgust when I saw that, though eyeless, one end of the tiny worm was equipped with a gaping sucker-like mouth.

"Behold the Siamese red leech," Holmes declaimed grandly, presenting it to us. "Not our murder weapon, Lestrade, but one of its kindred. Some of my own studies regarding blood led to a side interest in leeches, and this is one of the only deadly specimens in the known world. It possesses biochemical enzymes in its mouth which render its victims numb and dazed when attacked – and, after having bloated itself upon its unsuspecting meal, expanding to hundreds of times its size when unfed, the same chemicals shrink the wound until it is practically invisible."

"My God, that's hideous!" the inspector breathed, echoing my own thoughts. "But how did you – "

"Charles Cutmore and Michael Crosby were known to be the culprits in the Drummonds affair, but they went deep underground," my friend explained, setting down the deadly specimen. "Crosby had never been photographed, though his description was circulated – he was the faceless banker who enabled the inside job to take place at all – but Cutmore was already making advances in his studies of marine animals, marsh grasses, freshwater habitats, and the like when the theft was discovered, and his photograph was published by the Scottish authorities, which is how I came to know of him. The pair were at school together in Edinburgh. Much more was known about Cutmore than Crosby and, at the time of the robbery seven years ago, Cutmore was affianced to one Helen Ainsley, with whom we spoke. I never dreamed that Charles Cutmore and Horatio Swann were the same biologist until yesterday."

"It still isn't clear to me," I interjected. "You yourself asked him why he returned. Why ever should Cutmore murder Crosby, and after all this time?"

"There we enter the realm of conjecture," Holmes admitted, "and shall only know all after Cutmore is questioned. But here is what I propose: after the robbery, Cutmore made off with considerably more than his share of the profits – note comparatively the residences of the conspirators, after all. So. Cutmore fled to Siam, publishing under an alias and waiting until such time as he could return to the British Isles without his features being so recognisable. Crosby, meanwhile, disappeared into the great cesspool of

London and took Helen Ainsley with him, marrying her in Cutmore's absence and continuing to practice banking, from time to time mourning his lost fortune. They may well have believed that the man who betrayed them would never return. But suppose that Cutmore still harboured affections for Helen Ainsley and regretted the loss of her? The reunion last night may have purported to be a friendly one, and Cutmore may even have vowed to restore what he owed them – we have seen the results, however."

"You think this was a crime of passion?" Lestrade drew nearer, glowering.

"Of a sort. Of a very premeditated sort. You have met Charles Cutmore," Holmes reminded him, half-sitting on the desk. "He and Mrs. Wiltmore were once engaged. He does not seem to me the type to remain in hiding forever, supposing he desires to return to someplace, or someone for that matter."

"But what of her husband?"

"Surely you can see that her marriage to the man calling himself John Wiltmore was a matter of expediency – they knew one another's worst secrets and were very much thrown together. I do not claim to have any practical knowledge of the matter, but who ever heard of a married couple who *never* fought, as Mrs. Stubbs claimed? If they seldom fought, I should only have suspected a happy union, and the same goes for an unhappy one if they fought often. But never? It wasn't a union at all. In fact, I should lose no time arresting her."

"On what charge?" Lestrade demanded.

"That of ordering a bath for her freshly unsettled husband and placing a Siamese red leech in it," Holmes replied, his piercing tenor grown grave. "You don't suppose that Charles Cutmore marched up the stairs and dropped it in unnoticed? When I asked him why he returned, he refused to answer, though he had already given himself away – he was trying to shield his former fiancée. The urge was an honourable one, though she shan't escape the law. I haven't evidence enough lacking her confession to prove my findings in the mystery of the missing willow basket, but judging by her behavior at the house, she'll crack on her own once Cutmore is charged. The pair of them have been in contact for far longer than a day, I believe, probably since shortly after his return to England and his purchase of this estate."

"The missing willow basket? Make some sense, by George!"

"Where is the leech now, Lestrade?" Holmes spread his hands in a dramatic show of longsuffering.

"Good heavens," I gasped. "Holmes, you're right – you must be. They planned it together. You said she had been walking by the Thames and not in the park. She took the leech, wrapped it in the cloth, and made off with it in the marketing basket. It must be in the river now."

"Managing to make the most disgusting body of water in the history of mankind still more repugnant." Holmes chuckled, clapping once. "Well done, my dear fellow."

"To think that he left Helen Ainsley behind and then never forgot her, only to lose her again," I reflected. "It's a terrible story."

"And you claim," Lestrade hissed, advancing still further on my friend, "that you knew all this *yesterday*?"

Holmes glared down his hawklike nose at the inspector. "Can you be serious? Are you suggesting you would have believed me if I told you last night that John Wiltmore was killed by a Siamese leech?"

"I might have believed you."

"You might have laughed in my face. This relentless persecution grows tedious, Lestrade."

"Persecution?" Lestrade snarled. "I'm persecuting *you*? Oh, that's rich, Mr. Holmes. Very funny."

"Oddly, I don't find it the slightest bit amusing."

"Gentlemen – " I began.

"Let's have it out in the open then, shall we? Man to

man?" Lestrade's shoulders hunched above his clenched hands as if he longed to express his emotions with pugilism.

"By Jove, yes, let's," my friend hissed, standing to his full height. "Perhaps I had better give you some privacy." Fearing nothing for my friend's safety but feeling dreadfully awkward, I took a step backwards only to find that Lestrade was pointing at me furiously.

"That man," Lestrade snapped, "would – no, don't leave, Dr. Watson, you'd best hear my mind on the subject. That man there, Mr. Holmes, would have taken a bullet for you, I'd stake my own life on it."

Holmes said nothing as I gaped at them.

"And what do you do?" Lestrade was turning crimson with fury. "Instead of seeing it through together, you leave the doctor out entirely, and then you make him think you were *dead*. You stood up there at the altar with him on his *wedding day*, for the love of all that's decent, and do you suppose he enjoyed being written out of the picture? For that matter, how do you suppose *I* felt when I learnt about your demise from a common news hawker? Or when I discovered down at the Yard that Inspector *Patterson* was dashing about rounding up the scoundrels you had apparently been trying to capture for three long months? I should have thought we deserved better from you, Mr. Holmes, and you ought to know it."

Sherlock Holmes, always remarkably pale-complected, had turned absolutely pallid during this speech, though his face betrayed no expression whatsoever otherwise. Meanwhile, my heart was in my throat. I had hardly begun to speak when Holmes held up a perfectly steady hand demanding my silence and said frostily, "You want to know why I left the papers needed to destroy the Moriarty network with Patterson and not with you?"

"I'd find the subject of interest, yes," the small inspector seethed.

Holmes towered over him with that air of aristocratic

mastery only he can assume. "I selected Patterson for the task because he *was not* you."

"Of all the...." Lestrade spluttered in outrage.

My friend commenced idly examining his fingernails. "Professor Moriarty was proven to be directly or indirectly responsible for the murder of no less than 40 persons, though I suspect the true death count to be 52. Patterson is above the common herd, for a Yarder anyhow, but I had previously worked with him twice. You and I, Inspector," he continued, pretending to struggle for the exact accounting, "have worked together on...let me think, dear me, 38 cases, today marking the 39th. Now, I realise that so many figures in a row must be difficult for a man of your acumen to grapple with, but I shall add one more and have done. Ask me how many times I was shot at during the course of this very interesting little problem we are discussing."

"How many?" Lestrade inquired rather faintly.

"Nineteen," my friend reported, though this time fire underlay the ice of his tone. "And if you think I am not aware of the fact *that man*, as you referred to him, would take a bullet for me, then you are still denser than I had previously supposed."

So saying, Holmes checked the time on his pocket watch and swept out of the room.

We were silent for a moment.

"Oh, good lord," Lestrade groaned, rubbing his hand over his prim features. "I'm the biggest fool in Christendom. That was...God help me."

"I'm going to...." said I, gesturing helplessly.

"Yes, yes, go!" the inspector urged, pushing my shoulder. "I'll just confer with the constables while I reflect on the fact that Mr. Holmes is right to call me dense. Go on, quick march."

Hastily, I gave chase. Not imagining my highly reserved friend had any wish to remain in a house where such a scene had just been enacted, as his levels of detachment border upon the mechanical, I dove for the entryway and the faintly blue atmosphere of the mild spring morning beyond.

I found Sherlock Holmes some 30 yards distant, leaning against the ivy-draped stone wall. He seemingly awaited my arrival, although he confined his eyes to the smoke drifting skyward from his cigarette. When I had reached him, I halted the words which threatened to leap from my tongue, knowing this situation required more careful handling. Several tacks were considered before I settled on the one likeliest to succeed without causing further harm, and immediately, I breathed easier.

"Well, my dear fellow?" Holmes prompted in a strained voice when I said nothing. Crossing his sinewy limbs, he lifted a single eyebrow although he still failed to look at me. "Have you any salient remarks to add to this topic? Come, come, I am eager for all relevant opinions upon – "

"Holmes," said I, gripping him warmly by the forearm. "Everything I have to say has already crossed your mind."

He did peer at me then, searching my face with the sort of razor focus he ordinarily devotes to outlandishly complex and inexplicable crime scenes. After what seemed an age of this scrutiny, a sorrowful smile crept over the edges of his mouth.

"Then possibly my answer has crossed yours," he continued to quote in an undertone. "You stand fast?"

"Absolutely," I vowed.

A flinch no one save I would ever have caught twitched across his aquiline features; he then clapped my hand which still grasped his arm and broke away to stub his cigarette out against the wall.

"The inspector is sorry over – "

"He needn't be. As Charles Cutmore seems to have learnt to his detriment, the returning can be harder than the leaving."

"Holmes – "

"Do you know, as many features of interest as this case

held, I find I tire of it dreadfully, my dear Watson," he announced, wholly returned to his proud and practical self. "A ride back to London with our friend Lestrade and his men and our quarry I think is in order, then a pot of tea at Baker Street and a complete perusal of the morning editions on my part, whilst you work upon whatever grotesquely embellished account of our exploits you plan to inflict on the world next, followed by a change of collar and an oyster supper before Massenet's Manon at eight."

So it came about that the good Inspector Lestrade, whose opinion of Holmes's dramatic demise had been such a low one, came to look upon the matter in another light. Whether he ever again spoke to my friend of that impassioned conversation, neither man was gregarious enough to inform me; I highly doubt they broached the topic afterwards. To this very day, however, when Holmes requires a stout colleague or Lestrade has need of England's greatest detective, they call upon one another without hesitation. The horrible death of Crosby the banker was determined a murder by the Assizes and will be tried as such; though the fates of Charles Cutmore and Helen Ainsley have not yet been determined, they belong to that enormous criminal fraternity who have such ample cause to bemoan the existence of my fast friend, the incomparable Mr. Sherlock Holmes.

The Onion Vendor's Secret

by Marcia Wilson

"I suppose," said Sherlock Holmes, "you may as well write it up. It will keep you occupied for a few days. More, if you persist in supporting the sentimentalism that is infecting the common taste."

This prickly observation was finalised with a loud cough, and the Great Detective once again reclined upon his sick-bed, with his wrist over his eyes in the very picture of ailing petulance against the backdrop of his bedroom window and its view of his bees devouring a stand of blue tansy.

"My dear Holmes!" I exclaimed. "I was not even asking for such a thing – and my thoughts are more upon your health, which you have severely neglected."

"Neglect – what of it? The war is over, Watson and to that end I have funneled my energies. Now I rest as the world muses – give them something to celebrate over and perhaps they will leave me in peace!" He sniffed and added, "If you keep to the facts and not the window - dressing, you ought to finish before our guest arrives with Tuesday's milk-cart."

Although his tone and wording was strident, I understood the warmth of his feelings. The Great Game, which he had played so well, had cumulated with the Great War, and now he and the world were equally spent. They had both shared the miserable truth that large emergencies do not remove the smaller ones. That he was still alive was a wonderment to me, I who have felt this astonishment far too much in my life.

As I write with my pen in the past and my eyes upon the future, it occurs to me what an extraordinary life it has been to share it with such a friend as Sherlock Holmes. Long gone are the days when I was a shattered veteran of the desert, and he a young consultant on the verge of becoming an active force for justice. I have no regrets save in general: that of each case my readers saw, there were at least 20 left silent and unseen. Some patiently await their day in the vaults of Cox; some were remarkable for only a day – and became unremarkable just as quickly. These "Mayfly Cases", as Holmes once described them, were important for the intellectual exercise, and he viewed them with the absent respect a master musician gave to the importance of his warm-up scales. The most beloved of these must surely be that of the gentleman's hat, which led to the discovery of a precious stone within a goose.

But some cases fall into a category where they have taken on veritable lives of their own in the imagination of the public. These are what may arguably be termed "the immortal ones" for their continued attention and fascination. They remain as talked-about as they were upon the day they were emergent news. Most are our shorter adventures, such as the matter with the repulsive Roylott, and I have it on good authority that not a single British jeweler can pass the year without someone asking for a stone to emulate the aforementioned Blue Carbuncle. If Holmes bemoans my florid style, I admit that I am equally baffled by the never-ending pleas from my publisher, his wife, and even the random acquaintance upon the street, for these immortal tales.

By now my reader has suspected my intention: I am permitted at long last to break silence and offer them what they have so often begged to read – A return to Dartmoor.

I apologise now, for I will not satisfy the countless pleas for the impossible return of Jack Stapleton from a watery grave, or the marriage of his widow to Sir Henry, and it is certainly not about a return of a devilish hound. But I beg the reader's pardon one last time, and suspend judgment until they have read the tale through. Crime has been the livelihood of Sherlock Holmes with all the necessity of a knot into a skein, and some knots need time to untangle.

"Halloa!" exclaimed Sherlock Holmes, his interest sharp and his enunciation perfectly clear as he held his favoured cherrywood between his teeth. I looked up from my breakfast in time to see him leap from the table to the window to peer down his nose at the street below. "Now this is no light thing," he observed to me without looking away. "Onion Johnny is about to pay us a visit."

My old wounds were paining me, but I threw down my napkin and went to see this marvel for myself. This time of day, the city was choked with early news-chaunters, messenger boys, and rented cabs as the public strove to move between train stations. Against the swarm of obstreperous humanity, a little Frenchman stumbled with an exaggerated, uneven stride we knew well. Like all of his kind, he stood out by the unmistakable costume of his profession as an oignon vendeur: A short coat over his striped shirt matched a navy beret upon his dark head. Like a tiny fisherman's float in a great sea, he bobbed in and out of the confusion. He was hardly a prepossessing size to manage for himself, but he held a stout stick upon his shoulders, and upon that stick depended heavy braids of French onion, which slowly swung back and forth and encouraged others to make way.

"I believe this is a first, Holmes. I've never seen him at Baker Street before the end of his work-day."

"To be sure he has from time to time, but he is not unlike a pony in a coal-mine. If he deviates from his schedule we may blame the path, for he lacks the imagination to wander off it himself. His world is shaped by clocks and blinkers."

I studied the heavy weight of his cargo again, and attempted to use Holmes's methods. "He must have stopped selling his wares to come here." For it was clear that he was desperately making his way to us; his face kept turning up to reassure himself that our rooms had not vanished in the curling fog, and I was certain it was relief in his dark little face to glimpse our forms behind the glass. For all his efforts, he was stymied by the slow march of brick-carters that blocked his crossing. Despite the anxiety of his situation, we had to smile as he stamped his foot.

"And which of my methods have you used to determine this, Watson?" Holmes smiled around his pipe-stem and puffed cold vapours.

"It is the meagrest of observations, I fear. I remember he told you once that his bundles weigh up to 220 pounds, and it would seem he has nearly that much to carry."

"A simple observation is often the correct one, Watson. Bravo! And bravo, Johnny!" For the little man had abruptly nipped down the street in order to get around the parade faster. "He shows initiative today! Well, Watson! At the very least we can say our breakfast-time has proven diverting."

Before long, our guest was gasping by our low fire. His wares had been abandoned for safe-keeping in Mrs. Hudson's kitchen, and he strode in with his sun-darkened face flushed from exertion. A chapelet of the pink two-pound Roscoff onions swayed easily in his hand. Not for the first time I marvelled at how of a type he was. With his sharp- chiselled face and sable hair with piercing dark eyes, he could have been any man from the coast of France, all the way to the south of England.

Unlike the usual vendeur, ours was well-versed in the English tongue, and he often used it to good effect.

"I am aware that I am hours too early, Messieurs," he began with his beret twisting in his hands. "But a sorry matter has come to my attention and I have in turn come to you on behalf of my brothers in trade."

"Come, come." Holmes proclaimed generously. "The onions will keep. We are always glad to see you, regardless of the circumstances." He lifted his pipe to the mantle. "There is a bit of tobacco which you may enjoy if it helps your blood cool from your travels."

"Ah, and I thank you both, but my duties keep and must be on my way. There are many Captain's Heads that need their crew and I am to supervise the fleet." Johnny flashed a quick grin of teeth and tapped his rope of onions. "I promised to make a matter known to you, and I must keep my word."

"By all means, Johnny." Holmes smiled and leaned back, pressing his fingertips together. I have witnessed his management of the many different guests to his office, but Onion Johnny was a guarantee to put him in good cheer.

"Sir Henry Baskerville is paying penance for the lost soul that was his relative."

"That is hardly news, Johnny." Holmes said mildly. "It has coloured the papers and the gossip-halls since he returned from his constitutional."

"I know, Messieurs," he nodded to us both, "and we have heard how he has given a new well to that Boys' School, and money to the Madame Beryl's family. I am speaking of the four burglaries of your West Country, where my brothers sell their onions."

"Hum." Holmes opened his eyes and tapped his fingers. "As I recall from the news, Sir Henry prudently hired a detective for each of the burglaries to prove the culpability of the unlamented late Stapleton. All of them men of the law who can be trusted with such cases."

"It is Folkestone Court that concerns us." Johnny lifted his heavy weight of onions in his agitation. "And Sir Henry has hired that Lestrade to solve this one. But the damages, sir, and the damages are only for the loss of property, and no one is thinking of the little page coldly pistoled by the thief."

Holmes exclaimed in surprise. "Well, this is most unusual. Surely a loss of life would be part and parcel of the damages incurred!"

"The conversation was heard clearly by my kinfolk." Our guest insisted.

"Do continue."

"I cannot explain but if you were to go and see, we will pay you." Before anyone could protest, the little man had a purse out and slapped it upon the table with his rope of onion, cheeks bright with high colour in his Gallic fervor.

"You needn't worry about the fee, Johnny. My rates are fixed, and you have given Mrs. Hudson as well as the Irregulars your excellent onions on credit," Holmes murmured. "If you say I ought to go speak with Friend Lestrade, then I certainly can find the time."

"You must speak soon!" Johnny persisted. His urgency had not been appeased by this peace-making. He turned to go, and then stopped to wag a scolding finger upon my friend.

"And do not again use my onions for your mischief! The Roscoff is a sweet onion. The next time you make a plaster, use one of those rude Spanish friars!"

When we were alone we burst out laughing. "Rude Spanish onions!" I wiped my eyes. "So, he reads Dickens?"

"Many do, even the French." Holmes had recovered his breath and was lifting the chapelet to test its weight. "30 pounds! This may be diverting. Crime has been very unimaginative of late, and while this promises to be no different, at least we can be in the open air." He chuckled. "Perhaps I owe our little friend recompense for offending his vegetables. Never argue onions with a Continental, Watson. Their proverbs centre on peeling away problems even as they weep for them."

"Anstruther has my practice while I recuperate," I consulted the Bradshaw. "There is a train at two o'clock."

"Well, well. We have been cooped up like chickens in a rather dull London. A minor diversion in the open air with the famous Folkestone butter will be to our improvement." Holmes examined the onion rope in his long fingers. "Not a single blemish. And what a fine head is this captain!" He prodded the crackly bottom bulb, which was markedly larger than the rest. "The captain suits this crew. Remarkable, is it not, Watson? The secret to so much fine British cooking rests within Roscovite soil where Mary, Queen of Scots once set her contrary feet. One can hardly imagine England without these little entrepreneurs, and yet they are a new pigment on the bright canvas of our country."

Holmes's loquacity advertised a fine mood, which in turn led me to suspect this case may be more than a seeming plea to Lestrade on behalf of a legal fine-point. In this, I wisely bowed to his instincts, for I would not go against the observations of the expert any more than Holmes would deny my diagnosis as a physician.

We soon ticketed ourselves to the west. The London fogs cleared under a blue summer sky, and the city melted to silvery streams trickling across sloping greens by which droves of men and women drove flocks of geese to Leadenhall. I asked myself if Holmes expected the matter to stimulate his intellect in some way, for I knew nothing appealed to my friend so much as a thorny problem. After tucking the onions away to Mrs. Hudson's kitchen, he had fallen into a brief stupor of concentration from which I knew better than to intrude.

I distracted myself from the aches and pains aggravated by the train's movement by pondering our visit. "I confess I have been puzzled about the news, Holmes. Why did Sir Henry employ Lestrade for one of the cases? It cannot be because they know each other."

"You are correct. It is because of the current owner of Folkestone Court, Abraham Quantock, wants redress for Stapleton's burglary."

"The name means little to me."

"Did you glean nothing of him in the many newspapers, Watson?"

"Holmes! I have read the exact same articles as yourself, and none have said more than the fact that he is a retired expert in properties from London."

"The absence of news can be the most illuminating. He originally served the nobility, but greed created too many compromises, and he is retired for the betterment of all to Folkestone Court, owned by his Aunt Oriana Quantock, a sensible dame. Alas, the shock of Stapleton's attack contributed to her death, and this charming nephew took the estate.

"Hypocritically, he demands the highest conduct from all, as though he were as worthy as his clients. One false step in his presence and vituperative violence is his reaction. I had the delight of the man whilst solving one or two small matters for my brother." Holmes chuckled. "No doubt he thinks the title of baronet is still a young and upstart one, a purchased billet into the presence of his betters."

"Is Lestrade a bridge between Sir Henry and this fellow?"

"There is some finesse in the baronet. Quantock must be wondering with every ounce of his ferocious will if Lestrade is secretly conducting business for the Foreign Office – for they are not without their extensive spies, and his former office employed them heavily."

"You do not paint a rosy picture. I begin to feel sorry for Lestrade."

"By now Quantock knows why Sir Henry employed Lestrade: Our unimaginative friend has no fear of living man. He will not concede to a title nor flinch at a powerful name. No, Watson, Lestrade is an *excellent* bridge between the two opposing poles of Baronet and Buffoon. He may trust our assistance if he so needs it. For all his flaws, he is honest enough to admit them."

"It all seems peculiar. Sir Henry restores the honour of his family name by making restitution for Stapleton's crimes. Wouldn't Quantock reciprocate by only asking for the value of his lost property?"

"And that is the question that begs." In his lap rested his collection of newspaper clippings. "If one relishes irony, here is a feast. You will never see a province so charming and rich with creameries as Folkestone, where it is said the native-born cannot swallow his tea without butter. Quantock is as cold and thin as the lands are fat. He is pure puffery, Watson! Folkestone Court is respectable only by age and history. The family money begat itself in the Navy, but you will find this Quantock's feet high and dry. He would imply that the house and its holdings has always been his, but in truth he received it in exactly the same way as Sir Henry did Baskerville: there was no-one left to inherit. Here, Watson. What do you think?" He placed the open book in my lap.

On the collected front page rested the proud face of our friend the baronet, standing before seemingly endless rows of winged insects in tight glass frames. By coincidence or design, a small speckled moth matching his necktie sat on the wall behind his shoulder.

"SIR HENRY RESCUES RARE COLLECTION FOR SCIENCE."

The article itself was dull and rambled to tangents, but the gist was plain: As the owners of Merripit House had suffered for tenants after the scandal of the Stapletons, and Beryl Stapleton wanting nothing from her former life, Sir Henry had purchased the property. His first act was to rescue the collection of insects, for they were fragile in an unheated house.

The article included a quote from MRCS Mortimer, who was pleased that science would benefit. All that was left, he assured the readers, was the appropriate place for the collection.

Almost hidden in the far corner was a tiny legal missive: Sir Henry had successfully applied to have one Jack Stapleton recognised permanently as Jack Stapleton, and not as his former identity of Rodger Baskerville. The law agreed that it was highly unusual to change the name of a dead man, but as he had willfully changed it in life, they saw no reason not to accept Sir Henry's plea. As easily as that, the line of Rodger Baskerville vanished from the Baskerville records.

"I see nothing more than I did when I first read this."

"Exactly."

Holmes pulled back his book and wasted no time in raining copious notes upon the pages. I left him to it and amused myself in the countryside.

Our stops grew further apart as industry dissolved to agriculture. By the time we eased into Folkestone, there was little more to see than lazy slopes of rich green meads and herds of Folkestone's legendary White Cattle, peppered with small stone shelters freckling the greensward amongst ancient standing stones. The hedgerows were cleverly sculpted of ancient blackberry under bloom as white as the cattle itself. The scene was breathtaking.

Holmes prodded my arm. "That would be Folkestone Court."

I followed his gaze up the tallest of the gentle rises to see what I had presumed a large standing granite was actually a creaky stone lump of windows and bottle chimneys. Long ago its high rock walls must have been impressive; now it was an ageing dowager refusing to conform to her age, and clutching the pearls at her throat in the form of the strings of white cattle lowing upon the hill.

A herd of these cows browsed behind a lively country market against our stop. Under their placid eyes, two Johnnies laced their onions upon sturdy bicycles and took off, wobbling under the weight of their chaplets. A third held office before a swarm of sharp-eyed country cooks as a boy chalked the transactions on a blade of slate.

Before long we saw Lestrade, smartly dressed with a walking-stick under his arm. His lean face twitched, and his sly dark eyes glittered in amusement.

"Pale as a mushroom, Lestrade." Holmes scolded. "Of what use is country air if you cannot breathe it?"

The little Yarder drew himself to his full height and looked up at Holmes. "Easy for you to say," he complained. "I've been indoors!" He sighed and glanced about. "I got your wire just in time. Come. I've rooms."

"By all means. We look forward to an illuminating conversation." The little professional whistled up a waggonette. "The Candlebat Inn," Lestrade instructed. To us he muttered: "Abraham Quantock is possibly failing in his senses. He is obsessed with getting full value of damages from the theft that we believe Stapleton committed upon him, but his notion of reparation is...." He glanced about him, though by now there was no one to hear. "It was you who first suspected he was behind the Folkestone Court murder and theft."

"I still do."

"Well, Sir Henry agrees, and it should be a simple case of collecting the testimony of the damages incurred by Stapleton. But here Mr. Quantock wants the damages of the page's death to go to *him*, not the grieving family! He claims that as the page – Artie Baldwin – was in his employ, thus *he* is the one with reparations, as he had to do without a page thanks to Stapleton."

Lestrade rested his chin on his hand and we could see for the first time the hours of sleepless duty upon his face. "He refuses reason, Holmes, and swears if he is not satisfied he will sell and move to London, and the very thought has panicked the people. Quantock is the lifeblood of these people." Oddly as he said this, his eye fell upon a watching herder and he frowned.

"Does he own the cattle?" I asked.

"He rents the land for the cattle and the land is vital for the milk that makes their famous butter. The dairies need the wild grazing. Everything here is bound to the cows! It is the only reason why the train even stops here on the way to Coombe Tracey."

"This is indeed a problem. What of the page's family?"

Lestrade groaned. "The father is Charlie Baldwin, a retired seaman and an outsider, but well-liked for all of that. His mother's needlework at Court got Artie the post. They relied on his small income as a page, but upon his death the pressure is on to bow to let Quantock have all of the restitution...even though they are close to being evicted for their struggle to pay rent, because it was all on their head to pay for Young Artie's funeral!"

"Perhaps, you could explain Sir Henry's instructions."

"The baronet is leery of Quantock. He will pay full value to Folkestone Court all damages proven wrought by that wretched Stapleton, which is estimated at £3,000 and no more. He is content to pay for the glazier's time in the repair of the cut window used to gain entrance, you see, but not for the glass itself, which Quantock picked up and threw to the floor in his rage. Mr. Mortimer is the one who sewed him up when the shard caught his cheek."

"Forever charming." Holmes murmured. Although the news was sensational, I could not understand why he was in deep thought. Clearly there were facets of this case that escaped me, and I could only wait for the outcome. "Is Mortimer available?"

"He is at a dig on Lewis. I could try to contact him for you."

"Perhaps later. Would it be difficult to see this scene of old crime?"

"Quantock is expecting a final meeting of the scene tomorrow morning. And here we are."

We could now see the inn. It was a large cube built alongside a skeleton-thin road that by neglect had worn down to little more than ribbons in the grass. A broad man with a wooden peg-leg scattered barley for a flock of hens beneath a large painted sign of white moths before a lantern – the "candlebats" of the Inn.

"It looks pleasant." I offered.

"Be careful outside it. There are many ears." Lestrade murmured. His gaze, we saw, had never completely left off from watching the solitary herder in the fields.

Holmes left for a walk. My old wounds had drained me, so I spent the time jotting down my impressions and the facts of the case as I knew them. A stately country dame brought a tea tray, and even the skimmed milk held lumps of butter. Stories of the White Cattle were not exaggerated.

It was a pleasant place, not unlike Coombe Tracy. The thick Dartmoor mists were but weak wisps, easily taken by the fresh sunlight and the touch of the sea-breeze from the south. Instead of wild ponies and crags, I saw tame bovine and stone crosses. I knew Holmes saw the countryside as silent wells of horror, but here it was hard to imagine anything more violent than the inn's moths flying into the lantern.

Lestrade and Holmes returned and fell upon their portions. Afterwards, Holmes settled back upon the bed with his knees drawn to his chest, unconscious of anything but his pipe and the occasional question. I opened the window, and Lestrade filled me in on pertinent details that I would not have found without weeks of gossip: Quantock's anxiety over money, he assured me, was rooted in his purse.

"It isn't cheap to own a monster like the Court," he said over his own buttery coffee. "All that history means freezing rooms and tons of coal burning nonstop to keep the frost off the floor. It smokes like London year-round! Why, I'm certain he has a full staff just to keep down the mold. The Quantock fortune is bound up in legal knots, and he can't get at it or raise any rents."

"We are alone now. What else do you know about the Baldwins?"

"They rent this inn, and they are afraid to be seen talking to anyone," Lestrade said into his cup. By his actions, my friend had as much proclaimed his loyalty to the Baldwins. "Charlie is joked about as Folkestone's last Catholic. He met and married Miss Fern Runston when he was reduced from ferrying Onion Johnnies from Brittany into becoming one himself. Artie was their only son, but another has arrived since. Injuries keep Charlie from putting in a full day, but he is clever and makes string bags to sell to the dairies to carry the small tubs of butter. His style of stringing has become part of the signature of the area, and they would all grieve if the family had to leave."

"Something puzzles me...Mortimer knows Quantock?"

"He knows the Court's collection." Lestrade shuddered. "Simply all sorts of dead things on every wall – bones, skulls, feathers, stuffed and mounted beasts. The late Oriana was like most Quantocks and collected. Lichens and insects. Before the murder, her frames took up the entire library wall! The servants say Abraham is not a collector, unless one counts coins."

"If there are bones, Mortimer would visit. It sounds like a museum."

"It is! Do you remember when Ellen Terry played Lady Macbeth at the Lyceum back in '88?"

I said that was six years ago, but no one who had seen the fire- haired Queen of Theatre could forget her in her glittering green dress of a thousand wings of the Jewel Beetle.

"Miss Oriana was consulted for the dress design because she knew beetles so well. Discreetly of course – her people wouldn't like any connexion with actresses living arrears."

"How did you learn this?"

"Miss Oriana was the consultant, but Mrs. Baldwin's needle made the samples."

"I see."

"Miss Oriana hoped to make the Court a private museum. Folkestone approved because it would encourage the sort they like – moneyed temporary visitors who gad about with their nets and jars, breeze in and breeze out. The subscriptions would have modernized the Court and, of course, the butter would be sold on-site without the added expense of shipping it off to the city. But now it is all going to go to waste." Lestrade morosely toyed with his gloves. "And suddenly...Mr. Quantock has recently claimed the only that thing will satisfy this affair is the deed to Merripit House."

Sherlock Holmes had been calmly smoking, but at this news he sat bolt upright. "That is very odd, Lestrade!" His grey eyes glittered with a feverish excitement that I did not understand.

"The house is an eyesore, but would improve with a grazier, and the orchard comes with 20 hives of black bees. Lastly, the well has never dried up, and you know how valuable that is. Sir Henry may easily profit after a little work on it."

"There is something about this that tastes bad." I ventured. "I cannot quite put my finger on it."

"I know. Strangest of all is Quantock's insistence that Sir Henry *not* improve the House. He wants it as Stapleton had left it, in order not to 'ask more than his fair share!'" He scowled, and his dark eyes suddenly looked quite angry. "I can't prove it or provide an explanation to any court of law, Mr. Holmes, but Quantock's fiddling about was driving us mad. Yet, as soon as Sir Henry received the copy of Merripit's Deed on his desk...he changes his offer yet again, only instead of half-a- hundred itemised damages, it is just one thing – Merripit House, which is currently valued at less than half of the damages at the Court. For that matter, the rental properties are out of proportion; seven % of all the land is hedge! Wasteful, except here, where it is part of the key to the grazing that maintains the health of the cows. Rent has been fixed at 1.23/acre for 50 years. Quantock can't even pay his own tailor!"

"You are out of your depth, Lestrade. You should have summoned me."

"I am being watched." Lestrade said with grave dignity. "Poor folk, desperate and afraid to see the end of their livelihoods. I hold them no grudge, but I wish for restitution of my own."

"I daresay you will get your wish. And you will see Quantock tomorrow?"

"Early on."

"Sir Henry?"

"He said it is a low thing to be predictable to one's enemies. He has authorized me with full powers of decision if I must." Lestrade produced the necessary letter from the baronet.

"Sir Henry is a cunning fox." Holmes admired. "Very well. The three of us will venture out and gird this cave-lion in his draughty den."

"You should not mention the smuggling, Watson. It would not be in the best interests of the people in your sensationalist writings."

I set down my pen. "And I will not, I assure you."

"You practically have, my good Watson. A lantern painted on the Inn-sign! The proximity to Plymouth! The use of Bretons! The stone manse!"

"I did not mention the old shipwreck's lookout, or the unanswered questions about the root cause of the Quantock's original wealth, Holmes. I could not mention any of these things without being forced to comment on the local's surreptitious form of income."

"We are in agreement." Holmes riposted pettishly. Being feverish never helped his temper, and I ignored it. It was better to encourage him to health. "And do not put Lestrade in the ending."

"I would not dream of it."

"Do not be overly descriptive of Quantock. Put him down as the world's scrawniest toad and leave it at that."

"I am not sure that is possible, Holmes. There is no such thing as a lean toad."

"I was referring to his complexion."

"Holmes, you may read this for yourself when I am finished."

"Must I?"

Abraham Quantock allowed us entrance to his private study that was so poorly lit it gave him the impression of a lean toad. His flat, moist blue eyes glimmered at Holmes, who was the only one tall enough to meet his gaze, and he spared Lestrade an icy glare. Myself he dismissed as irrelevant.

Holmes found a corner by the window and puffed on

the pipe he had carried with him on our journey to the Court. Every inch of his lanky form exuded the boredom of a man who must be present for the sake of appearances but nothing more. As I watched, Lestrade struggled more and more for calm as Quantock's ugly amusement grew at Lestrade's expense.

For my part, I knew Holmes was often unfathomable, but there was no sense in trying to draw him out. He would speak when ready and not before, and Lestrade knew this as well as I. But the little professional was baffled at the seeming loss of his ally.

"My terms are clear." Quantock said coldly. "Sir Henry cannot disagree that it is against restitution if I am left the poorer from it. I only wish Merripit House."

"You wish to own it in its original condition," Lestrade countered doggedly. "That is not to put too fine of a point on it. The house needs work. Stapleton was more interested in netting butterflies than keeping it up. You could have purchased it at any time, but you waited until after Sir Henry bought it."

"My reasons are my own."

"And my duty is clear. I will accept your statement and personally deliver it to Sir Henry, but I cannot give you the guarantee that you desire."

"You shall remind your baronet those are my only terms."

"I will, but it would go well with you if I had some reason for your decision."

"No more than it was my Aunt's dream to open Folkestone to naturalists and collectors like herself. Stapleton damaged her original collection and contributed to her untimely passing; it is fitting that her memory receive the benefit of his residence." Quantock grew agitated with the force of his own words and rose up. "Merripit is ideal for the scientist with the desire to do more than take a pleasant stroll among the trout-streams. It is close to the wands planted for safe passage and one less burden I would have on my family's name."

"Not to mention your soul," Lestrade said, in one of his rare examples of dry wit. "You would need to maintain the property, Mr. Quantock. Sir Henry would not let you beggar yourself. Can you afford such a thing?"

"I would own Merripit House only long enough to restore it to fine condition, and then offer it free and clear to the Baldwins, on the understanding that they would host any visitors who come to visit the Moor."

Lestrade was as speechless as myself. He looked at Holmes, who continued smoking with a bored air, as though this were all a trivial affair. He looked back to Quantock and found his voice. "Is this your final word, sir?"

"It is."

"Then I will explain your position to Sir Henry immediately, but it would help if you also wrote your wishes down on paper, which I and any of these gentlemen would be content to sign."

"That we would," I said firmly.

Holmes shrugged. "Oh, I suppose if it pleases you," he drawled. Quantock sniffed. "It will do."

In short time, Quantock drafted a terse statement and we all signed it. Lestrade let no emotions escape his face, but I could tell he was simmering with rage under his calm mask. It was not until we were well outside shouting-distance from the Court that he finally opened his mouth.

"I've talked to brick walls with more sense!" he roared. "And if that man ever gave anything to anyone 'free and clear' it was a germ!"

Holmes was so overcome with hilarity he was unable to regain his composure for some minutes, during which he clapped the little Yarder on the back and leaned upon his shoulder. I thought it a rare sight, with long and lean Holmes bent over the small police detective.

"Be calm, Lestrade!" he cried. "Rest assured, you have done your duty. You saw my lackadaisical performance and responded beautifully to my rudeness, which delighted Quantock so well he assumed he had the upper hand in the debate. Now we shall make haste and inform Sir Henry of the latest development."

Sir Henry's promised electric lights perched like soldiers down the drive of Baskerville Hall, and the ragged greensward was neatened by the thrifty use of white-faced sheep. Small ponds cunningly crafted from the native stone dotted the landscape, shimmering like mirrors and populated by many gossiping birds.

What we took for a gardener proved to be Sir Henry himself, dressed for digging with a large straw hat. He grinned as he waved us over to the edge of a large, shallow circle sliced into the sod, barely more than two inches deep and filled to the brim with clear water.

"Just in time for dinner!" He laughed. "Come and see my dewpond – a real marvel, eh?" The Neolithic collection-pool was a testimony to the skill of Dartmoor's early forbearers, and the convenience of sweet water lured the wild ponies from an early death in the Mire.

"That, and my new mares," the baronet told us. "I've been improving the bloodstock." He turned to Lestrade with his hands on his hips. "I expect you have news for me. Come in and let's talk over a drink."

Lestrade sadly gave a summary as we walked inside the Hall. Stapleton's impressive collection of butterflies hung on the walls, but even I could tell Sir Henry planned to move them out as soon as he could.

Sir Henry was startled. "I knew he was contrary, but...Mr. Holmes, can you riddle this?"

"Perhaps. A separate party hired me to facilitate an equitable solution for all involved. Can you add anything?"

The baronet shuddered. "I've dealt with enough snakes that I can't help but respect them for being good at a job no-one else in Creation wants. But this...." He rose to serve a strong rye bourbon. "This out- Herods Herod, by thunder!"

With a troubled air, the young baronet turned to Lestrade. "I thought I was giving you a straight job, not a wild goose chase."

"Lestrade is capable of fulfilling his duty, Sir Henry," Holmes assured them both. "And the matter can still be resolved cleanly."

"I'll believe you, Mr. Holmes, but I wouldn't believe anyone else." Lestrade rubbed at his brow.

"No-one need believe. Simply tell Quantock to come here tomorrow to sign the agreement. Watson is a splendid fellow in a pinch, and he can be trusted to add his signature of witness to the agreement, am I correct?"

"Indeed," I said stoutly. "Although I have no more an idea of what you wish than Lestrade."

"Or me." Sir Henry lifted his hand like a boy in a schoolroom. "But I'll be ready for anything!" He grinned. "And I'll be glad to see this through!"

"Excellent!" And without further warning, Holmes turned and dashed down the Hall with the speed of a schoolboy, stopping by turns to peer up the walls and skipping down again. The three of us gaped, but at the very end we saw him grab something in the murk and run back with the object under his arm. It was the light-speckled moth next to the baronet's elbow in the newspaper clipping.

"Your job will be simplicity itself, Lestrade!" Holmes declared. "Merely place this on Sir Henry's desk like so – there! Right next to where the deed shall rest. A delightful conversation piece, is it not?" He beamed with his hands on his hips and admired his handiwork as we again looked at each other, baffled.

"This is one of your tricks, is it not, Mr. Holmes?" Lestrade asked in resignation.

"Not at all, Lestrade. Simply remember," he lifted his hand, "'I swear to you that The Merripit House Collection is complete!' Every specimen that rightfully belonged to Jack Stapleton will be returned to its walls so that Mr. Quantock can accept the deed on his terms. Mr. Quantock agreed before witnesses that he would personally repair Merripit as part of his concession to the plight of the Baldwins."

"Why am I thinking of a pony and a potato right now?" Sir Henry muttered with smile upon Holmes. "I've seen your look in a man's eye before, friend, and it was always right before someone got their comeuppance."

"You give me too much credit, Sir Henry." Holmes pursed his lips. "And now, you spoke of dinner?"

Here my pen falters, for though I have often devoted my thoughts to this crucial scene, I still cannot give full description to how Quantock strode proudly into Baskerville Hall, only for his swagger to crumble like sand under rain as his eye fell upon Sir Henry's desk. He paled before our eyes, and his greeting quivered in his throat.

"Good morning, Mr. Quantock," the baronet said. With his fingers laced together upon the blotting-paper, and his large hazel eyes unblinking upon the newcomer, our friend smiled. "I believe you wished to own Merripit House?"

With a shaking hand, Quantock signed his agreement to Sir Henry, and Lestrade, Holmes and I added our witness. Merripit House thus passed from Baskerville Hall to Folkestone Court, and Quantock was promptly beggared in the repairwork that was past his means. He was close to penniless when he passed the house to the Baldwins. That good couple promptly sold it back to Sir Henry for no more than the value of the Candlebat Inn, and reside comfortably there to this day. It was a far better fate than Quantock's, for he soon was forced by penury to do as he had sworn in revenge, and had to sell what he could and return to London. Allow me to say that the purchaser would have made Miss Oriana proud, for they thought her dream of a Museum a sensible one, and Folkestone breathed fresh relief at a new source of money.

"Sentimentalism, Watson!" Holmes protested. "And of the basest kind. You would have them think it was purchased out of the kindness of the heart!"

"I doubt the Foreign Office would like it if I mentioned their interest in the property, Holmes. They do like to keep their eyes on private entrepreneurs."

"Bah," Holmes sneered. "In any case, your tale is missing large chunks. You will have to splice in a build-up of atmosphere with our journey to Folkestone and keep up an over-inflated account of my behavior to unsettle Lestrade."

"I thought to put that in later. Tuesday is almost upon us."

"At least there will be fresh milk."

"All right, Mr. Holmes." Sir Henry had gathered us all before the fireplace, for even summer in Dartmoor is chilly. He gnawed on the stem of a new pipe in a seeming picture of content. Only the gleam in his eyes and the smile on his lips said otherwise. "You played a long game, and you came out on top again, but it is done and time for the magician to spill his tricks."

Holmes bowed with a pleased mien to be compared to a magician, and bowed again as Lestrade and I leaned forward.

"Quantock only pretended to be callous of his Aunt's work. In reality, he was quietly replacing choice specimens and selling the originals. He could do this because of her failing eyesight, and he started with the pieces high up, knowing she would be content with examining her paintings and sketches. But the real plum, the prize specimen, was the Vandeleur Moth, which you so kindly placed on Sir Henry's desk, Lestrade."

"What!" Sir Henry stared wildly at the silent moth. "You mean that Moth named after Stapleton back when he was passing as Vandeleur?"

"The same."

"By thunder!"

"Yes. I asked myself if it was indeed that worthy moth, but although my suspicions were strong, I had no confirmation until Lestrade gave me the proof I needed with the news of Quantock's sudden desire for Merripit House.

"Stapleton knew from his friendship with Mortimer that the Folkestone Collection was worthy of a visit, and one day he did just that. He must have felt as though his secret days were numbered when he saw the very moth credited with his old name from East Yorkshire was under glass! If its presence became common knowledge, eventually a Yorkshire expert would come to visit, and his disguise would be circumspect. He did not think that his distinct hobby was already a danger to his identity, but we have established his 'hazy thinking' in the past. Naturally he had to have the moth, but he could not ask overtly – Miss Quantock's dream of a museum was public. No, he had to recover this specimen covertly.

"Thieving was on his mind that fateful May, but not just for the silver. The moth was his true goal, though he was already dangerous with his need for money. Little Artie may have seen him take down the case; we will never know. He shot him down in cold blood and fled with silver and moth, leaving behind a wreck of the specimens on the wall.

"What with the loss of her closest confidant's son, which Miss Oriana felt responsible for by securing the child's post, and the devastation of her beloved collection, she was not far from the grave. Stapleton must have thought himself safe, for even he had no idea Abraham Quantock was a savvy moth-man, chafing at the believed destruction of the rare moth.

"For this *was* a very rare moth indeed with reverse-patterned wings. This happens less than three times in five thousand specimens – which Stapleton had estimated but had never been able to personally collect."

"I still can't imagine it." Sir Henry's expressive face was clouded. "All of this for a little moth."

"Do you know the root of entomology, Sir Henry? From the Greek entomos, 'that which is cut in pieces.' The entomological world is as complex as the creatures they study. The fanciers of moths alone will guarantee you a fair share of rivalries, destroyed careers, and thefts of far more than specimens.

"Sadly for Mrs. Baldwin, in helping restore the room of her son's murder, she discovered the forgeries within the cases. With Miss Oriana's failing health, she had taken over for her mistress more than anyone could guess. She knew it could have only been the nephew's work. But what could she do? The shock of learning her Abraham was a thief would surely reduce the old lady's life further. In miserable silence, this poor woman kept watch over her friend, but grief is difficult to mask, and Abraham not only learned she had his secret, but that she was very easily bullied into submission. It was the work of a minute to remind her of the slender financial thread upon which their livelihood hung at the Inn. It took only a minute more to force her to swear to silence. And so this sad affair continued through Miss Oriana's decline into death. Unable to bear the strain, Mrs. Baldwin consciously cut her income by moving back to the Inn, and Quantock's greedy soul must have thrilled that she had by choice ran away. She had sworn never to speak, and he firmly believed in the superstition of the peasant against breaking their word.

"Alas for his schemes! Stapleton's perfidy was exposed the moment Quantock saw the newspaper photo of Sir Henry by the rescued Merripit Collection! For there by his arm was his aunt's Vandeleur Moth, a spectre from the past! In a single stroke, Quantock thus gasped Stapleton's blow and plotted frantically to get the moth back.

"Quantock hit upon the idea of using Sir Henry's need to clean Stapleton's stain from Baskerville honour by ploy of Merripit House. If he had the full collection of Stapleton's plunder, he would have the precious Vandeleur again, sell it, and easily do as he vowed in repairing Merripit. But he dare not tell Sir Henry his true goal, for his greedy soul could not imagine so much honour in a baronet. His need for the moth and its verified price on the market was 20 times that of Merripit House, and almost equal to that of Folkestone."

Sir Henry exploded. "I wouldn't sell him his own family's moth back to him!"

"Be calm, Sir Henry. It is no slur on you that a morally destitute man viewed you with his own limited lens." Holmes soothed. "One may very well ask an ant's opinion of a pine tree."

"Maybe so, but all this effort to lie when they could have just kept to the truth!" But the baronet quieted, his fists thrust into his pockets as he listened.

Holmes continued his explanation. "His foggy scheme, which is only slightly better contrived than Stapleton's theft, would have been successful had he remembered Mrs. Baldwin. Her sense of duty was no less as strong as a Ghurka's, and when she saw the same newspaper article, she recognised the moth for what it was. Suddenly there was a shard of her beloved lady's legacy – survived! She had to protect, and so she wrote her grief to her husband, circumventing her oath to never talk. Together they hatched a clever plan to avoid Quantock's spies using the Onion Johnnies.

"The Onion Johnnies are a stout brotherhood, and word passed amongst the ranks in their Breton tongue until they found a rather clever one with the idea of directly appealing to Sherlock Holmes." Holmes paused for a moment, his grey eyes twinkling, and we saw Lestrade straighten in surprise. "I was soon on my way to Folkestone. The Johnny did not need to know much. He was simply an Onion Seller who happened to know a consultant able enough to go where Sir Henry and Mr. Lestrade could not. It was a moment's work for the Baldwins to slip a detailed confession to me within the head of the largest onion – the Captain's Head, as it is called in the vernacular, and according to the proverbs of these folk, *the Head keeps all secrets*. By these means, I was able to learn of the Baldwins' plight without anyone else the wiser."

"I was certainly not the wiser!" I breathed. "I heard a crackle when you lifted the onions up, and thought it was only the papery skins! It was the message, wasn't it?"

Holmes bowed again.

"All this made possible by an Onion Johnny!" Sir Henry whistled. "Well, I knew I liked the fellows for a reason. Good with delivering mail when you need them to, and honest to a fault."

"So I've heard," Lestrade agreed evenly, and it was all Holmes and I could do to keep our countenance intact. "Mister Holmes, this is one of your queerest cases yet, but it seems to be what you excel at. Still, solving a case backwards is amazing even for you."

"Why, thank you, Lestrade." Holmes glanced at his watch. "But I fear the congratulations must be cut short. We have just enough time to return to the Inn and pack before the next train leaves Folkestone."

And here I have paused. Holmes is finally asleep. I do not pretend I aided this step to recovery; doing nothing is worse for him than doing too much, and keeping him occupied with my poor writings has served this cause before. He rests when he is busy, and frets when he is not.

But it is my sincere hope that with this sleep he will overcome his illness and rise up, as our equally weary England struggles to rise from her sick-bed. I do not lie when I say my friend is indistinguishable from England.

But I must stop now. I can hear the milk-cart rattling up the shell drive, and with it our long-awaited guest.

"Halloa the house!" A familiar cry makes me smile. As I limp outside with my cane on the uneven earth, the milk-man hurries his cargo to the cool-room for the housekeeper. Our guest is lowering a small bag to the earth, and despite his considerably advanced years compared to mine, he remains as stubbornly spry and active as ever. Only the bright silver wings sweeping from his temples suggest his age, and a jaunty beret perches upon his touseled head.

I cannot but laugh to see an Onion Johnny here in the Sussex Downs, but they seem to be everywhere, now that there has been just barely enough time for the first crops since the War. And the Bretons will not choose in their loyalties of England or France – it is like asking a child to say which parent they love the most.

He limps unevenly to me, and his own stick is no longer for show. A chapelet of Roscoff's finest droops over his shoulder.

"What is this?" I exclaim. "I thought you had retired!"

"Lestrade has retired, Doctor Watson!" is my response. "But Onion Johnny still works."

I laugh out loud and take the chapelet. "For himself or for the Foreign Office?"

"They are much the same." This old friend reassures me. "You are looking better! I take it Holmes finally gave you permission to write about that last mess with the moth? Why else would he 'put in an order' for onions?"

And the truth strikes: I had thought I was seeing to Holmes's health, but all this time he was seeing to mine. He kept me from fretting over him and the wake of the War by concentrating on a long-awaited tale.

"I had thought to hide my health from him, since his was so much worse."

"Hum." Lestrade snaps a cigarillo alight between his lips. "Well, anything I can do to help?"

"Only answer how you could turn from browned Johnny in London to pale Inspector in Folkestone so quickly."

"No great secret. Most stains come right off, but it was a bit close. I took the chance. People were watching a late-napping Inspector Lestrade, not the in-and-out Johnnies at the inn."

"I am glad."

"As am I." We pass the tobacco between us and nod to the departing milk-cart. "Come. Holmes will wake soon, and if he hasn't improved, I am making him a plaster!"

"Not from my onions, you won't!"

"Certainly not. There is always a rude friar in the kitchen...."

About the Contributors

The following contributors appear in this volume
The Verse of Death and Other Stories

Matthew Booth is the author of Sherlock Holmes and the Giant's Hand, a collection of Sherlock Holmes short stories published by Breese Books. He is a scriptwriter for the American radio network Imagination Theatre, syndicated by Jim French Productions, contributing particularly to their series, The Further Adventures of Sherlock Holmes. Matthew has contributed two original stories to The Game Is Afoot, a collection of Sherlock Holmes short stories published in 2008 by Wordsworth Editions. His contributions are "The Tragedy of Saxon's Gate" and "The Dragon of Lea Lane". He has provided an original story entitled "A Darkness Discovered", featuring his own creation, Manchester-based private detective John Dakin, for the short story collection Crime Scenes, also published by Wordsworth Editions in 2008. Matthew is currently working on a supernatural novel called The Ravenfirth Horror.

J.R. Campbell is a Calgary-based writer who always enjoys setting problems before the Great Detective. Along with his steadfast friend Charles Prepolec, he has co-edited the Sherlock Holmes anthologies Curious Incidents, Curious Incidents 2, Gaslight Grimoire: Fantastic Tales of Sherlock Holmes, Gaslight Grotesque: Nightmare Takes of Sherlock Holmes, and Gaslight Arcanum: Uncanny Tales of Sherlock Holmes. He has also contributed stories to Imagination Theater's Radio Drama The Further Adventures of Sherlock Holmes, and the anthologies A Study in Lavender: Queering Sherlock Holmes and Challenger Unbound. At the time of writing, his next project, again with Charles Prepolec, is the anthology Professor Challenger: New Worlds, Lost Places.

Carole Nelson Douglas is the author of sixty New-York-published novels, and the first woman to write a Sherlock Holmes spin-off series using the first woman protagonist, Irene Adler. Good Night, Mr. Holmes debuted as a New York Times Notable Book of the Year. Holmes and Watson have been Douglas' "go-to guys" since childhood, appearing in a high school skit and her weekly newspaper column. Seeing only one pseudonymous woman in print with Holmes derivations, she based her Irene Adler on how Conan Doyle presented her: a talented, compassionate, independent, and audacious woman, in eight acclaimed novels. ("Readers will doff their deerstalkers." – Publishers Weekly) Those readers pine in vain for a film version of the truly substantial and fascinating Irene Adler that Holmes and Sir Arthur Conan Doyle admired as "The Woman." Now indie publishing, Douglas plans to make more of her Irene Adler stories available in print and eBook. www.carolenelsondouglas.com

Lyndsay Faye, BSI, grew up in the Pacific Northwest, graduating from Notre Dame de Namur University. She worked as a professional actress throughout the Bay Area for several years before moving to New York. Her first novel was the critically acclaimed pastiche Dust and Shadow: An Account of the Ripper Killings by Dr. John H Watson. Faye's love of her adopted city led her to research the origins of the New York City Police Department, as related in the Edgar-nominated Timothy Wilde trilogy. She is a frequent writer for the Strand Magazine and the Eisner-nominated comic Watson and Holmes. Lyndsay and her husband, Gabriel Lehner, live in Queens with their cats, Grendel and Prufrock. She is a very proud member of the Baker Street Babes, Actor's Equity Association, Mystery Writers of America, The Adventuresses of Sherlock Holmes, and The Baker Street Irregulars. Her works have currently been translated into fourteen languages.

Jeremy Holstein first discovered Sherlock Holmes at age five when he became convinced that the Hound of the Baskervilles lived in his bedroom closet. A life long enthusiast of radio dramas, Jeremy is currently the lead dramatist and director for the Post Meridian Radio Players adaptations of Sherlock Holmes, where he has adapted The Hound of the Baskervilles, The Sign of Four, and "Jack the Harlot Killer" (retitled "The Whitechapel Murders") from William S. Baring-Gould's Sherlock Holmes of Baker Street for the company. He is currently in production with an adaptation of "Charles Augustus Milverton". Jeremy has also written Sherlock Holmes scripts for Jim French's Imagination Theatre. He lives with his wife and daughter in the Boston, MA area.

Ann Margaret Lewis attended Michigan State University, where she received her Bachelor's Degree in English Literature. She began her writing career writing tie-in children's books and short stories for DC Comics. She then published two editions of the book Star Wars: The New Essential Guide to Alien Species for Random House. She is the author of the awardwinning Murder in the Vatican: The Church Mysteries of Sherlock Holmes (Wessex Press), and her most recent book is a Holmes novel entitled The Watson

Chronicles: A Sherlock Holmes Novel in Stories (Wessex Press).

William Patrick Maynard was born and raised in Cleveland, Ohio. His passion for writing began in childhood and was fueled by early love of detective and thriller fiction. He was licensed by the Sax Rohmer Literary Estate to continue the Fu Manchu thrillers for Black Coat Press. The Terror of Fu Manchu was published in 2009 and was followed by The Destiny of Fu Manchu in 2012 and The Triumph of Fu Manchu in 2015. His previous Sherlock Holmes stories appeared in Gaslight Grotesque (2009/EDGE Publishing) and Further Encounters of Sherlock Holmes (2014/Titan Books). He currently resides in Northeast Ohio with his wife and family.

Robert V. Stapleton was born and brought up in Leeds, Yorkshire, England, and studied at Durham University. After working in various parts of the country as an Anglican parish priest, he is now retired and lives with his wife in North Yorkshire. As a member of his local writing group, he now has time to develop his other life as a writer of adventure stories. He has recently had a number of short stories published, and he is hoping to have a couple of completed novels published at some time in the future.

Sam Wiebe's debut novel Last of the Independents was published by Dundurn Press. An alternative private detective novel set in the Pacific Northwest, Last of the Independents, won the 2012 Arthur Ellis Award for Best Unpublished First Novel. Sam's short fiction has been published in Thuglit, Spinetingler, Subterrain, and Criminal Element, among others. Follow him at @sam_wiebe and at samwiebe.com.

Marcia Wilson is a freelance researcher and illustrator who likes to work in a style compatible for the color blind and visually impaired. She is Canoncentric and her first MX offering, You Buy Bones, uses the point-of-view of Scotland Yard to show the unique talents of Dr. Watson. She can be contacted at gravelgirty.deviantart.com

Vincent W. Wright has been a Sherlockian and member of The Illustrious Clients of Indianapolis since 1997. He is the creator of a blog, Historical Sherlock, which is dedicated to the chronology of The Canon, and has written a column on that subject for his home scion's newsletter since 2005. He lives in Indiana, and works for the federal government. This is his first pastiche.